RUBINE RIVER

DAVID RAY SKINNER

Printed in the United States of America.

Library of Congress Control Number: 2020912099

ISBN	Paperback	978-1-64803-262-2
	Hardback	978-1-64803-263-9
	eBook	978-1-64803-264-6

Westwood Books Publishing LLC
11416 SW Aventino Drive
Port Saint Lucie, FL 34987

www.westwoodbookspublishing.com

CHAPTER 1

The Bridge in the Desert

As Clay drifted into consciousness, the overwhelming white-hot brightness of the October morning forced him to quickly shut his eyes with a painful grimace. He lay frozen on his back, brushed back the wisps of blond hair cascading over his damp forehead and listened hard for the heavy rumble of approaching choppers in the sky overhead. *Where's my unit?* he thought, *That blasted desert sun is cooking my head like a microwave meatloaf TV dinner, and yet my boots are all iced over. Guess the elements can't make up their mind how they want to kill me.*

His thoughts were drowned out by a low *whop-whop-whop* roar above him.

"It's about time," he said to himself, "But that chopper sounds like an old Chevy with a rusted-out muffler."

Then, with his eyes still closed, he did a mental assessment of his physical state. *Just my luck—it appears as if I've landed in medical no-man's land*, he thought, *not serious enough to be treated and carted away by the medics, but bad enough to make me not want to move.* There was a metallic taste in his mouth, and a sharp stab of pain began surging up and down his ribs to join with the already pounding throb in his head, the after-effect of a night of way too much cheap bourbon. *What was I thinking? Actually, what was I drinking?* A stinging drop of sweat rolled into his right eye and, as he began to force open his eyes, he saw the desert sky morphing into a massive interstate bridge above him.

The high autumn sun had angled over the bridge, catching his head in its path, but leaving the rest of his ragged body in the dirty shadows. Somewhere, close by, the sound of rushing water softly gurgled.

"What tha—?" he said out loud, *"How'd a bridge get stuck in the middle of the desert?"*

"'Cause it ain't the desert, brother," a voice from the shadows answered. "You're in South Care-o-lina, and there ain't no desert in Carolina—'least not one I ever heard of. How you feelin' anyway? Heard you 'bout got yerself kild last night. 'Least that's the word on the street. Well—the word on the *ground under the bridge*, rather. Said they done rolled you pretty good, brother. Or you rolled yerself. Either way, *you rolled!* My friend, Percy over there said you came flying out of an old redneck pickup truck like Superman, and you and yer bag came a-rollin' down the hill toward the river. An' I'm guessin' you feel it 'bout now. Percy here said he couldn't tell if you jumped or were pushed."

Clay squinted toward the voice and made out a black man about his own age—early- to mid-thirties. He had a friendly smile, and he moved with the grace of an aging athlete as he paced on the red-dirt bank above where Clay had landed. The man wore a bright yellow polo, and although he was dressed casually, he was too well-dressed—*and his yellow polo was much too clean*—for him to have spent the night under the bridge. Clay figured the man apparently was a new arrival to the scene; *a cop, maybe?* If that were the case, he would have been an undercover cop, because he definitely wasn't in uniform…unless the *under-the-bridge* cops wore bright yellow. *Plus,* Clay thought, *based on past experience, if he was a cop, he would have most likely already accused me of something and would have already thrown me in the back of a cruiser.*

"Ain't that about right, Percy?" said the man in the yellow polo gesturing toward an older white man sitting in the shadows of the bridge. "You said he looked like Superman flyin' from a redneck truck."

Percy laughed, "Yep, thas 'bout right. Coulda been Superman or Batman. Whichever one don't got a cape." Although he was sitting on the muddy bank next to the yellow-polo man, he couldn't have been more different in appearance. His clothes were not torn, but they were old and worn enough to successfully hide any kind of dirt or debris he could have picked up during a stay under the bridge. His weather-beaten cap had a rusty bill and was adorned with a logo that had long-since been rendered useless and nondescript. The cap, however, served its purpose; it protected the old man from the sun and bathed his face in shadows, embossing the furrowed winkles on his forehead, temples and cheeks as he gestured.

Clay slowly sat up, and as he did, he realized that the old man had been correct in his description of his previous night's adventure—tiny-but-sharp bursts of pain jabbed him from all over his body, like angry bees. Percy held up a water bottle in salute. "Welcome to Sunday, my man," he said, "How you feelin' this fine day? Your friends in the truck were concerned 'bout you."

"Ow. Uh, they weren't exactly my friends."

"I figgered. An' I'd be using that term *i-ron-i-cal-ly*. Satire-ically, actually. Can't really say they wuz *concerned* 'bout your welfare, but they wuz definitely *interested* enough to stop on down th' way. Then they backed up, all swervy-like. Idiots. I guess it's lucky that it's only an overpass bridge up there and ain't no exit, 'cause they woulda most likely driven down to check on you. Fact is, I thought for a minute there, they *wuz gonna try and drive down anyway*, exit or no exit. An' as you say, they weren't your friends, so you may have had somewhat of a problem, seein' whereas you were off to dreamland at that point."

"Did they get out?"

"Not all of 'em. They sent a lil' ol' pudgy scout to check on ya, but all he did was up-chuck half-way down the hill, so he never got to where you landed after you flew out the truck. I'm pretty sure he weren't the leader, 'cause he looked to be even more idiot than the rest o' the idiots, so I don't think they woulda made him king of the moment. I don't know if he was trying to be all stealthy-like, but if he was, he failed miserably—he made way too much noise crashing through the brush. An' they ain't that much brush up on this hill, so that numbskull had to go outta his way to find some brush to crash through. We like it nice and quiet here under the bridge. It's one thing to have Superman come rollin' down the hill—*you were quiet and polite.* Well, at least once you came to a stop. It's quite another thing to have some blowhard bellowing like a beached whale. So, I admit I did some hollerin' back at him. An' possibly some bad language." Percy put his hand to his mouth as a mock gesture of an apology.

"Didn't take much to spook 'im, though," he said, continuing. "He scampered on up the hill like a big ol' rabbit an' jumped back in th' truck. Actually—*an' this wuz purty funny, though purty mean*—they locked 'im outta' the truck at first and started takin' off without 'im. He was a-screamin' and cryin'—*and I mean boo-hooing, tears an' everthing*—so they finally stopped—in the *middle* of the bridge, can you believe it?—an' he waddled over an' they finally let 'im in. I don't blame you for not havin' 'em as friends. They was extremely disreputable. An' irresponsible. Buncha mo-rons."

"'Preciate you lookin' out for me, since I was somewhat... *indisposed*."

"If that's what you wanna call it, son. Fancy ol' word for your condition, as it were." Percy cackled.

Out of instinct and habit, Clay sat up and did a quick check of his surroundings, just in case he needed to utilize a contingency plan. He probed the back of his head until he found the dried blood and, as he rolled over to get his bearings, a dull blast of pain from his chest told him he had a least a couple of bruised ribs. However, past experience also told him that nothing was broken.

The *whop-whop-whop* above him continued, and he squinted up at the bridge and realized it was the sound of the traffic rushing over a loose metal plate on the overpass.

"Right, that makes a little more sense than a chopper," he said as his memory started returning. *Oh yeah, now I remember,* he thought to himself sarcastically, *Yesterday was a fairly action-packed day with so many wonderful adventures.*

"So, let me guess," it was yellow-polo man again. "I suppose this wadn't your planned destination, was it?"

"Uh, no," Clay said, "I don't even know where *'this'* is. Can you enlighten me?"

"Well, it's nowhere, really. As you discovered last night, it ain't even an exit. That road up there—*at the top of the hill, where my car is*—that road goes under the interstate an' eventually ends up in Rubaville. That's where I was headed when I saw Percy. I think ol' Percy musta been trollin' for more superheroes bein' thrown from pickups when I saw him from the road this morning. Hey, Percy, thanks again. Thanks for keepin' watch under th' bridge."

"Yeah, thanks, Percy," Clay said, still rubbing the back of his head.

"And that there river you almost landed in?" Percy said, "That's the Rubine River."

"That really doesn't mean anything to me. No offense. There's lots of places I've been that I had never heard of before I got there. So no, I never heard of the Rubine River. And no, I never heard of Rubaville."

"Well, the proper name is *Rubineville.* But, if you want to fit in with the locals, you butcher the pronunciation like the rest of us."

"I'm not sure I'm gonna stick around long enough to fit it with the locals. And again, I never heard of the river or the town."

"No surprise there. Rubaville ain't even a town anymore…more of a community.

"Let me guess—more of *'a state of mind,'* right?"

"I don't know about that. It's just not so well known. It and the river don't do much advertising these days. No Chamber of Commerce. No 'Welcome' signs."

"If that's the case, then why were you headed to it?"

"Oh, I do appreciate people with intelligent questions and inquisitive minds."

"Yeah, well," Clay said, feeling the back of his head, "I'm just hopin' my inquisitive mind is still intact in my inquisitive skull."

CHAPTER 2

The Long and Winding Interstate

That Saturday morning had started with such promise. Clay had used the last of his money for a hot meal and a place to stay the night before, but he was used to being totally broke, and the day had begun with hope and a cool-but-sunny day for hitchhiking. He had found a motel just off the main drag of the town, where his last ride of the day had dropped him off. It was a no-frills, mom-and-pop place, but it was clean and inexpensive. Plus, there was a hometown diner between the motel and the interstate, and he was able to eat a big breakfast before he hit the road. He knew that it might be a while before his next meal, so he ordered the biggest omelette on the menu with all the trimmings and asked for extra biscuits. As he finished his last cup of coffee, he dumped the last basket of biscuits into some paper napkins, along with some packets of grape jelly, and carefully placed them down into a pocket inside his duffel bag. *That may be lunch, dinner and tomorrow's breakfast,* he thought. As he paid his bill, he noticed the picture of the local Little League team the diner sponsored on the wall behind the cash register. There was a shelf below the picture with a couple of trophies. *That was me not so long ago,* he thought. *Funny how everything changes.*

As Clay exited the diner, he pulled on his heavy Army jacket, and he noticed that the smell of the restaurant had clung to his clothes and followed him outside. He had dressed warmly for the day—a khaki shirt over a charcoal grey t-shirt, tucked into his faded jeans, along with waterproof hiking boots—and checking out his reflection in the diner's window, he brushed his straw-blonde hair out of his eyes and adjusted his sunglasses. *Crap,* he thought, *I look like a sniper.* The observation made him flash back to an incident that had happened during his military days. The memory made him inadvertently shiver, but he shook if off and folded his sunglasses and put them into the pocket of his khaki shirt. He figured the drivers of potential rides would feel more comfortable if they could see his eyes. At least he would look a little less like an assassin.

By the time he got to the interstate ramp, the sun was high and the morning had warmed up, so he took off his jacket and stuffed it into his duffel bag as he put out his thumb. Back at the diner, he had spent the last of his change on a pack of Wrigley's, so as he waited on the interstate ramp, he patted the left pocket of his khaki shirt and fidgeted briefly with unbuttoning the flap. He pulled out the pack and extracted a foil-wrapped stick of gum, and as he replaced it, he tucked the flap into the pocket to give him easier access. *How lazy can I get?* he thought, laughing at himself, *I don't even want to bother with buttoning and unbuttoning my shirt pocket. Gotta have that immediate access to chewing gum!*

As he scanned the highway which crossed the interstate, he could see an approaching copper-colored SUV. Inside was an old hippie, and he pulled over on the ramp just beyond where Clay stood and motioned for him to hurry up and get in. Because of the man's wrinkles and grey-white hair pulled back into a long ponytail, Clay guessed that he was most likely about the same age as his own father back in Illinois.

"You military?" he asked Clay once the SUV started rolling down the ramp to merge in with the sparse, southbound interstate traffic.

"Ex-military," Clay told him.

"Thas cool. Thought so. You got that look. Ain't the same military now as it was in my time."

"Oh, where'd you serve?"

"Me? No. No way, man. I did my best to stay *out* of the military! I had no desire to get my head blown off in Vietnam."

Wow, that sounds a little too familiar...how many times have I heard that? Clay thought, but he listened politely. "Spent my 20s in Canada," the man continued, "But that wudn't exactly a picnic, either. Canada's too cold for me, man. Alls I'm sayin' is that it's a lot hipper to be military now than it was then."

"Yeah, that's me in a nutshell. I'm all about hip," Clay replied. "But don't sell yourself short, dude—there's a lot to be said about chillin' on a comfy couch, versus the prospect of getting your head blown off crouching down in a crappy foxhole." Clay realized he probably should have filtered his response, because he saw the man's face tighten, and a few exits later, he pulled up off the interstate and let him out.

"Here's my exit, man. Good luck to ya," he said.

"Yeah, thanks. Thanks for the lift," Clay said, climbing out with his duffle bag. He then watched the SUV cross the highway and pull back down onto the interstate entrance ramp. Clay sighed and crossed the highway himself and stuck his thumb out on the same ramp. He could see the copper SUV disappearing over the horizon, gleaming in the sun.

"It figures," Clay said out loud, "One of these days, I'm gonna learn how to keep my stupid mouth shut."

Fifteen minutes later, a big golden Buick eased over to the side of the ramp with the passenger window rolled down.

"Where you goin,' partner?" asked the man behind the wheel, leaning over the seat to call out from the passenger-side window.

"South," Clay said.

"That makes sense," the man laughed, "Nice to know you can read the signs! Get yourself in, partner. Make yourself at home!"

The man, although older than Clay, appeared to be a bit younger than the old hippie that had dropped him off at the exit. He was bald with a salt-and-pepper mustache.

"Glad to meecha. Hank Thoreau. I'm a plastics rep."

"Hank Thoreau as in Henry Thoreau?" Clay asked, as he climbed in with his duffle bag.

"Yeah, like *'the'* Henry Thoreau," Hank said, "My old man always claimed he was kin, although neither one of us got any poem-writing smarts from that side of the family. Well, any side of the family, that is. Sure, the name caused me maybe a little bit of grief in my younger days—back in school. The good news was that the kids that were tough enough to effectively bully me about it didn't know squat about Henry the poet, and the geeky ones who always had their heads in a book—the ones that *did* know who the original Henry Thoreau was, they wouldn't dare say anything. Well, one of 'em did, back in seventh or eighth grade, but I made an example out of him. He said something like, 'Hey Thoreau, what about Walden?' What a tool. We were in P.E. Ain't no teachers or coaches in P.E. Well, at least in our boys' P.E., back then, that is. The coaches were probably monitoring the girls' P.E. Haw, haw, haw! Anyway, there wasn't anyone to help little Mr. Smarty Britches when he gave me the business about Walden. I picked him up—with one hand, mind you—by the back waistband of his underwear, and held him up for everone in the P.E. to see just what happens to smartypants. All the other geeks just stood around horrified, so I finally said, 'My mistake…I thought he said, "What about wallopin'!"' So, that nipped it in the bud!"

Clay smiled. "Interesting conflict resolution," he said.

"Yessiree. By the way, I can take you a few hours on down the road," Hank said.

"That's great. I appreciate it."

A few hours and several hundred miles later, the man nosed the big Buick down an exit ramp to get some gas. "So, partner," he said to Clay, "You're more than welcome to continue down the interstate with me, but I got to tell you—all exits down this a-ways ain't created equal. Look around. There's an Arbys, a Motel 6, this gas station and a Starbucks. Now, admittedly, it ain't Grand Central, but it's lot busier than the next few exits, especially the one I need to get off at. This is a four-lane federal highway here, so there's a fair share of traffic getting on the interstate. The exit I'm getting off at is like 'Nowheresville,' population negative one-hunderd. Like I said, you're welcome to get off there. Actually, you can go with me all the way to the plant, if you want. You any good at selling plastics? I can get you fixed up with the company…"

"Nah, sorry. I know nothing about plastics…maybe a little about plastic explosives, but that's from the military."

"Well, these I'm sellin' don't go boom. Well—allegedly."

"In that case, I guess I'll get out when you get off the interstate. I'm enjoying our conversation."

"Me, too. I just thought it would be fair to warn you that there's not a lot of traffic on that entrance, and the state troopers wouldn't take too kindly to you hitchin' down on the shoulder of the interstate."

"I got it, but I prefer the bird in the hand. Well, the Buick in the hand," Clay told him, "So, if it's alright with you, I'll take my chances."

"Okay. Last chance to get off here. You're missing out on an Arby's. And a Motel 6. And a Starbucks."

"I had a big breakfast. And, I sure ain't sleepy, and the coffee would just keep me awake."

"Hmm. You're a walking paradox, aren't you?" Hank said.

"That's the point. I don't have to walk, long as I can ride in your fine Buick, here."

"Suit yourself," Hank said, "And, it's nice to meet a man that appreciates the finer automobiles. Yessir, I am a Buick man. This is my eighth one, actually. And, boy what a deal I got on it. Yessir. But before I forget, consider yourself warned. I'm down through here every month, and there's never anybody at that exit. So, I'd be remiss if I didn't at least give you the facts on that exit. Don't say I didn't warn you! As much as I'm enjoying our conversin', I don't want you to feel that I led you on and then let you out!"

"Got it. It's all good, man. Drive on!"

"Splendid! That's what I was hopin' you'd say. Even though that works to my advantage—I don't often have a travelin' partner that I can converse with! By the way, there's some cheese and crackers in the glove box. Help yourself."

"Thanks."

Hank pulled the Buick up to one of the pumps in front of an old convenience store. It was freshly painted, but there were burglar bars in the window which had a bunny rabbit logo. Clay laughed to himself. *Looks like the bunny is in jail,* he thought, *wonder what he did?*

After Hank finished filling the Buick and paying, he jumped back in and directed the big car back onto the interstate. They drove a hundred miles or so down the road, and though the conversation was pleasant enough, the scenery became more and more boring and nondescript. When Hank finally nosed the Buick down the exit off the interstate, it really was the middle of nowhere, and he guiltily shoved a ten-dollar bill in Clay's hand as he climbed out of the car with his duffle bag. Clay gave the door a quick shove to shut it, and Hank rolled the window down.

"Take it easy, partner," he said, "If you're still here when I come back through, I'll give you a ride."

"Sounds fair. When you comin' back through?"

"Next week sometime," Hank said, and the two of them laughed. Hank hesitated for a moment and then continued, "Uh, something I need to tell you."

"Okay?" Clay said, leaning over into the window to hear.

"I was kinda stretching the truth about how I handled the kid that gave me a hard time about that Walden thingy."

"Okay."

"Yeah, I didn't really grab him by the back of his underwear and hold him up with one hand."

"Okay."

"I did report him to the principal and he got a stern talkin' to, so he never did it again."

"That's all that really counts, ain't it?"

"Yeah. Sure. Now that you put it that way. Well, thanks."

"Sure. Thanks to you for the ride."

"Oh. Yeah, my pleasure. Hope you're here next week when I come back through."

"Uh, sorry, but I hope I'm not."

"Oh. Right," Hank said, "That might be a little unpleasant, heh, heh. Okay. Well, good luck to ya. Take care." And with that, Hank gunned the big Buick and it disappeared down the highway in a cloud of exhaust. Clay sighed and crossed the road to the interstate entrance ramp to wait for the next car.

CHAPTER 3

TRUCK OF FOOLS

After a few hours of standing—and sitting on his duffle bag—at the side of the entrance ramp, Clay found himself seriously regretting his decision about getting out at the exit. *Never thought I'd miss a rabbit behind bars,* he thought. Both the sun and the October temperature were going down, and Clay was trying to figure out how and where he was going to sleep. The October day had been fairly warm—shirtsleeve weather, actually—but he knew that it would not be pleasant once the sun was down. It had been at least an hour before the last vehicle had passed, and, it being a minivan packed with a family, he had known better than to expect it to stop as it rolled down the ramp onto the interstate.

Then, as he watched the sun disappear behind a distant grove of trees, he kneeled down and upzipped his duffle bag to retrieve his heavy coat, but before he could take it out of his bag, a beat-up, four-door pickup slammed on its brakes and slowed to a stop, just past him on the ramp. Actually, he heard it coming long before it clattered into sight, but he figured it was a farmer or another local. Consequently, he was surprised—albeit relieved—that someone had finally pulled over to offer him a ride, especially since it was getting dark. He certainly wouldn't miss that *middle-of-nowhere* interstate exit. However, his first impression of his rescuer's truck was that it was some sort of clown machine—*not that it mattered*—at that point, he would have accepted a ride in Bonny and Clyde's death car, so he quickly zipped up his bag and threw it over his shoulder. As he sprinted toward the truck on the shoulder of the ramp, he noticed a torn and faded rebel flag decal on the back window and the tires had black wheel covers. The front and back fenders had begun to corrode over the wheel wells, and against the dirty tan shade of the truck, it gave an appearance of rusty eyebrows over the cartoon-black eyes of the wheels. Although the four of them—*one black and three white kids*—were a seedy lot, they looked more comical than threatening. At any rate, Clay didn't have any concern for his safety. Climbing into the backseat, he noticed the inside smelled like sweat, cigarettes and stale beer. There was a time when he could have easily dispatched the lot of them without raising a sweat, but it would have been a while ago, and he would have had to have been stone-cold sober. The last few years had taken a toll on his physical strength and reaction time, and that was even if he wasn't drinking. Once alcohol was added to the mix, it made him even more vulnerable.

A couple of exits later they got off—in another middle of nowhere—and pulled into a QT to get some gas, along with some chips and cigarettes. About a hundred yards down the road from the QT—*to their whooping delight*—stood a falling-down-shack of a package store. The driver—Rocko was his name, or at least what they called him—took off his dirty cap and passed it around the truck for contributions. It was a dirty and (formerly) yellow hat with a CAT DIESEL logo stitched onto the front. Someone—most likely the wearer, Rocko, himself—had taken a black magic marker and run a top-to-bottom line through the "C" to crudely make it read: ¢AT DIESEL. *Cat cent? Cat scent? Cat sense? No sense? Wonder what message he's trying to communicate?* Clay wondered as he threw in his last ten—the parting gift from Hank to assuage his guilt for dropping him off on the deserted ramp.

The designated buyer was the plump kid occupying the front passenger seat; at first, Clay thought they were calling him Gerbo, which he thought was a creative and interesting—*if nondescript*—name or nickname. However, as Rocko continued to harangue him for a myriad of minor offenses, it became increasingly apparent that they were calling him "Gerbil," and it was, indeed, a nickname and actually more accurate than nondescript, because he continued to stuff his puffy face with chips and sunflower seeds, chewing them quickly and rodent-like. Gerbil's hairline was already receding and he appeared to be the oldest of the bunch, so Clay surmised that he may have been the only one of the bunch who could have legally purchased the alcohol, other than Clay, and it was clear that they hadn't yet accepted him into the club. *They probably don't even check IDs*, Clay thought. From the looks of the store's exterior, Clay figured they probably played fast and loose with any sort of regulation.

Gerbil disappeared into the building, and minutes later, he emerged with a large, electric-blue bottle of some no-name whiskey. The large bottle jutted out of a plain paper bag like a big blue possum trying to escape from a tote sack. When he climbed back into the passenger's seat and pulled it out of the bag, Rocko scowled.

"Gerbil, you idiot, what is this? It looks like something out of an antique store."

"It was the biggest and cheapest whiskey they had," Gerbil said, defensively, "I thought that was what y'all ast for."

"It's prolly home-grown and'll make us all blind," Rocko said derisively. "Then, who's gonna drive, genius?"

In an attempt to diffuse the situation and act as the only grownup in the vehicle, Clay came to Gerbil's defense. "I'm sure it'll be okay," he said, "You're thinking of home brew. Moonshine. Hooch. Sure, there's a lot of that to be found, but the law watches places like this, and they most likely wouldn't sell home brew to a stranger. Besides, after a couple of rounds, this stuff'l taste the same as Jack."

"Right—*same as Jack*. So you do know *Jack*," Rocko said, his eyes narrowing.

Hmm, it appears that I'm not making any friends here, Clay thought.

After an awkward moment of silence, Rocko opened the blue bottle and took a long slug and passed the bottle to the black kid behind the driver's seat. And then, rattling past the QT, they squealed onto the entrance ramp and were back rolling southward down the interstate. Rocko pulled an almost-empty cigarette pack out from behind the visor, and lighting the last cigarette, wadded up the pack and threw it out the window. "So, how'd you get to be a whiskey conner-sewer?" Rocko said, taking a deep draw on the cigarette and squinting at Clay in the truck's rear view mirror.

"Nah, I'm not anything close to an expert," Clay deflected, "I *can* say that I've had everything from moonshine up to 14-year-old *Wild Turkey*, and, when I was in the service, one of the officers shared a few glasses of some of his *Pappy Von Winkle's* with some of my squad—I later learned *that* stuff was about 65 bucks an ounce. Point is, the goal—the destination—is always the same; it don't matter to me whether it's with a McLaren or a Yugo—the main thing is to *get to that state*," he said, pouring a drink from the blue bottle into a styrofoam cup.

"Huh. That state, eh?" Rocko said.

"What's a Yugo?" Gerbil asked, chewing on the last of the sunflower seeds.

"What's McLaren?" asked the kid sitting next to Clay.

"It's names-a whiskey, you idiots," Rocko said. Then, he turned to look at Clay. "Service, eh?" he said, "You still in? Active?"

I wouldn't be bumming rides off of greasy low-life morons like you if I was still active duty, Clay thought, but he politely said, "Nah. I've been out a while. I elected to not sign on to another tour."

At first, there were the usual questions. *How long were you in? How many tours? Did you see a lot of action? How many kills did you have?* A ride is a ride, Clay figured, so he tried to answer the questions patiently and non-condescendingly. However, by the time Clay figured out that they didn't really care about his military service and were just trying to distract him into drunkenness, he realized—*all too late*—they had succeeded, and he was unfortunately much more vulnerable than he should have been. However, what really frustrated him about the situation was that he knew he was in a bit of trouble, but *he just didn't really care.* In fact, he found himself actually enjoying the feeling of being out of control, even though it was overriding his instinctual perception of impending danger. It was that brief moment of reckless abandon that he so often sought, as of late. *Mixing alcohol with adrenaline again*, he thought.

All of the warning signs had been there, flashing like a big blue electric neon sign: *Danger, danger, danger,* and he fed on it and let it flow throughout his body like a drug. It had long since gotten dark, and the conversation had gotten less and less friendly. Rocko had begun addressing him as "Soldier Boy." By then, they were all in various stages of inebriation, but the two in the backseat seemed the least affected. Clay hadn't noticed it at first, but sometimes when the bottle was passed to the backseat, he had been the only one taking drinks from it. Gerbil in the front seat, however, apparently hadn't gotten the memo; he had taken more than his share of swigs of the *gnarly-but-potent* blend and was paying the price—he was throwing up into the paper bag that had previously held the big bottle of whiskey.

"You okay, Gerbil?" Rocko laughed, "Do we need to pull over? You blind, yet? How many fingers am I holdin' up? Just one, maybe? Which one, Gerbil? Haw, haw, haw!"

"Shut up."

That only made Rocko laugh harder, and as Clay observed him in the rearview mirror, a sense of dread ran down his spine. He thought that Rocko resembled a braying donkey as he laughed with squinty eyes and crooked yellow teeth that reminded him of an old Confederate cemetery.

"There may be some food places at the next exit," Clay said, "That might make you feel better."

"Uh. No, no, no, I don't think so." Gerbil said, rolling his window down and throwing out the bag. "Please just shut up."

Marquis, the black kid sitting in the back seat directly behind Rocko added, "Sign back there say there's a Dairy Queen and a Captain D's just up ahead."

"No. Stop it. Ugh," Gerbil swooned, "I done tossed my barf bag."

"An' your cookies," Rocko said, gaffawing, "How 'bout some deep-fat-drippin'-fried catfish Captain D's?"

"No! Shut up!"

"Drippin' in big ol' yeller-green globs of grease!"

"Shut up! I mean it! Jerks!"

"You could get a milkshake next door at the DQ and mix it all up."

That set Gerbil off again, this time into his hat, and the other three howled.

What a bunch of idiots, Clay thought. But, at that point, his main concern had become the very real possibility that they might be pulled over by a Carolina trooper, and he had already collected his share of priors. Nothing like weaving and littering to attract unwanted attention from the law. The last thing he wanted was to spend the night in a small-town jail cell with these morons.

"Keep your window down," Clay said, "Take some deep breaths. It'll pass."

"Yeah, it'll pass, Gerbil. Listen to Soldier Boy. He's our official medic tonight and he's jus' full of useful information," Rocko said, turning his attention to Clay, "By the way, Soldier Boy, did we ever thank you for donatin' that ten to the cause?"

"Forget it. It was nothin'," Clay said, although he instinctively knew that Rocko wasn't seriously thanking him.

"Yeah, that's what we wuz thinkin.' Right? It wuz nothin'."

The two in the backseat beside Clay nodded in agreement. Gerbil was distracted and didn't comment.

"So how 'bout a nuther donatin'?" Rocko said.

Here we go, Clay thought. From the backseat, he looked up and saw Rocko's narrowed eyes in the rearview. That was the point where the mood inside the pickup's cab shifted, and Clay remembered instinctively clinching his fists and feeling down on the floor for his duffle bag, and waiting for the scene to begin to play out. Sizing up the four of them, he figured that Rocko would keep driving, and Gerbil was totally occupied throwing up into the plastic bag. That left Darryl and Marquis as the main threats; they were next to him in the back seat. Clay's warrior instinct began to drunkenly kick in, and he slowly slid his right hand under the strap of his duffle bag, which lay on the floor between his leg and the back door of the pickup. With his other hand, he closed his fingers tightly around the neck of the empty big blue bottle that had only moments earlier held the cheap whisky. He was grateful that they hadn't thrown it out of the truck, like the rest of the litter and cigarette butts. He also surveyed the horizon ahead to try and devise an escape plan. They had been rolling down the interstate in relative darkness for the past hour, with an occasional streetlight at exits and interchanges. As he squinted through the windshield at the horizon, he could see a flicker of light a half-mile away. *Finally, a convenient exit,* he thought, gratefully.

"Fork it over, Soldier Boy," Rocko said, "Darryl, as treasurer and sergeant-at-arms, what don't you collect Soldier Boy's dues?"

"What'ya mean, treasurer and sergeant with arms?" Darryl asked.

"I mean get his money, idiot!" Rocko said.

Darryl, who was in the middle seat, began drunkenly digging in his pockets, and Clay figured he wasn't looking for spare change. However, he saw that they were quickly nearing the flickering interstate streetlight and what he hoped was an exit…it was less than a quarter-mile away.

"Well that's a funny thing, Rocko…" Clay said, smiling, hoping to stall just for the half minute or so it would take them to reach the interstate streetlight. "Really, really funny, but that money that I gave y'all—"

His intent was to patiently and calmly explain that the ten-dollar bill that he had contributed was the *only* money he had to his name. But, before he could finish his sentence, to his surprise, an unexpected elbow to the side of his head was delivered by Gerbil from the passenger's seat in front of him.

Crap, he thought, *Blind-sided by a drunken Gerbil.*

"Shank him, Darryl! Get his money—his bag!" Rocko said, twisting around in his seat.

By then, the pickup was nearly under the bright streetlight. *Here's the exit,* Clay thought, *it's now or never.* He weighed his options in a split second, although it seemed as if the whole scene materialized in slow motion. In one quick sweep, he observed two flashes of metal—to his left was the shiny blade that suddenly appeared in Darryl's clumsy hand (*so that's what he was digging through his pockets for*)—and, to his right was the metal handle of the door on the rear passenger side. Clay went for the latter, and the last thing he remembered was throwing open the door with his right hand (still holding the duffle) and with his left, shattering the empty blue bottle over the top of Darryl's head in a twinkling cascade of electric-blue glass, illuminated by the interstate lighting. *It's almost like big shards of magic dust,* Clay thought, as he delivered a solid kick with his heavy boot, straight between Darryl's blood-shot eyes, flattening the hapless youth's nose with a sharp crack. The kick not only dislodged the blade in Darryl's hand (sending it spinning in the air like a circus juggler's shiny knife), it also launched Clay out the door like a floppy acrobat. A split second later, he was sailing out of the pickup, and then hitting the pavement and rolling down the dirt-grass-and-mud hill beside the bridge. *Oops, not an exit ramp,* he thought, *guess I'll make my own exit.*

Due to Rocko's drunken state, he was probably only doing 30 or 40, Clay thought as he recalled the event, *I don't know if I could have survived if he had been doing the speed limit or anything close to it. Thank goodness for cheap whiskey.* That was the last thing he remembered. He wasn't sure if it was the whiskey or some obstruction that he hit with the back of his head rolling down the hill. Either way, the end result was a deep sleep—*not totally without nightmares*—at the bottom of the hill beneath the bridge.

CHAPTER 4

DOWN THE LAZY RUBINE

"So. Brother. You hungry? You wanna join me for a bite?" It was the black man in the yellow polo, standing in the shadow of the bridge and snapping Clay back into his present reality.

Clay slowly surveyed his surroundings. The interstate traffic hummed and pounded on the bridge above him. It traversed a sparkling river at the foot of the hill where he had landed the night before. At the top of the hill, also in the shadow of the bridge, he could see a single car parked, apparently on the shoulder of the road the man had mentioned.

"I'm guessing you're countin' your lucky stars, 'bout now," the man said, grinning, "Like Percy mentioned, you coulda kept right on rollin' down the hill and right down into the Rubine. Splish, splash. Guess while you were playin' Superman, you were lucky you didn't bang your head on a big ol' Kryptonite rock."

"Actually, with the way my head aches and the way my ribs hurt, I don't really feel that lucky. But thanks for filling in the pieces of the story, uh, Percy," Clay said nodding to the older man. "And thanks for stopping and prying the story out of Percy, Mister—"

"Oh. Yeah. Silas. Name's Silas," the man said, helping Clay to his feet. He was still a little wobbly. "Sorry, sometimes I forget to introduce myself."

"Glad to meet you, Silas, I'm Clayton Maddau. Call me Clay."

"Did you say '*Maddau*?'" Silas asked, surprised.

"Yeah, Clay Maddau. Is that a problem? I mean, I'm not on any 'Wanted' posters in your local post office, am I?"

"No. No, uh, 'course not," Silas said, but he still seemed startled.

"...and no, the name 'Maddau' is not French, if that's what you're wonderin'," Clay said, "'Least as far as I know. Ow, my head. If 'Maddau' *is* French, it probably means 'someone who accepts rides from pimply punks in pickups.' Say that five times."

"That's too much of a tongue-twister for me this early in the day," Silas laughed, "I was just going to say *'Maddau' as in 'Maddau Acres'*?"

"Sorry. 'Maddau Acres'? I don't know what you're talking about," Clay said, rubbing his eyes.

"Maddau Acres. It's a gated community right up the river. Maddau ain't exactly a common name like Smith or Jones. French or not. 'Course Maddau Acres sounds a lot classier than Smith Acres."

"I ain't from here. In fact, I'm a long way from home," Clay said, brushing back his blonde hair and brushing the grass and dirt off his shirt.

"Where's home?"

"Illinois."

"Well, Illinois Clay, welcome south!"

"Thanks. Chicago Clay, to be more precise. But, uh, 'Chicago Clay' kinda sounds like something you'd find on the banks of Lake Michigan. So, 'Clay' will do. I gotta be honest, though—I can't exactly say that I have the greatest first impression of here. 'Course, now that I think about it, those yahoos in the truck weren't from here, either, so I really shouldn't hold that against Rubine."

"*Rubaville*," Silas said. "The river is the *Rubine*. Thas th' one you almost ended up in."

"I can swim."

"Prolly not so good when you's sleepin'."

"Yeah. Well, you have a point."

"Jus' simple logic, brother. So, Clay Maddau, when did you serve? How long you been out?"

"I didn't realize it shows."

"Been there, done that. Takes one to know one." Silas laughed, "Also, your duffle was a big clue."

"To answer your question, enough tours to have my fill of the military. I've been out a few years now."

"Welcome home, brother."

"Thanks."

"So. As I mentioned, how 'bout breakfast? Coffee, eggs, pancakes, maybe? You hungry?"

"Yessir, I could eat and that sounds pretty good. I'm sore, but that's never shut up my hunger before. I suppose I can still eat with a headache and sore ribs. I don't think anything's broke. Well, except for me. I'm pretty broke."

"Don't worry 'bout that. *I* invited *you*. In fact, a nice hot cup a joe may help your head feel better. Can't vouch for your ribs. Can you make it up the hill? My car's right up there."

"Sure. I've been in tougher scrapes."

"Somehow, Clay, I'm not surprised."

"Wow, you already got me figured out. In just a few minutes, even. I must be pretty transparent."

"Nope, not at all. Let's jus' say I been around awhile, and I've gotten to know a lot of people."

"Okay. I'll accept that. But I do have a question for you."

"Go for it."

"You obviously don't live or sleep under the bridge, so exactly *what* are you doing here, uh…"

"Silas."

"Right. What you doing here, Silas?"

"I came looking for you."

Clay stared at him quizzically.

"…or someone like you," Silas added.

"I see."

"Actually, I was intentionally drivin' by this morning. As I may have mentioned, I was on my way to Rubaville. This ain't the most direct way, but I do like the scenery. I'm especially partial to the river, specially this time-a year with the nuttall trees going all red on the banks. An' this road eventually catches up with the river and runs parallel with it most the way into Rubaville. This morning, once I went under the bridge, I saw Percy, and pulled over. I've been knowing Percy for several years now. Sometimes he takes me up on my offer of breakfast. Sometimes, he shines me on. Percy—you hungry?" Silas said, turning his attention to Percy. "We gonna get breakfast. You wanna come along?"

"'Preciate it, Sy, but I'm gonna pass," Percy said, smiling, "I better stay here and watch out for more superheroes flying off the bridge. Haw, haw, haw!"

Silas and Percy chuckled, but Clay was not amused.

"Oh, by the way. Are these your glasses?" Silas asked, holding up Clay's sunglasses, "I found these on the bank leading down to where you landed."

"Oh. Yeah. Thanks, man," Clay said, rubbing his head with one hand and putting on his sunglasses with the other.

"Yeah, I pulled my car over, and Percy says, 'Hey, Sy, check out that white boy—see if he's still breathing.' It's funny. You were obviously a white dude, because your hair blended right in with the weeds down there on the bank."

Clay squinted at the man to determine if he was making fun of him. If he was, Clay figured, it was untentional. *This guy is just painfully blunt,* Clay decided, *but that's not so bad; at least I know where I stand.*

As he and Silas climbed the hill up to Silas' Ford, Clay glanced back at the river below. It didn't appear to be all that deep or wide, but the interstate bridge spanning it was long and weathered. There was a row of rusted bolts lining the bridge—just under the overhang from the road—dripping copper-brown steaks of rust. Then, he noticed that it appeared as if two rivers merged together on the far side of the bridge. Actually, it was just a spit of land dividing the river—*an island in the stream.* On the other side of the river—beyond the *island*—there was a thick grove of trees on the bank and beyond. Silas was right—the red trees lining the branches were stunning. At the far end of the grove was a huge oak that towered above the rest of the trees. Above the giant oak, the sky was a brilliant blue with a myriad of clouds. Silas followed his gaze to the clouds.

"I love clouds like today...when they look like they're in some sort of art gallery," Silas said.

"Yeah, I was just lookin' at them," Clay said.

"I used to spend hours, jus' watchin' clouds," Silas continued, "Sometimes when I wuz 'sposed to be doing some sort of chore. Got me more than a few whuppins. But, I was always fascinated by the shapes as they turned into buildings or people or animals."

"I guess that one could be a tiger," Clay said pointing at a large puffy cloud just overhead, "Or a witch on a broom. I actually prefer a tiger—it matches my tattoo." Clay pulled up the sleeve of his khaki shirt to reveal the head of a snarling tiger on his left bicep.

"That just proves you're biased," Silas said, "...and you got tigers on the brain. And your arm."

"Yeah, well, this tiger is the permanent reminder of a bad decision rather than an obsession."

"How's that?"

"I had a crazy ex-girlfriend that was an LSU grad and fanatic."

"Guess you figured that out *after* you got the tattoo."

"The crazy part, yes."

"So, forget about tigers, then. That there cloud looks more like a lion to me. Look, see that clump is his mane and that wispy cloud is obviously a tail. You, my friend, picked the wrong jungle animal."

"Okay. Lion it is. Scissors cut paper, rock beats scissors, lion beats tiger. Never argue with someone who's promised to feed you."

Silas laughed, "Good philosophy, after all, the lion is the king of the jungle, but with that bein' said, I ain't gonna be the one feedin' you; I'm jus' takin' you to where the food is."

CHAPTER 5
WILD ANIMALS

On the other side of the river, on a sweltering hot summer afternoon many years before the interstate was even a concept, beyond the same grove of trees, Neemy stared at a similar lion-cloud floating over the huge oak. The boy cupped his hands around the old tarnished dipper and tilted his head up, letting the cool water roll over his lips and down his parched throat. The Carolina sun was pulsing with the afternoon heat as the passing clouds above painted a patchwork quilt of shadows on the lawn beside the plantation's big house. The pump was on the south side of the house, a couple of dozen feet from the wrap-around front porch, in the cool, inviting shade of a century-old oak tree. Although the boy knew that the pump was off limits, and it would not be wise to be seen deviating from the trajectory of his assigned task, the hot July sun and the overhead cluster of clouds slowed him long enough for him to be distracted by the thought of the relief that a refreshing drink of water could bring. Besides, there didn't seem to be anyone around, or at least certainly not anyone who could chastise him for stealing a cool drink of water.

The clouds appeared to be rising out of the distant line of trees, beyond which was the river. It was not visible from the house, but the sound of its current rushing over the large stones in its center was a constant, if faint, reminder of its presence.

"Look at 'em clouds," he said silently to himself, "They's look like a passel-a wild an-mals done 'scaped from they's home. Lions and el-fants. They be lookin' down at the river. They thirsty, like me."

Neemy had actually never seen any of wild animals that he perceived the clouds to be imitating, but they had been described in detail by his Uncle Jobe, in many a late-night story session. Jobe was the older brother of Neemy's father, Gabe. And, although Gabe and Jobe had grown up together, working that same plantation, Jobe had been "loaned out" to the owner's uncle, who was a ringmaster in a traveling circus, and he spent some of his early adult life traveling the country. Jobe's days with the circus had left him with an equal number of tales and scars, as well as a significant limp. The latter was the result of a near-fatal accident that had ended his days with the circus and had landed him back in the fields with his brother and his brother's family. It also left him with a well-worn wooden cane with a lion's head skillfully carved into it, the parting gift of one of his fellow circus workers.

Uncle Jobe's stories had both thrilled and terrified Neemy, and he was never sure what was truth and what was the truth stretched. But, he and his older brother, Jonathan, never tired of their uncle's description of the wild lions and tigers that would "tear up a man from *hair t' toe*," and the massive elephants that had "curved teef, big as a hoss and red, red eyes the size-a wagon wheels, blowing steam and water out they long noses."

"Whoo whee, Unka-Jobee," Neemy would squeal, "Tell us! Tell us!"

"They's el-fants, they's tigers, they's leperds. They's all wild wild animals," Uncle Jobe would say with wide eyes, "They'd jus' as soon eat you up as look a-chu, boys! Yassuh, theys carry dem silver fork 'n' knife and theys put you on they's tiger table back in they's cave. Then theys come rite back for some pie!"

"Pie?" Neemy would always ask, because the answer always changed, "What kinda pie, Unka-Jobee?"

"*'Nother Boy* pie! Haw haw haw!"

"Your leg hurt, boy?" Neemy's father would then ask.

"No, Pa, why?" Neemy would ask, even though he knew the answer.

"'Cause your Uncle Jobe be pullin' it mos' ferocious!"

Looking up at the clouds, he could almost hear Uncle Jobe describing them, and he felt a rush of excitement. The boy watched with fascination as the afternoon sky turned itself into a deep blue jungle with the big cats, giant elephants and hissing snakes swimming over his head, and morphing into even stranger and more wonderfully terrible white, puffy animals.

"They's lookin' for pie," he said to himself, laughing at the thought.

As he shaded his eyes and squinted dreamily at the clouds, his reverie was suddenly shattered by the sharp crash of one of the hand-thrown flower pots on the front porch. Dropping the dipper, he spun around to see the young son of the plantation owner, Jack, on the front porch steps with an identical look of surprise on his pale face. He brushed his blonde hair out of his pale blue eyes as he leveled his gaze at Neemy.

Although Neemy was startled, he marveled briefly at the strewn pieces of the former pot as they glittered in the afternoon sun like tiny jewels. He could even make out the scattered remnants of wavy red lines that had snaked around the pot before its destruction. However, before either boy could speak, there followed the mistakable sound of Charles Maddau's boots on the boards of the front porch. He had come around the corner on the opposite end of the house carrying a heavy wooden box, which he let drop to the ground as he approached his son. He was a big man with an imposing presence, even when he wasn't angry. His blonde hair had long since gone grey, and he wore the work clothes of a wealthy farmer; the sort of clothes that would be considered fancy by a man of lesser means.

"What did you do now, Jack?" he scowled in a booming, irritated voice, standing over the broken pieces and scattered plants on the front steps and pushing his hair out of his eyes and off his sweaty forehead.

"Never mind. I see what you've done. You done broke one of your mama's pots and most likely ruint these flowers."

Jack pointed at Neemy, who still stood by the pump, big-eyed and frozen like a cornered animal.

"You best take it up with the boy," he said, "I came out the house when I heard it knocked over."

Neemy still stood frozen motionless by the pump. He was amazed at the ease at which Jack could lie, but his amazement quickly turned to fear when Maddau jumped down beside him and began shaking and smacking him back into reality. Grabbing the boy by his dirty collar, he dragged him away from the pump like a limp doll as Jack watched with no expression from the porch.

From the front room inside the house, Elizabeth watched with dismay through a cracked pane in a corner window. "It was just an old pot," she whispered to herself.

"You know you're not supposed to be here, boy," Maddau said, "Where you supposed to be?"

"Fetchin' a sack-a seed," Neemy said. Although he was determined not to shed any tears, he also knew that being stoic would only worsen the situation.

Maddau dragged the boy across the side yard, beside the large house, from the front lawn to the back yard. With one hand clutching the boy's shirt, he began pulling his own belt off, but before he could strike the boy with the belt, he heard a loud tapping from a window in the house. When he looked up, he saw Elizabeth in the window. She was slowly shaking her head, "no." Maddau sighed. He hated to yield to his wife in front of the boy and Jack, who still watched from the porch, but he also didn't want to endure the days of silence from his wife that he knew he would suffer if he continued. So, in compromise, he shoved the boy in the direction of the barn, which lay just beyond his wife's make-shift pottery shed, to the rear of the big house. Stumbling, Neemy instinctively knew that if he let himself fall, it would most likely satisfy Maddau. "You better hurry, boy," Maddau said, standing over the boy, "Or Mister Palmer will give you a real what-for when you get back to the field for being too slow. And, Mistress Elizabeth won't be around to save you, then."

As Maddau turned to go toward the fields, he glanced up at the house to see if Elizabeth was still behind the window. He felt gratified to see her slight smile as she looked beyond him at Neemy. She watched as the boy passed her pottery shed and proceeded on up to the barn and hurried inside. A few minutes later, she waited for him to reappear, and as he did, he was carrying two large burlap bags in each fist. She watched the boy's progress as he traversed the large front lawn and through the main gates, disappearing through the trees and over the rise to the waiting fields beyond.

CHAPTER 6
VESSELS

The morning brought a welcome rain. As the sun came up, the drops started, initially big and scattered, kicking up puffs of dust as they hit the dry soil. Within minutes, the downpour turned the sky into a dense metallic grey, but by mid-morning, it had calmed to a gentle summer mist. The rain had cooled the inside of the pottery shed as Elizabeth began to shape the pot on the wheel. She was wearing her apron over a floral-print, cotton dress that she used as her work clothes; like her husband's attire, it would have been considered fancy by most of the women in town. Her red apron was splattered with old and new splotches of clay.

Also, like her husband, her dark hair had strands of gray, but on her, they offered a rich, textured effect. Her eyes were pale blue, the color of an early summer sunshiny morning sky, with flecks of gold that were only visable by close inspection. With the exception of some laugh lines at their edges, her light blue eyes had changed little in the last 20 years. Her dark hair and pale eyes were complemented by a rosy complexion that had also changed little from the days of her girlhood. In fact, by most accounts, she would be considered an attractive woman. The truth is, in her youth, she had been considered to be stunningly beautiful by everyone who came into her presence. She also had had a wide range of suitors, and her eventual choice of Charles Maddau as the one to marry seemed suitable by most and even a perfect match by others. However, those who knew her best questioned her choice, as she, herself, would one day do.

That morning as she focused on the spinning pot, out of the corner of her eye, she saw movement, and when she looked up, she was startled to see Neemy standing silently in the doorway.

"Massa Palmer say you sen' fer me," he said quietly.

"As a matter of fact, I did," Elizabeth said, letting the wheel slow on its own and wiping her hands on a cotton towel. For a brief moment, she sized up the boy. She guessed his age to be 11 or 12. He was small and wiry, but about the right size for that age. His hair was cut short and his skin was the color of rich molasses and butter. His eyes were bright and inquisitive, and he looked as if he would break into a smile at any moment, were he not apprehensive about being summoned to the workshop.

"I could use an extra hand in here, and it *is* raining, so I hoped you could help," Elizabeth said.

"Yassum."

"First of all, I'm Miz Elizabeth, and you are—" she said, waiting patiently for the boy to respond.

"They's call me Neemy."

"Hmmm. Neemy. That's a real nice name, but something tells me that's not your given name, Neemy. It sounds more like a nickname. What's your real name? Your birth name?"

Neemy hesitated before speaking. "Nehemiah, ma'am," he finally said, shyly.

"Ah," she said, "That's a name from the Bible."

"Yassum."

"Your people must be godly people."

"Yassum."

"Your mama is—Belle, right?"

"Yassum," Neemy answered, surprised that Elizabeth knew his mother's name.

"Bring me that towel and that jar of water and sit over here by me on the bench."

The boy obediently brought the jar to Elizabeth, and she wet her hands and started kicking the wheel up again as he settled in beside her at a respectible distance on the bench.

"Did Mr. Palmer tell you why I asked for you, Nehemiah?"

"No'm. He jus' says come over here."

"I need a helper, Nehemiah," she said, "Do you think you could help me?"

Neemy looked at her and then at the door and then back at her blinking and hesitating as if it were a trick question.

"Yassum, if theys say so," he said.

"Do you know what I do in here? In my shed?"

"They's look like pots, ma'am."

"That's right. And do you know how pottery is made?"

The boy thought a minute and then realized he'd never really wondered about where things like bowls and spoons and forks and buckets and lamps and wagons came from; they always seemed to be there when the folks in the big house needed them. It was a ponderous moment for the young boy.

"No'm," he finally said.

"I'm making a new flowerpot right now...on this wheel," she said, before he could answer. "Mr. Klein, over at the general store in town, has been selling some of my pottery. In fact, he's asked me if I could make even more than I have been; he says they sell as soon as he puts them on the shelf."

The boy stared at her, blinking. "Yassum," he said.

"Look over there, beside the door," Elizabeth said, "See that pot? That's what this one will look like, once I've finished shaping it on the wheel here. And, of course, once I've added my design and glazed it and fired it."

Neemy stared at the pot beside the door. It was beautiful, but a tinge of discomfort came over him as he recognized the interwined wavy red lines that circled the center of the vessel and remembered seeing the same design in pieces at his feet, glittering in the sun, right before the master dragged him away from the pump.

"But frankly, Nehemiah, I'm going to have to have some help," Elizabeth finally said as he stared at the pot, "I need you to help me."

"Yassum. Um—"

"Yes?" Elizabeth asked smiling.

"Waz dose snaky lines?"

"Oh. You mean this line?"

"Dose two snaky lines," Neemy repeated.

"That's what distinguishes my pottery," Elizabeth said, "This red thread. It's my mark. My brand. You know how Mr. Maddau puts a mark on his cattle?"

"Yassum."

"This is my mark. My brand. This red thread."

Neemy looked confused. "Dere's ***two*** snaky lines," he said, finally, scratching his head.

Elizabeth laughed and wiped off her hands as she stopped the wheel. She leaned over and took a finished pot off the shelf. "Do you mean this thread?" she asked.

"Yassum. Two lines. Crossin' over each other like fightin' snakes."

Elizabeth smiled and shivered. "Well, I've certainly never thought of it as…*snakes*! Here, take this pot and put your finger on the red thread."

"Which un?"

Elizabeth laughed again and pointed to the shelf behind Neemy. "Either one," she said, "Look over there on that shelf and grab that slate pencil."

Neemy followed the direction of her pointing finger and picked up the solitary pencil on the shelf. "Put the point of the pencil on one of the red threads and follow it around the pot. Draw a pencil line on top of the red line," she said. The boy sat down on the ground and slowly followed one of the red threads around the pot as instructed. As he slowly turned the pot, tracing the thread, his pencil crossed over the starting point that he had initially made.

"Keep going, Neemy," Elizabeth said.

Once the boy turned the pot for the second time, to his surprise his pencil stopped at the point where he had started. He looked up, eyes wide, mouth open. "How you do that?" he asked.

"See! It's just one thread!" Elizabeth said.

"It's lack magic," Neemy said.

"No, it's not magic," Elizabeth said, smiling and trying not to laugh at the boy's wide-eyed wonder. "It's just a, well, special kind of wavy line. A rubine red thread." She then turned back to the wheel and kicked it up to a fast spin. Then, she leaned over the spinning pot and deftly shaped it as it spun.

"You know," she said, "Nehemiah, *with a biblical name,* there's pottery mentioned all through the Bible, from Genesis all the way through to Revelation."

"Yassum," the boy said, but he was still looking at the red thread circling around the pot in his hands.

"Do you know the Bible?"

"Yassum," Neemy said, putting down the pot.

"What do you know about the Bible, Nehemiah?"

"I know God and Jesus and Moses and Abraham and Noah and Jonah and David..."

"All the famous Israelites, right?"

"Ma'am?"

"Israelites. Children of Israel. Do you know about Israel?"

"Ma'am?"

"Israel was a country, like America, only they were a people...like a tribe of people. United people."

"Where's Is-rel?" the boy asked.

"Sadly, Israel is gone...at least for the time being."

"Did Is-rels have pots like dis?"

"Yes, they did, but they used them for many things, not just flowers. They used them for water, and wine, and grain and oils of all kinds. They had all sorts of vessels."

"Fessels?"

"Vessels. Va, va, va, vessels. It's just an old-timey, fancy catch-all name for vases, cups, bowls, pots."

"Did da Bible Ne-miah have fessels like dat?" Neemy asked, pointed at the glimmering pot beside the door.

"That's a good question," Elizabeth said, looking up and slowing down the wheel, "I'm sure he did. Do you know about Nehemiah, Neemy?"

"He wuz a Is-rel chile?"

"That's right." Elizabeth knew that he wasn't allowed to learn to read, so she caught herself before she asked the boy if he had ever read about Nehemiah. Instead, she took her hands off the spinning pot and wiped them again on her apron as she pushed away from the wheel, which gradually slowed to a stop. Brushing off her apron, she reached up to the top shelf on the shed's back wall and pulled out a spattered cloth which had covered a large Bible. The Bible had a well-worn, black leather cover, which had been speckled with bits of clay that had escaped—both in a fine mist and as a light splattering—from the various pots that Elizabeth had shaped on the potter's wheel over the years, before she learned to cover it with the cloth. There was an engraved golden cross on the cover above Old English lettering that spelled out "Holy Bible." The light speckling of clay gave the black leather cover an appearance of a misting of snow on a dark winter night.

"This is my 'Shed Bible,'" she said, sitting down beside the boy on the old bench. She thumbed through the worn pages—some were torn and some had corners missing, and there were detailed engravings depicting Bible stories. The intricate illustrations were mixed in with the various books, chapters and verses, and Elizabeth paused at a few, so Neemy could study them. He had never seen anything like them, but he knew some of the stories that they chronicled; he had heard them from his parents, his Uncle Jobe and at the secret "church meetings" that he had grown up attending, mostly in the dead of night.

"Do you know the story of David and Goliath?" Elizabeth asked, "The shepherd boy and the giant?"

"Yassum."

"Here's a picture of that." Elizabeth said, pointing to the picture.

The engraving depicted a young boy standing over the fallen giant with a large sword. The contrast between the two couldn't be more drastic. Although the boy held the sword over his head, ready to slash the giant, he was dressed as if he had just wandered out of the field after tending a flock of sheep, while the giant, who lay at his feet, was girded by armor from head to foot, all gleaming in the sun. The artist had used dozens, if not hundreds, of intricate lines to fully convey the expressions on their faces—David looked confident and the giant looked wide-eyed and stunned with a darkened indentation in the center of his huge forehead. Neemy stared intently at the illustration and shivered.

"Glad dat wadden me," he said with a slight smile.

Elizabeth continued slowly thumbing through the yellowed pages until she came to the book of Nehemiah. "Here's where it talks about Nehemiah—the *Bible* Nehemiah."

"Dere a pitcher o' th' Bible Ne-miah?" Neemy asked, excitedly.

"I don't think so, Neemy," Elizabeth said, and noticing the boy's obvious disappointment, she added, "If it's any consolation, even if there *was* a picture depicting him, that's all it would be—*an artist's depiction.*"

Seeing that her explanation didn't remove Neemy's frown, she continued, "Look, see these pictures of Moses, and Abraham, and Daniel, and even Jesus? The artist that created these engravings—he wasn't alive to actually see what they looked like. He just used his imagination to create the scenes."

"Why day in th' Bible if dat ain't dim?" Neemy asked, still disappointed.

"It's just an interpretation, Neemy, like the Bible, itself. Do you believe that the Bible tells us what Jesus said?"

"Yassum.'Course."

"But Neemy, Jesus didn't speak English. There wasn't an America when Jesus walked the earth."

Neemy looked even more confused, so Elizabeth continued, "It's the same thing, Neemy. Just as these pictures are interpretations of what Moses, and David, and Daniel and Jesus looked like, these English words are educated interpretations of the words of Moses and David and Daniel, and even Nehemiah." She could see by the boy's changing expression that he was beginning to understand. "Just as there were no cameras to take the pictures of these Biblical figures, there were no English-speaking scribes to write down the words of Jesus—they were born much later. What's important is the *meaning* of the words and pictures and how they reach our hearts.

"For example, talking about Nehemiah. He lived hundreds and hundreds of years ago. Even many years before Jesus was born. And he was an important man in the Bible."

"Not as 'portant as Jesus."

"No, you're right, but he was still important. Nehemiah was a servant to a powerful king," she said.

"Servant?" the boy asked.

"Yes. He worked for the king."

"*Slave,*" the boy said, the significance of the Nehemiah name dawning on him.

Elizabeth saw the boy's expression change and quickly added, "He was the king's cup bearer. The king loved him. And trusted him."

Neemy seemed impressed. He smiled, but still seemed puzzled. "Whut's a cup bear?" he asked.

"Well, the king was very important. Very powerful. And with power, comes enemies. So, there were always evil people who wanted to kill the king."

"Did Ne-miah keep da king safe?"

"As a matter of fact, yes. You asked if Nehemiah had vessels. I'm sure he did, since he was the king's cup bearer. Nehemiah would taste the king's drink before the king drank...just to make sure there was no poison in the drink."

A cloud came over Neemy's face. *So da slave die,'stead the king*, he thought, *that's about right.*

"Nehemiah was a great man," Elizabeth continued. "His job was highly prized and very important to the king's empire. Look here, in my Bible."

She pointed to the faded words on the old torn page, moving her finger along each line, "Look, here's what it says: *'And it came to pass in the month Nisan, in the twentieth year of Artaxerxes the king, that wine was before him: and I took up the wine, and gave it unto the king…'*"

"Don't say nuthin' 'bout no Ne-miah havin' or makin' any pots," the boy said, arms crossed.

"Well, Nehemiah, you are correct about that," Elizabeth said, smiling, "But sometimes you have to read between the lines."

"Ma'am?"

"I mean, somehow, I don't believe that anyone would dare serve an important and powerful king any sort of drink out of their bare hands!"

Elizabeth watched as Neemy seemed to ponder this image and paint it in his imagination, and she smiled as the boy bent over double with infectious laughter.

CHAPTER 7
HAPPY DAY

When Neemy stuck his head into the doorway of the cabin, his mother, Belle was standing by the cookstove, wooden spoon in hand with a part-relieved, part-angry look on her face. Even after the bearing of children and the decades of hard work in the fields, the wrinkles of anger in her forehead still couldn't completely erase her beauty. She was slightly more rounded than she had been in her teens and early 20s, but the spark in her soft brown eyes was still there when she laughed or when she was irritated at her children or husband.

Both boys had inherited Belle's soft brown eyes, but beyond that, the differences between the two were obvious. Neemy's quick smile was constantly on his molasses-colored face; Jonathan's darker face often reflected his mood; it was as if there was always an oncoming storm brewing.

"Lawdy, whar you been, chile?" she asked when Neemy entered the cabin, "And don gimme none yo stories."

"Uppa da big house. With Miz 'Lizbeth." Neemy said, sheepishly.

Neemy's older brother, Jonathan stood by their mother at the stove. He looked up at their mother and then, back at Neemy. "Whoo whee, boy! Wuz you da guest-a honor at their big ol' dinner table? Howja like all that ham and cake?" he sneered.

"I din say 'in'…I say 'at,'" Neemy said, defensively, "Heppin' Miz 'Lizbeth widder pots."

"Pots?!" Belle asked, wiping her hands on her apron.

"Pots an' fessels," Neemy said.

"Pots?" Belle repeated, suddenly concerned, "Did Palmer know 'bout this? He'll skin you alive, chile!"

"Palmer know. He done tole me go up dere."

"Is they chocklit cake they gib you at da big house?" Jonathan asked. He was irritated that his younger brother had gotten attention from both his mother and the owners in the big house.

"Hush up," Belle said, with a sidelong look at Jonathan. As unbelievable as the story sounded, she knew that Neemy, although usually creative, was not creative or brave enough to conjure up that big of a tale.

"You say *pots*?" she asked again.

"Yassum," Neemy answered, "She makes da pots…like in da Bible. She knows 'bout my Bible name. *Ne-hem-iah*. The Bible Ne-miah wuzza servant…a *slave*. He wuz the wine taster fo' th' king!" He looked carefully at his mother's face to gauge her reaction.

"That ain't why you named that," she said, guessing his next question.

"You ain't no wine-taster," Jonathan said, laughing, "You named dat 'cause you da fool."

Whap! Belle brought the wooden spoon down on Jonathan's shoulder. "I already tole you hush," she said. She turned to Gabe, the boys' father, who had been silently observing the conversation from his rickety chair in the corner of the cabin. "You hearin' dis?" she asked. The man nodded slowly, but didn't comment. He wasn't sure he wanted to get involved.

"Gabe?" she said, "Whutju think?"

Gabe sighed. "I think white folk is gwine be white folk," he said, "Thet's all it ever gwine be. But. I would speculate pot-makin' be better'n sweatin' in the hot sun all day."

"She gotta big Bible in her pot shack," Neemy said, trying to sway the direction of the conversation. "She show me 'bout the Bible Ne-miah."

"Da slave," said Jonathan, scooting away from the reach of his mother's wooden spoon.

"Das right," said Neemy, pausing to choose his words, "But he's a 'potant man. Not jussa slave. He change hiss-ta-ree. Miz Lizbeth show me th' words."

"You can't read, Mr. Wine Taster," said Jonathan.

Belle started to say something, but caught herself. "So whutju do widda pots?" she asked.

"I hep Miz Lizbeth make 'em."

"Hmm. That is curious. You gwine back? This be yo' job now?"

"Yassum," Neemy said, shooting a glance at his brother, "Miz Lizbeth say fo' me to come when all she need me. She say th' man in town buyin' her pots. She's gwine learn me how to pot-make."

"Well. That's fine," Belle said. She knelt down and took Neemy's shoulders in her hands and shot a quick glance at Gabe. "Jus lissen, son. You always, always, always be on ya bes behaver. Don git to thinkin' you sumpen you not. 'Member who you is. I don know Miz Lizbeth that much, an' I ain't ever been in her house, but I knows white folk, an' I know they's can turn quick as a wink. An' den, watch out. Don git to thinkin' you sumpen you not."

"Yassum," Neemy said.

"Lawdy, I near burnt our supper!" Belle said, wiping her eye and quickly turning back to the stove to stir the bubbling and hissing stew. "You boys go outside and wash up."

Once outside, Jonathan raced ahead of Neemy, but quickly stopped with his leg out to trip the younger boy, who sprawled into a muddy patch a few dozen yards from the cabin.

"Well, would you lookee dere," he laughed, "Dere's one mo' 'potant slave wid a suit-a mud. An' all trimmed wid grass 'n' pebbles! Good thang you ain't carryin' no fessels fo' de king. They be breakin' all over yo' fool haid! You be spillin' th' king's wine all over th' place! Fo' you gits to taste it, even. Th' king be taken a stick to you, boy! Haw, haw, haw!" Jonathan bent over double, laughing. "Yassah, you be spillin' th' king's wine all over th' place fo' you gits to taste it!"

Neemy stood up, brushing himself off. Even though both of his knees were bleeding from his fall, his brother's laugh was infectious, and he found himself laughing along with his brother, who was making his way down toward the pump. "You's right, Jonathan," he called after him, "Dat iz a funny sight. Dat ol' king's 'potant slave be wearin' a suit-a mud. Glad to make you laugh," Neemy called, cupping his hands to his mouth, "Dis a happy day fo' ever-body and ever-body needs a happy day!"

Neemy craned his neck and listened to his brother's peels of laughter as the last rays of the sun sunk behind the big oak trees and the gentle hills.

"Yassuh, dis is a happy day!"

CHAPTER 8
A DIME A POT

"What exactly are you doing with that boy?" Charles Maddau was sitting in the shadows of the house's parlor, smoking a clay pipe when Elizabeth came in. She didn't immediately answer, but as she untied her clay-covered apron, she waited for the next question that, knowing her husband, she knew would follow.

"You ain't teaching him letters, or anything foolish like that, are you?"

Elizabeth sighed, "I needed someone to help me with the pots, Charles, and Jack clearly wasn't interested."

"I can make Jack be interested, if that's what you want."

"Actually, that's *not* what I want. If Jack's not interested, then he'll be more of a hindrance than a help. I think Nehemiah has the interest and the ability to be a real help."

"Hunh," Charles grunted, "Nehemiah, is it? Palmer told me about that boy. In fact, that's how I knew you had him there in the shed with you. He made a special point about telling me this afternoon."

"What did Mr. Palmer say?"

"He said all that boy's good for is fetching and delivering. They won't miss him in the fields. Or fetchin' a bag o' seed. You remember. I caught him drinking out of the side yard pump in the middle of the afternoon when he was supposed to be working. Just staring up at the sky and breaking your pots. I don't know whether to be irritated or glad that you found a place for him. I just hope he don't look at it as a reward." Charles brought it up to subtly remind her that he had honored her wishes by letting the boy go. However, if Elizabeth understood his intent, she chose to ignore it.

"Oh, Charles, that was just a silly ol' pot," she said with a frown. "Totally replaceable. I'm sure it was just an accident."

"We can't be having accidents like that to destroy our home and grounds. Next thing you know they'll be knockin' over a fence or 'accidentally' settin' the barn on fire."

Elizabeth sighed. "But there's a bigger issue here," she said, "An opportunity."

"Opportunity?" Charles said, curiously. He put down his pipe and brushed a lock of graying blonde hair out of his eyes. "This I gotta hear. What sort of opportunity could there be with you and this boy?"

"Well, as it turns out, I had a long talk with Mr. Klein over in town last week."

"Klein?! That little four-eyed, bald-headed Jew?! That's as bad as dealin' with free Negroes!"

"Mr. Klein is a good and decent man. And, he loves my pots. He appreciates them. He's always complimented me on their artistry. And, in fact, he's been selling them for quite a while. Actually, they've sold, and fairly quickly. But now he wants even more of my pottery to sell. He says they fly off the shelf."

"I'll tell you for sure—they don't fly," Charles said, smirking, "They crash into pieces when they fall. Your boy proved that the other day up on the front porch. I guess Klein just hadn't dropped one, yet. When he does, he'll see that they definitely don't fly."

"He's paying me a dime a pot," Elizabeth said evenly.

"A dime a pot?" Charles said, surprised and mouth open, "You're separating Klein from his coins? Now that *is* something. That's the same kind of money we get for our cotton. And our cattle. You sure you heard him right?"

"Wait here," Elizabeth said. She went up the stairs and returned with a floral carpetbag. She flipped it upside down on the dining room table, and pennies mixed with dimes and nickels gushed out like water from an overturned pot.

"Well, now," Charles said, reluctantly, "I guess I can't really argue with cold, hard cash. Let's see how that boy does…and if he really can help you. But you better keep an eye on those coins. And also, you make sure that Klein pays you for ever single pot. It would be just like him to 'forget' to pay for a pot or two."

"There hasn't been a problem, Charles," Elizabeth said, evenly.

"Hmmm," Charles said, relighting his pipe, "You just keep your eye on him…and that boy."

Elizabeth refilled the carpetbag with the coins and returned it upstairs to her closet, where it stayed. Once she returned downstairs, she headed into the kitchen to start their dinner. She lit the fire in the cook stove and pumped water into a large tin pot with a red wooden handle. She retrieved a jar of tomatoes that she had put up earlier in the season and dumped the contents into the tin pot. As it began to boil, she added onions, carrots and a few other vegetables she had picked out of her garden and began to stir it all into a soup.

Charles went out on the front porch and watched as the setting sun painted long dark shadows on the massive front lawn. There was a hawk flying in low circles around the giant oak tree. *Funny how life works*, he thought, as the hawk's circles tightened around the tree. *There's a squirrel somewhere in that tree enjoying his supper, totally unaware that he's about to be supper, himself.*

Charles possessed a no-nonsense disposition, and he wasn't totally convinced that his wife had made a wise decision when she had taken the boy under her wing. Had it not been for the coins spilling out onto the table, he would have told Palmer to rescind the assignment; maybe not immediately, but definitely before the end of the summer, when the harvest was at hand. But, as he had told Elizabeth, you can't argue with success.

As for his son, Jack, the older the boy had gotten, the more of a disappointment he had become. The house and fields had been in Charles' family for more than a few generations, and he was afraid that

Jack wouldn't have the smarts or enough ambition to take over for him, once he was too old to deal with the day-to-day operations of the farm. *Oh, well,* he thought, *there's time to figure that out.*

The crickets and frogs from the river's bank joined together in a meadowland symphony as the Carolina sun set behind the trees in colors of dark orange and green. Taking a deep draw on his pipe, Charles leaned his chair back on two legs to take in the scene, and at the same time, he breathed in the fragrances of the early summer evening. The thick and delicious aroma of Elizabeth's soup had already wafted across the house and through the front screen door. When it reached Charles, he closed his eyes and smiled as it swirled and blended in with the pungent smells of the smoke from his pipe and the twilight in the nearby field.

CHAPTER 9

TALES OF THE BIG TOP

Although it was early evening when Jonathan and Neemy made their way from the fields back to their cabin, the sun was still high enough above the horizon to cast long shadows across their path. Elizabeth had spent the day nursing a sick neighbor, so after a week or so of working with her in the pottery shed, Palmer had returned Neemy to his role as a field hand for the day.

When they reached the cabin, the door was closed, but Belle was not inside. The boys figured it would be a while before Gabe would be home—rarely did he make it home in the daylight—but they were surprised that their mother wasn't there. Even more surprising was the apple pie—*still cooling*—on the sill of the kitchen window.

"'Least ma left us apple pie for supper," Jonathan said.

"I don'ts recall her sayin' nuthin' 'bout no pie for supper," Neemy said.

"Then you ain't hungry as me. No s'prise. You don't works hard as me. You in the big house half the time, anyway."

"You don'ts have to be hungry to want that pie," Neemy said, "Jus' smellin' it's like eatin' a big ol' slice. I could have five ham dinners in a row and still wanta piece o' dat pie. I's jus' sayin' Mama din say nothin' 'bout us havin' pie t'night."

"Maybe she wants to s'prise us! Whoo whee! Still warm!" Jonathan said, poking the pie and cutting a slice using his pudgy finger as a makeshift knife. He pulled up a chair at the table beside Neemy and let the pie slide down his throat. "Whoo-whee!" he said, repeating the process, "I gwine have a nuther!"

Neemy had a bad feeling about the pie, and he was glad that Jonathan had not cut him a piece of his own, because he knew he wouldn't have been able to resist. It was then he heard someone on the path outside and recognized his mother's voice.

"Thanky fo' th sugar, Flor! I will tell you what the preacher sez," he heard Belle say as the door latch lifted. Behind her, just outside the cabin, the boys could see Belle's friend, Flora heading back down the path to her own cabin.

"Oh, good, boys, y'all home," Belle said, but just as quickly, her eyes darted over to the window sill.

"Tell me y'all didn't get into that apple pie!" she said, even though she instinctively knew before examining the evidence. She paused at the window, her back to the boys.

"That pie was for th' preacher," she said, slowly fumbling on the counter for a large wooden spoon, "What would make you boys do such a thing? That's the same as stealin'. Actually, it's wust than stealin' 'cause it was fo' de preacher!"

Jonathan was wide-eyed and frozen, but Neemy stood up as she angrily made her way over to the table, wooden spoon in hand.

"My fault," Neemy said.

Jonathan's look of fear turned into one of astonishment, as their mother dragged Neemy from the table, whapping him with the spoon.

"An' that's just for starts 'til your pa gits home," she said, finally, releasing him after one more solid slap to the side of his head from her open hand.

"Now I gots to go git more sugar from Flor," she said, storming out the front door and heading down the path to catch up with her friend.

"Why'd you do that for, fool?" Jonathan asked as Belle was safely out of the cabin. "I gits the pie an' you gits the beatin'," he laughed. "You sure sumpin'."

"Thing is," Neemy said, wiping his eyes, "I don't even know why I said nuthin. 'Sides, I didn't tell Mama I et it; I jist sez iz my fault."

"How you figger dat? How it yo' fault if you don'ts eats it?"

"I figger I shouldn't-a not tol' you how good it wuz gonna taste, an' I shoulda been better at talkin' you out of eatin' it."

"Fool!" Jonathan laughed even harder at the irony.

"Or maybe it's 'cause I's more used to whuppings than you is. It's almost quit hurtin,' anyway."

"Wait 'til Pa gits home. That oughta start the hurtin' all over. That is, if you don't tells on me."

"If I tells on you, I gits a whuppin' from Pa and a 'nother from Mama fo' not tellin' on you to b'gin with."

Then, suddenly, they heard Gabe's angry voice on the path outside the cabin. "*What?!* He et *what?! Preacher's pie?"* The two boys sat up straight at the sound of his voice.

"Jus' yo' luck. Pa early tonight," Jonathan said.

Gabe had met Belle on the path and had gotten the news. He burst through the door of the cabin and snatched Neemy by the collar, hoisting him off the ground by the scruff of his neck, not unlike a bad dog.

"What you thinkin' boy?" Gabe said, slapping the hapless Neemy with his other hand, still holding him up by his collar. "You thinks the whol' worl' owes you a pie? You thinks 'cause you heppin' Miz Lizbeth wi' her pots, you th' king o' th' pie eaters?"

"No suh!" Neemy said, trying to cover his face to ward off the blows. "I didn't know it wuz a preacher pie." Jonathan had slowly moved to the far end of the cabin, just in case his father took a notion to include him in on the punishment. He watched guiltily from the shadows.

"Well, maybe you'll learn to ask, next time!" Gabe said, still furious.

"Gabe, let loose-a dat boy!" It was Gabe's brother, Jobe, standing in the cabin door. Gabe had left the door wide open when he charged in.

"Whud he do?" Jobe asked, "Burn de cabin down?"

Gabe sputtered, but quit striking the boy. "If he burn th' cabin down, yo' wudden be standin' in it would you?"

"Did he poison th' well?" Jobe asked, smiling.

"Don't be givin' him any mo' ideas," Gabe said, still holding Neemy aloft, "He et the preacher's apple pie!"

"What?!!!" screamed Jobe in mock horror as he limped over to where Gabe stood and, putting his lion-head cane under his arm, grabbed the boy with both hands, jerking him out of Gabe's grasp. "No! Oh lawd, no, no, no! Not de preacher's apple pie! Iffen only he had jist burnt down de cabin! *Hold on, hold on. That boy's not de cabin-burner!* I recolleck dat was another boy dat done near burnt his cabin down once upon a time."

Gabe reluctantly smiled a sheepish grin and rubbed his chin. Jonathan and Neemy were looking at each other and at the men, trying to decide if it was okay to laugh.

"Itz a-comin' to me! Hol' on," Jobe said as he playfully shook Neemy in mock anger. "Wait! Wait," Jobe continued as he suddenly stopped pretend-shaking Neemy, "Nosuh, that weren't no Neemy that wuz-a firebug. It wuz my own lil' brudder, a-playin' wid-a candle! You boys ever hear dat story?"

"They don't needs no ideas 'volvin fire or candles," Gabe said.

"Or wells?" Jobe grinned.

"You did your own share of mischief, as I r'call," Gabe said.

Jobe pretended not to hear. "You boys ever made animals outta shadows?"

Jonathan and Neemy shook their heads. They were just glad the subject had been changed and there was good humor in the air. Gabe was also glad the subject was changed.

"Gimme dat candle," Jobe said, "Neemy, hol' dis candle right there."

As Neemy and Jonathan watched, Jobe created the shadows of flying birds and roaring animals. As the boys stared in delight and amazement, Jobe growled and cawed in tandem with his shadow creations.

Just then, Belle returned with the sugar and apples for the replacement pie. Seeing them laughing at Jobe's antics made her angry again.

"Would you jes' look a' this pie?" she asked.

"I heard all 'bout it, Belle, honey. Don't git me wrong, girl," Jobe said, "I loves the preacher as much as you. I helps him out as much as I can wi' his preachin' and his gittin' around, but he's gittin' on and he don't have much teeth left, so I don't think he'd mind sharin' this here pie with all us."

"You ol' fool," Belle said, "I ain't givin' the preacher a half-eaten apple pie!"

"Now yer talkin,' girl," Jobe said, "Jes take him a slice. We can take care o' the rest."

"No! It means I gots to start all over wi' a new pie!"

"Whoo-whee!" Jobe said, gleefully, "Thas even more fo' us!"

"Not fo' Neemy," Belle said, slicing the pie, "He sure ain't gonna git any good from his sin."

"Then I'll take his slice an' have it fo' breakfast," Jobe said, winking at Neemy.

As Jobe, Gabe, and Jonathan sat around the table finishing their pie, Neemy sat a few feet away, sitting backwards, leaning forward on the back of the chair. He loved his mother's pies, but he loved his uncle even more; just his presence took away the sting of his disappointment at being left out of the pie-fest.

"Unka-Jobee," Neemy said, "You got any stories t'nite to pull our legs?"

"What chu talkin' 'bout, boy?" Jobe said, smiling as he finished the last bite of his slice of Belle's disappearing pie. Belle wrapped up Neemy's forbidden piece of pie in a linen rag and put it down in front of Jobe.

"Gabe, light that stove fo' me," she said. When Gabe got up to light the stove, and with Belle's back turned, Jobe figured it was safe enough to slide the wrapped piece of pie into Neemy's overall pocket.

"So, Unka-Jobee?" Jonathan asked.

"Yas?"

"Youse gwine tell a story 'bout tigers and el-fants?"

"It's gittin' late, boys," Gabe said, "Unca Jobe don'ts haf time fo' pah-formin'."

"Hol' on, brother," Jobe said, "You don't know what I gots time fo' an' what I don't gots time fo'. I allus gots time fo' dese boys!" Then, turning to the boys, he asked, "Y'all know how I gots this leg?"

"God made it?" Neemy said, earnestly.

Jobe almost fell over laughing. "'Course, God made it! I means what happened to make it useless?"

"Tiger bit it?" Jonathan said.

"Whoo-ee, thas a good answer! How you know that, boy? Yassuh, you leaves the cage door jes unlocked, not even open. Ol' Bengal takes his big ol' paw and sticks it 'tween door an' cage, an', bang, he's out lik' lightnin'. He's lookin' here and there, 'cause he's hungry. Ol' Bengal wuz born hungry. Oo, dere goes th' lil' ol' poodle-dog wi' the girly dress, rite down his throat. One bite. Ol' poodle goes, 'Yip, yip, yip' all the da way down. Din Bengal spits out dat silly ol' girly dress."

"He eats da dog?" Neemy asked.

"Bye, Mr. Poodle," Jobe says, continuing, "Then he see the slippery seal. Oh, I loves the ol' seal. He ain't never hurts nobody. He jes' goes his own way, bouncin' his ball on his nose. Such a gentle critter. I loves the 'ol seal. But dat ol' Bengal, he luvs 'em even more. I sees de ol' seal as a gentle critter dat likes to balance his big ol' ball on 'is nose, but ol' Bengal sees him as a fine steak dinner."

"Whut does da seal do?"

"Wal, he looks 'round fur help, but they ain't none. He's a water critter, so's he cants run so fast o'er da land."

"So, the tiger gits 'em?"

"Yassuh. Seal steak for Mr. Bengal."

"So, din, did he bite yer laig?"

"Wal, he wuz lookin' at it, an' lickin' his lips, but din, he sees th' poison cobra snake, and-e makes a bee-line o'er to him. Dat ol' poison cobra snake is wrapped down in da basket, waitin' fo' de charmer to musicate 'em out. But dat ol' Bengal thinks he dun beat de charmer to da snake. So he pounces on they baskit and he grabs that ol' snake wi' his big ol' paw and slaps it in his mouth, purty as you please. An' din, dere goes th' poison cobra snake rite down th' tiger's throat, wigglin' lik a big ol' worm. Oo—"

"But, Unka-Jobee," Neemy asked, "Wooden da poison cobra snake kilt the tiger wi' 'is poison? Wooden he bite the ol' tiger inside his mouth?" Neemy shivered at the thought.

Jobe sighed. "Yessuh, Neemy. You is true. An' thas 'zactly whut happened! The ol' poison cobra snake sings hiz big ol' teefs down on th' inside of the ol' Bengal's throat."

"Whut happen din?"

"Wal. The ol' Bengal's eyes get really big…lik dis!" Jobe opened his eyes as wide as they would go and leans menacingly toward the boys. "An' din, he grabs his throat wid both his big ol' paws…lik dis!" Jobe grabbed his throat with both hands. "Din, he coughs, hack, hack, hack! An' din' he spits out dat ol' poison cobra snake. Ptu! Ptu! But it's too late fo' dat tiger, 'cause dat poison starts-a killin' 'im. So, plunk, ol' Bengal fall over daid!"

"Din whut?"

"Din, dat ol' poison cobra snake looks o'er at me, an' he is mad, mad, mad."

"Why's he mad, Unka-Jobee?"

"'Cause he jest got half-eat by a tiger, 'course! I din eat 'im, an' he done kilt th' ol' Bengal, but he don't care—he ain'ts satisfied wi' jest killin' dat ol' tiger. He starts slitherin' toward me, fast as he can go. He ain't even a full snake no mo' 'cause the tiger eats part o' 'im. Thets what makes 'im so mad. I runs and he slithers. I runs faster and he slithers faster. Even tho' he's jest half-a snake, he still can slither faster'n I kin run. I runs through the woods and he's rite b'hind me, slitherin' as fast as I runs. I look 'round and dere he is, and he sees his chance an' he jumps fo' all he's worth and catched me by my laig."

"Dats whut happen to yo' laig, Unka-Jobee!" Neemy said.

"Who tellin' dis story, boy? You o' me?"

"You is."

"Thas right. So this ol' poison cobras snake wraps hisself 'round my leg. Din he opens he's big ol' mouth, lik' he's a-sayin' 'Yum, yum, yum, I's got me some laig o' Jobe', an' he sinks his big ol' teeths into my pore, pore leg! Chomp, chomp, chomp!"

"Din whut happen, Unka-Jobee?"

"It kilt me, 'course! Jes' lik dat ol' dead Bengal. You don't live thru a poison cobra snake bite, boys!"

Jonathan and Neemy sat there wide-eyed, and then Jobe started guffawing, along with Gabe and Belle.

"Don't know if dat ol' snake got Unca Jobe's leg," Gabe said, "But Unca Jobe shure 'nuff pulled bofe o' yurn! Jes' like you ast him to. Now, you boys git in bed fo' I bites yo' laigs lack dat ol' snake!"

CHAPTER 10
THE YELLOW-HAIRED GIRL

The crescent moon was high above the field when Belle climbed into bed beside Gabe after checking to make sure the boys were fast asleep.

"Jobe sho wuz ona tare t'nite," she said.

In the dark, Gabe couldn't tell if she was amused or annoyed, so he chose a neutral response. "Sho wuz," he said.

"You ever hear dat snake tail b'fore?"

"'Course not. He jes' makes it up as he goes 'long. Dat silly tale din even exist 'til t'night!"

Belle paused for a moment, then asked, "Gabe, whut happen' to Jobe's laig, fo' real, an' I don't want no snake story."

Gabe didn't say anything, so Belle continued. "I means I 'member him as a young boy, runnin' this way and that. As I recall, he wuz 'bout as fast as they wuz…'least 'round these parts."

"Thas true. He wuz."

"Then, I knows he wuz gone fo' all those years wi' the circus carnval. Then one day he shows back up wi' a limp and a lion-head cane. Th' boys wuz babies, so I din hav' time t'even think on it then. I guess that silly tale tonight gots me a wondrin' how it happen, an' mostly why I don't knows th' real story. Does you even know?"

"Yas, I do."

"Is it some secret?"

Gabe sighed, "Not 'zactly. Is just one them things peoples live through an' jus' as rather let lie in th' past."

Gabe waited for a few seconds to see if Belle would move on to another subject, or would roll over and go to sleep, but she did neither.

"So—?" she said.

Gabe sighed. "You mays remember—or maybe not—but Massah Maddau's daddy use-da run this place, fo' Massah Maddau took charge," he said, "An' his ol' daddy had dis ol' rel-tive, uncle or sech, who runned de circus carn-val. Ever year or so, since I was a boy, dat show come to town. One year, theys in town, an' the massah sets up some deal wi' his uncle to loan out Jobe. I don't know iffen he sells him outright or jest borrows him out, but it upset Mama and Daddy to no end. Oh, Mama carried on, an' I thought Daddy would take an ax to da massah, but Jobe calms 'em down. Says he wants to do it. See da world, he sez. I don't know if thet wuz true, or iffen he says it jest to calm dim down, but he makes 'em b'lieve it.

"So, off he goes wi' da circus. Bye, bye, Jobe. I guess it's excitin' for 'im, at fust. Theys got 'im runnin' back 'n' forth, feedin' dese animals, feedin' dose animals, washin' they el-phants, cleanin' they cages, an' all dat."

"So, he actually *did* git in de cages wi' de lions and de tigers?"

"No, no, no. Don't be tellin' me he still got you b'lievin' that snake 'n' tiger tale, girl!"

Belle playfully hit him in the chest with her open hand. "'Course not!" she said.

"No," Gabe continued, "They gots trainers fo' dem wile animals, an' they'd take 'em out fo' trainin' and send in Jobe to clean they cages. An' fo' you ast again 'bout dem poison Cobra snakes, de answer is no, Jobe never feed o' clean up after no poison Cobra snakes. They has 'em dere, but Jobe sez theys got dis man who plays da flute an makes 'em come up outa theys baskit fo' de circus crowd. An' I think th' flute man takes care o' da snake. Fo' sho' no poison Cobra snake never latched onto Jobe's laig." Gabe shook the bed with laughter at the thought of Jobe running around with a snake hanging onto his leg by its fangs.

"Din, dere was dis girl dere in da circus…"

"Here we go," Belle said. "The truth is comin' out."

"Yassum, she wuz a pretty little yellar-hair girl."

"Oh, Lawd!"

"Yassum. Her daddy was a big ol' white preacher an' he worked wi' th' circus."

"Why do a preacher hav' anything to do wi' th' circus? Lawdy, do I wants to hear dis?"

"I don't have to tells you any mo'," Gabe said.

"You better. You gots me curious an' now, I rilly gots to know."

Gabe took a deep breath. "So, dis preacher likes to drink."

"Uh oh."

"*Uh oh* is right. He lose his church o'er his drinkin'. So it's jus' him an' his lil' yellar-hair girl."

"Whut happen to Miz Preacher, his wife?"

"She dead."

"Whut happen?"

"I don't know, woman! Do you wanna hear th' story?"

"Go on."

"So, everbody gotta have a job in th' circus, even th' lil' ones. So th' preacher, he tends to an-mals and sech, and the lil' girl, she carves an-mals outta sticks. Pieces o' wood. Jobe sez they look like da real thing. But they ol' circus man says they cants make no money offa wood animals, so she better learn somepin else. So she learns how to do tricks on a high swing. Yassum, she'd sit up on a swing, way high up in da air. An' dat swing would go back 'n' forth, higher and higher, an' she'd hang by her laigs, an' by her feets, an' by her toes, whilst that swing goes back 'n' forth. Jobe sez da crowd would cheer an' scream and cheer an' scream, an' she'd jest go higher 'n' higher 'n' higher, her yellar hair flowin' all 'round her face. Jobe sez she looked like a angel up dere. He sez sometimes she spinnin' dis metal stick with fire on it while she swings."

"Lawd!"

"So, by the time Jobe join th' circus, dis yella-hair girl wuz already a star. Jobe sez everbody, both in they show and in they audience, love her. Someun' like that—you'd think they'd be all high and mighty an' not have anythin' to do with a Negro, but she an' her daddy took a likin' to Jobe. Jobe wuz 'bout her age."

"But she white."

"Things different in they circus."

"Not dat different."

"Well, her daddy—th' preacher—as I sez, he rilly take a shine to Jobe. They talk religion an' the Bible all th' time. That's where Jobe got his Bible learnin'. Jobe still can't read th' Bible, but he gots it all up here." Gabe pointed at his own head, and even in the dark, Belle understood.

"Never thought a circus could be a blessin'," Belle said.

"Never know, I guess. Th' Lord be workin' in differt ways. Back when we's growin' up, Jobe be a wile one. He be vexin' my mama. She cry an' cry. Din he go off to th' circus. He be a differnt man when he gits back. Talkin' 'bout Jesus all-a time. Jesus dis. Jesus dat."

"He talk 'bout that yella-hair girl?"

"No. Jes when he tell me dis story."

"He sweet on her?"

"I don't know."

"Wonder if that ain't why he don't never marry."

"I don't know, Belle!"

"Uh, uh, uh. That yella hair girl. White folks. Always some sorta mischief."

"Does you want to hear 'bout Jobe's laig or not?"

"Yassuh," Belle sighed in the darkness, "Whut happen t' Jobe's laig?"

"Dat *wuz* whut we's talkin 'bout, after all. *Anyway*, as I's understands it, one night, the show gits started, an' they'd been late gittin' to town an' theys be hurried to git the big tent set up, and someun' missed sumpin' when theys settin' up they swing. A bolt or screw or sech. Funny how sech a little bitty thang like a bolt kin cause sech a big ol' problem. Anyways, this yellar-hair girl gits to swingin' like ever other night. She's hangin' by her feets, when alls-a sudden, part o' da swing comes apart, an' she's hangin' by one feet, swingin' back 'n' forth. The crowd is screamin.' They knows it ain't parta da act. The circus folks on the ground are frozen'—theys as scared as da yellar-haired girl—maybe even mo.' But th' yellar-haired girl ain't screamin.' She's swingin' back an' forth wi' her eyes wide open, an' she's hangin' by one feet. So, while everone's standin' 'neath they swing, twiddlin' theys thumbs, Jobe jumps up on they ladder, goin' up to they swing. He climes all th' way up, an' he reach out to da swing. He misses once. He misses twiced, but on th' thud time, he grabs hold-a thet yellar-haired girl. He gots one hand on they ladder an' th' other hangin' on to th' yellar-hair girl. She able t' grab hol' of da ladder jest below where he's climbin'. Wal, by then, some o' they circus fools git they wits an' they climes up an' gits that girl an' gits her safe on they ground. But that ladder wuzn't made fo' so many peoples climbin' it at they same time, an' it starts to shakin.' They gits the girl down, safe 'n' sound, but as Jobe an' the man b'low him tries to git down, that ladder lets loose an' comes down to th' ground wi' da both o' them. It kilt da man 'neath Jobe an' it drives his laig into th' groun' wi' da man, and busts it all up."

"Lawd! Where that girl's preacher-daddy durin' all this?"

"He drunk."

"What on earth? Durin' th' show?"

"He done his part already. He wudn't part o' th' show. He'd seen her up there a hunnerd times. He had no reason to think that night would be different."

"So, did they blame Jobe for that man gittin' kild?"

Gabe sighed. "He sez no, but I think he think they probly does. Theys go on to have a nice funeral for th' dead man—the preacher wuz sober 'nuff to do th' funeral—an' theys jest leave Jobe there in that lil' town. Din even take him fo' da doctor. They jest move on without him. No money, no clothes, no nuthin'."

"It's a wonder Jobe din loose dat laig."

"Almost did. Someun' took him to th' horse doctor, an' dat horse doctor fixed his laig. Wouldn't say 'good as new,' but 'least he gots to keep it to walk on. That circus. All his years he spend in it. All he had to show fo' it was a bad laig an' a lion-head cane."

"Where'd he git that cane, Gabe?"

"That yellar-hair girl, she carve it fo' him. Guess she feel grateful he save her life. She be leavin' it wi' dat horse doctor to give to Jobe. He din see her. She jus' leave it wi' dat horse doctor."

The two of them lay silent in the bed for a minute or so, and then Belle whispered, "Guess it's lucky for Jobe, dat horse doctor din shoot him."

Gabe laughed out loud, "Das jest meaness, Belle! *Shoot him?* Woman, whut am I gwine-a do wi' chu? *Shoot him?* Lawd. Don't you be sayin' dat to Jobe. *Shoot him?* Woman!"

CHAPTER 11
RUBINEVILLE

It was a warm fall morning, and Neemy was so excited about the trip into Rubineville that he had been unable to sleep the night before. It was the first time he was to be allowed to accompany Elizabeth into town with a wagon load of pottery. Belle had made breakfast for him and had packed a lunch for him to take with him. When Neemy got to the big house, the sun was already up, the horses had already been hitched, and Elizabeth was overseeing the loading of the wagon. The pots were packaged with hay in sturdy wooden crates that she and Neemy had carefully constructed, and they had been carefully packed into the back of the wagon for the journey into town.

Neemy had never been beyond the confines of the plantation, so this trip was more than a typical chore for him—he knew it was to be one of the first big adventures of his life. The road to Rubineville took them through deep woods and across swift-flowing streams. Neemy was careful to watch and make sure the crates were secure as they bumped over the rocky road and through the creeks. When they emerged from the woods and the modest skyline of the town came into sight, Neemy thought that Rubineville looked like something out of a fairytale that his Uncle Jobe would have told around a late-night campfire. All it was missing was a few wild animals.

Actually, Rubineville was just barely a town; in fact, it was more like a four-block village. Still, its citizens thought of it as a town and themselves as proud townspeople. Since it wasn't the county seat; there was no courthouse, just a row of shops and businesses lining the two main dirt streets, which met in the center of the town. The Rubine River ran parallel on the eastern side of the street that ran north-to-south; the land behind the buildings on that side of the road sloped down with a gentle grade that became the high western bank of the river.

The businesses included several two-story buildings; these included the hotel (and restaurant), a doctor's office (and makeshift infirmary), and Klein's General Store. Sprinkled among them were the smaller buildings that housed the post office, café, and barber shop.

There were two churches—one on each end of town. The churches were on the main street that ran north-to-south, and they both had church cemeteries beside their buildings. The church on the south end of the town was a whiteboard building with a small sanctuary and modest steeple, but the other one—the one on the northernmost end of town—was an anomaly. It was set close to the river, but unlike the church on the south end of town, the river didn't run behind the church. Rather, almost in deference to the church, the river chose to bend from its south-north path to a sharp turn, heading east for a bit before reverting back to its south-north direction. The church's red brick façade rose above the town, revealing a magnificent steeple, which housed a bright brass bell. In addition to summoning the congregants to worship, the bell ushered in every new year, celebrated Christmas Eve and Easter, and set the hours for the school, which was positioned on the south end of town. Also, in the event of a fire in the community, the bell was the first line of alarm.

But as important as the bell was to the town and the church and its congregation, the crown jewel of the church was its stained glass window that was in the east wall of the church, behind the altar. The stained glass had been an expensive gift from an anonymous wealthy couple in Charleston—some said that the wife was a former resident of the town. The truth is that nobody in town really knew the details behind the window, and in the absence of the facts, many stories had been manufactured and distributed.

One thing was for certain—the window had been imported from Munich in the late 1850's, and it had been carefully installed, piece by piece by craftsmen that came over from Europe with the window, itself. They had stayed in Rubineville for the duration of the installation—several months, in fact. And, once the window was finished and in place, the workmen disappeared as quickly as they had arrived. The only thing they left behind were the stories of what happened in the hours after they finished their workdays. The common denominator of the tales was that the catalyst of all of the unfortunate events appeared to be the German beer the workers had brought with them to help them more enjoy their leisure time. The unpleasantness that resulted from these incidents was a striking contrast to the beauty they created in the daylight hours in the form of the stained glass window.

The window had been created and shipped in dozens—if not hundreds—of pieces, much like that of an intricate puzzle. It colorfully depicted Jesus—with His arms down and hands out, but not so far apart—in a scene with sheep grazing beside a pastoral spring in the distance. It looked as if it was a moment in time, captured as the Good Shepherd was about to rescue an orphaned lamb. On Sundays, when the sun rose over the river and the pine forests in the distance, the rays would shine into the window, scattering thousands of gleaming shards of light throughout the sanctuary in a glorious quilt of shimmering colors.

Approaching the town from the south—as Elizabeth and Neemy did with their wagonload of pottery—the dirt road twisted through various groves of trees, running past large fields of barley and cotton before the town was ever in sight. Wide at some points and narrow at others, the old dirt highway ran parallel to the Rubine River in an interesting relationship; sometimes it ran right beside the river—almost on top of it—but on other stretches, the road was separated by a large field or clumps of trees, or both.

However, as the road got closer to the town, it nestled closer to the river, and on the south end of town the two were separated by the town's large cotton mill, which was the economic engine for the entire county.

Like the church, it was a massive brick building; in fact, the bricks were the same color and size as the bricks in the church, and appeared as if it had been built at the same time. The mill was nestled on a hill, shoved up against the river, whose rapids spun the giant wheels and gears with a deafening hiss of industrial glory. It ran day and night, so it was always a beehive of activity, both inside the building and on the roads leading to its loading doors. The mill not only provided cotton to local businesses, but nationally and internationally, as well. There were continuous shipments from the plant to Charleston and from there, to foreign ports around the world. It's no wonder that when the coming war finally broke out, the mill would become a vital asset for one side, as well as an important objective for the other.

CHAPTER 12

KLEIN'S GENERAL STORE

As Elizabeth steered the wagon down the street, Neemy couldn't help but stare, open-mouthed, at the glistening windows in the town's shops. And the shop with the biggest and most glistening window of all was Klein's General Store. As they passed the store, Neemy craned his neck and leaned out of his seat to see the display in the main window. There were farm tools and burlap bags surrounding a brightly-painted wooden bench beside a bedside table, all on a bed of hay. On the table was a Bible and a vase of flowers lit by a polished gold oil lamp. Neemy's eye was quickly drawn, not to the flowers in the vase beside the Bible, but rather, the vase itself—it was one of Elizabeth's pots. The intertwined dark red threads of color that circled the pot stood out above the flowers and the farm tools.

Elizabeth pulled the wagon into the dirt alley behind the store, and knocked on the back door until Abe Klein answered. When he threw open the door, his look of irritation changed immediately to one of excitement and anticipation. He was short and stocky with thinning hair and wire-rim glasses, which he removed when he saw it was Elizabeth at the door.

"Mrs. Maddau," Klein said, helping Elizabeth down from the wagon's seat, "Thank goodness! I thought it was one of those pesky salesmen. They've been hounding us for the past week, now, and once I chased them out of the front of the shop, they started showing up back here. But, you, my dear, are a welcome sight for these tired merchant eyes! We ran out of your pots two days ago! In fact, I've had to take orders for some. I put them on back order. I told them to come back next week, so thank goodness you're here!"

"Oh," Elizabeth said, "I'm sorry it's taken so long for me to get here. Charles—my husband—has been out of town off and on for the past month, and when he's away, I need to stay and manage the place."

"No, no, don't apologize! I'm just glad to have you here, now! Have your boy unload the crates here in the back room, and you come with me up front—I've got your payment for the last shipment." He then stuck his head out into the main room of the store and called out to his assistant—a balding young man with big teeth and bigger ears—who had been arranging cans of fruit on a shelf toward the middle of the store with the help of a young boy.

"Mr. Mullens, could you handle the register, please? Show Andrew what you were doing. Andrew, just continue stacking, please."

Klein then beckoned Elizabeth to follow him to the front of the store, leaving Neemy to unload the boxes and carry them into the back room, where an area had been cleared and set aside for their delivery. Inside the store, there were a dozen or so shoppers, including the mayor's wife and daughter and the minister of the stained-glass church on the north end of town, who was buying candles for his church's sanctuary. The minister was dressed in a black suit, as if it were Sunday or a funeral. He had dark hair, greying at the temples, and intense green eyes. His skin was paler than most of the townspeople, a tell-tale sign that he spent most of his waking hours indoors.

"Parson Barre," Klein said, addressing the man, "Meet Mrs. Maddau. Mrs. Maddau, Reverend Barre just moved here from Richmond. He is the new minister, since the death of Reverend Shubert. His youngest, Andrew, has been helping me here at the store, and he came to check on him."

The reverend smiled and stuck his hand out, "Mrs. Maddau!"

"Please. Call me Elizabeth," she said, returning his smile and offering her gloved hand, "Welcome to our town, Parson Barre. Are you related to Rufus Barr and his family up on the north trace?"

"No ma'am," the minister replied, "By coincidence, I did have the pleasure to meet Rufus a few weeks back, and he was asking the same question!"

"The Barrs have been in this part of the state for as long as anyone can remember," Elizabeth said.

"So he told me," the minister laughed, "I'd love to claim him as kin, but we spell our name with an 'e' on the end, and I'm fairly sure our ancestors came from different parts of Europe."

"That's wonderful that your son has been helping Mr. Klein," Elizabeth said, "How has your wife and family adjusted to our little town? Especially after living in a big city like Richmond?"

"My two sons seem to be getting adjusted…somewhat," the minister said, "Mr. Klein was kind enough to offer my boys a chance to earn some spending money. My oldest declined, but Andrew jumped at the chance. But, it's just me and my two boys. My wife passed away a number of years ago. In childbirth, actually."

"Oh," said Elizabeth, "I'm sorry."

"You couldn't have known. With my son, Andrew. But he was born healthy and has thrived."

Sensing the awkwardness of the exchange, Klein interjected, "Andrew has been a big help here in the store! Er, Reverend, last week you were asking about the pots in the window, Mrs. Maddau here is the potter, herself. The artist."

"Oh," Rev. Barre said, "You do beautiful work! As Mr. Klein said, I'm an admirer of your work and was disappointed when I came in to purchase some, only to find that they had all been sold. When will there be more in stock?"

"As a matter of fact, Reverend," Elizabeth said, "We're delivering a shipment this morning."

"Excellent! Maybe I can secure some for my church and my home before they all get grabbed up!"

"Would you like to see one?" Elizabeth asked, "I'm sure Mr. Klein wouldn't mind if I uncrated one before they hit the shelves."

"Of course not," Klein laughed with a wink, "I always charge a little more for the first ones out of the crate! Pick out the ones you want and I'll put it on your ledger. Go on back and take a look…Mrs. Maddau, I'll join you there as soon as I get what I owe you."

Elizabeth and the reverend navigated the store's crowded aisles and made their way into the back room, where Neemy stood guarding the crates.

"Oh," Barre said, "Hello."

"This is Nehemiah, my helper," Elizabeth said.

"Nehemiah was a cup bearer," Rev. Barre said.

Neemy squinted to see the parson in the dim light of the back room, "Yassah," he said.

Elizabeth took out a pot from the top crate and stood in the doorway of the opened backdoor. The pot—with its distinctive *wavy red thread* design—gleamed in the morning sunshine, the tiny pieces of the glaze sparkling like the stars of a cloudless winter night.

"This would be perfect for communion wine," the reverend said, looking back at Elizabeth for agreement.

Elizabeth smiled and shrugged. "I suppose," she said, "We attend the Baptist church on the other end of town." She stopped short of mentioning that it was usually only her that attended, and that was on the rare Sundays that Charles didn't require her presence at the house.

"That's a lovely church," the reverend replied, "I had the honor of meeting your pastor just last week. He was putting out flowers in front of your church. We also have beautiful flowers—in our sanctuary, and your pots would also be worthy holders; they're as beautiful as the flowers. I could use at least a dozen of these beautiful vessels!"

"Thank you, Pastor," Elizabeth said, smiling.

"Thank *you*, Mrs. Maddau," the minister said before turning to the shop owner. "Mr. Klein, maybe you could just send Andrew home with the pots and the balance of my order when he finishes his work for you this afternoon. Would that work?"

"Of course. If you think he can carry them. Actually, I have a small wagon I can let him use."

"Perfect. Thank you so much!" With that, Reverend Barre bade them goodbye and turned and found his way to the front door and out of the store.

"What a nice man," Elizabeth said once the pastor exited the store, "And he is replacing Rev. Shubert?"

"Yes," Klein said, "I think he will do well in Rubineville, although it is a different sort of parish than Richmond."

"He seems…conscientious, but with a twinge of sadness, somehow."

"Hmm. I agree. I think he has experienced his share of life's hardships."

"Oh?"

"Well, as he said, it's just him and his sons, since his wife passed away—"

"In childbirth. How awful."

"Yes. Awful. But also…"

Klein looked around to make sure no one was listening to their conversation. "If not an abolitionist, he at least is sympathetic to that cause, and that has brought his share of…unpleasantries to be heaped upon him," he whispered. "Truth be told, I got the impression that is what got him ejected from his previous pulpit."

"I see," Elizabeth said. "Does he preach in that direction?"

"I wouldn't think so," Klein said. "Especially, if that is what got him in trouble at his church in Richmond. So, in that respect, I would surmise that he is much like Rev. Shubert before him, in that he treads that fine line very carefully."

"Rev. Shubert was an honorable man," Elizabeth said. "I was sorry to hear that he had passed."

"Yes. It was a shock to the church and to the community."

"I've never been inside that church," Elizabeth said, "But everyone in town is always quick to mention its stained glass window."

"You can't help but be overwhelmed by the window," Klein said, "Even those of us of another faith. Its color and detail. Even on rainy days, its beauty is astonishing. But on sunny days, when the light shines through the glass, it's like being in another world..."

"I don't know that I've ever taken the time to stroll around to the back of the church to really study it. It depicts Christ, right?" Elizabeth asked, "With His hands extended out?"

"Ah, yes. The Messiah. Beckoning sinners," said Klein, smiling and peering over his wire-rims which were pushed down on his nose.

"Beckoning sinners," said Elizabeth, glancing over at the shop owner to see if he was being serious or facetious. "That is all of us, Mr. Klein."

"I suppose you are right, Mrs. Maddau. I suppose that is all of us."

Just then, the front door bell jingled, indicating someone had entered. When Klein peered back into the main part of the store, he was startled to see that Rev. Maddau had returned.

"Mr. Klein," he said, "I had a thought. Could you go ahead and let me have one of the pots from my order? I'm afraid I'm too impatient to wait for Andrew to bring it. I'd like to see what it looks like placed in the sanctuary. And, it's not that I don't trust my boy, but I would like to make sure at least one of Mrs. Maddau's beautiful works of art makes its way to our church...uh, intact!"

Klein chuckled. "That's not a problem. Beauty has a way of affecting us, doesn't it?"

"Quite right, Mr. Klein."

"Speaking of beauty, Mrs. Maddau and I were just discussing the stained glass window behind the alter in your church"

"Really?"

"Yes, and she confided that she has never seen the glass from inside the church."

"Well, we can certainly solve that dilemma. Mrs. Maddau, would you care for a guided tour of my sanctuary?"

"I would love that, Reverend," Elizabeth said, "Neemy, you stay here with Mr. Klein, if that is acceptable by Mr. Klein."

"Certainly."

"We won't be long, Mr. Klein," the minister said.

"No hurry, folks. We'll be fine right here. In the meantime, let me get you one of your pots," Klein said.

Klein hurried to the storeroom and quickly returned with one of the pots the minister had selected. Then, with the pot in hand, Rev. Barre left the store with Elizabeth, heading up the dusty street, and Klein returned to his spot behind the store's main counter.

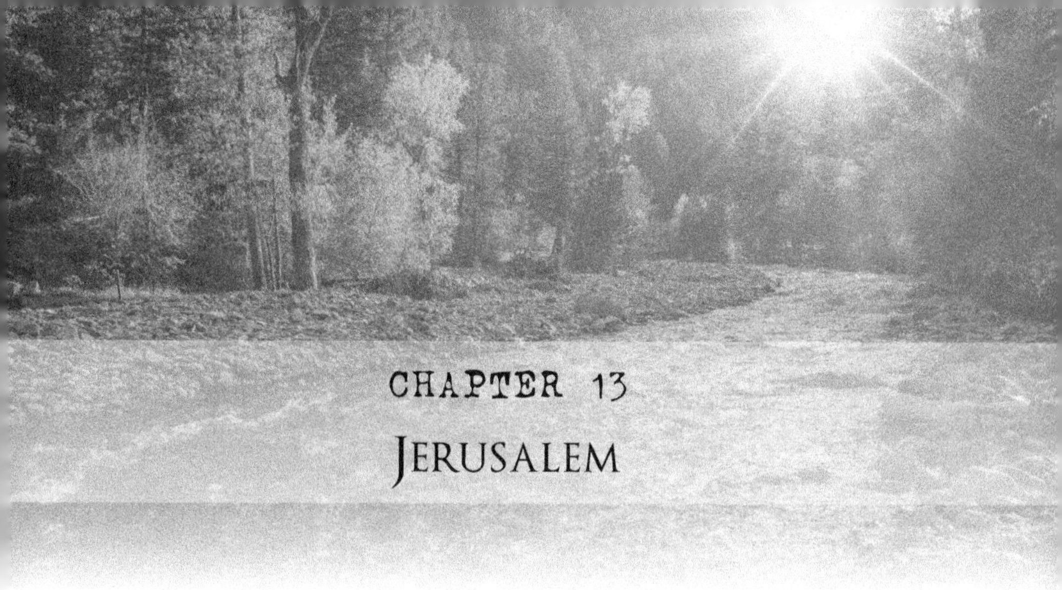

CHAPTER 13
JERUSALEM

From the store's front window, Neemy watched as Elizabeth and Rev. Barre disappeared up the road. After a few minutes, Klein called to his assistant, who had returned to arranging a selection of cans in the center of the store.

"Mr. Mullens, please watch the front for me, and Andrew can keep stacking. Good work, Andrew," he said, and then turning to Neemy, who was anxiously peering out the front window, "Young man, could you be so kind as to help me move some books?"

"Yessah, Massah," Neemy said.

"And you don't have to call me that. In fact, I'd rather you just call me 'Mr. Klein.' I'm nobody's 'master.'"

"Yassah," Neemy said, cautiously following the store owner into a smaller room behind the storeroom. He was not used to being asked so politely to help with a task, so he wasn't sure what the man's motive was, but he still knew better than to ask or decline. At the far end of the windowless room, there was an old sturdy table, laden with several dusty wooden boxes of books. Klein had lit a lantern and it cast eerie shadows on the various boxes and objects scattered throughout the room.

"I believe I heard Mrs. Maddau say your name was 'Nehemiah.' Is that right?" Klein asked.

"Yassuh," Neemy said, obediently.

"That makes sense. As Rev. Barre said, Nehemiah was the king's cup bearer."

"Yassuh."

"Oh, you know that, I suppose," Klein said.

"Yassuh."

"Well, Nehemiah, I realize that helping an old storekeeper isn't as glamorous as tasting a king's wine, but I really appreciate the help. If you could move that small box to that far wall over there, I'll get this other box," Klein said.

When Neemy picked the box up from the table, a large book fell from behind the box. Neemy immediately wheeled around to face whatever wrath would be thrown his way from the shopowner.

"Are you alright?" Klein said, making his way over to the frightened boy.

"Yassah, it fell," Neemy blurted.

"No worries. If it came apart, then its not worth hanging on to, anyway. Right?" Klein said, smiling as he held the lantern above the book, which had fallen and opened on the wooden floor.

"What ho! What have we here?"

"Don't know, suh."

"I've been looking all over for this! It must have fallen behind your box!"

"Yassah."

Klein knelt beside the book and hoisted it, still opened, to the table. "Have you ever in your life seen a book like this? Have you ever seen pictures like this?" he asked Neemy, and held his lantern above the pages. Neemy truly had never seen a book like that. Yes, he had seen tintypes and photographs before, mostly of the Maddau family, but he had never seen photographs on the pages of a printed book or anything like what the lantern revealed. Unlike the engravings in the shed Bible, these were not illustrations, but rather actual photographs. As he turned the pages, he instinctively scratched at one of the pictures with his fingernail to see if it was pasted down on the page.

"Don't worry, they won't come off the page," Klein chuckled, "They're photogravures. And they're not etchings or drawings; they're genuine photographs printed on the page. It's truly remarkable. Look at that!"

Klein held the lantern closer to the book and traced the lines of a gated wall on a rolling hillside in one of the pictures. "These are pictures of the Holy City of Jerusalem. They were taken by a French photographer, a man named Salzmann. Friends of mine in Charleston are in awe of his talents. Look! Here's the Arch of the Solomon Bridge. And this one is of the Damascus Gate. Look, these structures are literally thousands of years old. Look! You can almost see King David walking in front of this wall. Can you imagine?"

Neemy reflected on the illustrations in Elizabeth's Bible and remembered the one with Jesus riding into the city on the back of a donkey. "Jesus wuz there."

"Yes, He was. Jesus and King David. They were right here!"

"Fo' th cameras made."

"Yes. Before the cameras," Klein laughed, "That's something to think about, isn't it? Can you imagine a photograph or tintype of King David?" He excitedly flipped through the book and ran his hand over some of the images. "There are pictures from all over Jerusalem. Look at this—here's the Gate of David. Here, look at the detail on the arch on this one. We are truly living in the future. There is no way a simple man like myself could ever be able to see pictures of Jerusalem—the Holy Land, the homeland—without a book such as this."

Neemy was mystified by the beauty of the photography. "Dat's Druse-lem? Is-rel? Like from the Bible?" he asked.

"Yes, exactly. Israel is in the past, and hopefully, in the future," Klein said. "Do you know about the Children of Israel?"

"Yassah. They 'scaped ol' Pharoah. His army men got drowned."

"That's right. The Children of Israel escaped from Pharoah. They were..."

"Slaves," Neemy said.

"Yes. Just shows you that there is nothing new under the sun… especially when men have evil motives and a lust for power…especially over other people or peoples. But. It should also show you that there is always hope. There's always a glimmer of light in the darkness."

Klein held the lantern up between his face and Neemy's. As the lantern swung in his hand, the flickering light animated the shopowner's face and reflected in his wirerim glasses.

"Yassuh."

"I mean, those people were *my* people. My ancestors. Pharoah chased them across the sea, until it swallowed his soldiers all up. And then, we were free. At least for the time being. We've been scattered all over the world. But right here, right now, my people are free. We're free today, as you will someday be."

"Yassah," Neemy said. He wasn't sure if he should agree with Klein or dispute his declaration.

"And, if you take a good look in your Bible, and in my Torah, one of these days—and it may not be in my lifetime—but one of these days, my people—and hopefully, your people—will once again walk in the shadow of these holy shrines. Touch the stones. Feel their coolness in the noonday heat."

"Yassah," Neemy said, but secretly he thought that dream seemed more than an ocean away, and he sadly doubted that the ornate and detailed pictures in Klein's book could make any sort of difference in his freedom or destiny.

CHAPTER 14
GONE HUNTIN'

It was still a few hours before sunrise when the boards creaked on the big front porch as Charles and Jack quietly emerged from the house, both holding a rifle and a haversack that contained food and ammunition. "Those eggs and that coffee should hold you until mid-morning," Charles said to the boy, who rubbed his eyes and trudged sleepily behind his father. They found their way in the dark, across the great lawn and into the stables, where their horses were saddled and waiting. There was a chilly breeze in the air, but it was not altogether unpleasant, and the two were dressed warmly. The Maddau's land stretched for a number of miles. It was split by the Rubine River and included a number of multi-acred fields, as well as several thick forests and prime hunting locations.

Charles had wanted to make a weekend of hunting with Jack and to take him even beyond their property, deep within the woods, mainly so the boy wouldn't be whining to go back home for the night. Within a few minutes, the silhouettes of the man and boy on their horses could be made out against the big house, which had a faint glow about it as it stood bravely against the darkness of the late-autumn sky.

The two of them paralleled the river and were nearly a half-mile from the house when they turned off the main road onto a side trail. The trail meandered through a patch of woods, at the end of which was a pleasant clearing that bordered the large field that held a portion of their cattle. They followed the fence line for a bit, and then stopped at the gate, which was shrouded in darkness.

"Get that gate for us, Jack," Charles said to the boy.

"Why do we always have to cut through this pasture?" Jack said, "If we stay on the trail, it will take us to the same place. I'm always afraid we're going to step on one of the cows. It's too dark."

"Come on, Jack, why do we always have to have this discussion? You know it's a convenient shortcut," Charles said, bristling, "And it gives us a chance to admire our stock. Don't you want to save a little time? Time is money, son. And you outta be proud that we own cattle like these. Besides Jack, they may not be the most intelligent of beasts, but they do know to get out of the way of a couple of horses and their riders, especially in the dark. If I didn't know better, I'd say that Ol' Thor is the only cow you're afraid of stepping on," he chuckled. "You don't need to worry, son—that's why I let you ride ol' Mooneye, and I'm thinkin' he can outrun Ol' Thor any day of the week and twice on Sunday, day or night. After all, that's why we ride horses and not bulls. B'sides, chances are, they're all still asleep, especially Ol' Thor—he needs his beauty sleep so he can keep up with all his girlfriends."

Jack could feel his face redden in spite of the coldness. He was glad of the darkness, so that his father couldn't see his reaction. But, he also knew that his father was right; he was very uncomfortable in the field, whether on foot or on horseback, because of Ol' Thor. The old bull had sired most of the cattle in the field that he still ruled over, and his advanced age had not seemed to slow him down. When Jack was a young boy and fond of exploring, he had an unpleasant encounter with the old bull. He couldn't remember exactly why he had wandered into the field, only that he had been on foot and by himself. At some point, out of the corner of his eye, he saw a massive black shape a few hundred feet away moving slowly—but with determination—in his direction, and he knew immediately that it was the old bull.

His father had always warned him not to run from the bull, telling him that only encouraged a chase, and it was one that the boy could not win. Jack backed slowly toward the gate, careful to not trip and keeping the bull in sight. Ol' Thor turned his side toward the boy and snorted, pawing at the ground. When Jack figured that he was a little closer to the gate than the bull was to him, he turned and ran for all he was worth. Behind him, he could hear the thundering bull as he picked up speed. The only thing that had saved Jack from Ol' Thor's horns and hooves was his panic-driven fleetness of foot and the fact that he had accidently—*but fortunately*—left the gate open. Once on the other side of the gate, he quickly slammed it shut and saw that he was eyeball-to-eyeball with the old bull, who had managed to stop just short of the gate, kicking up a cloud of dust in the process. Jack was in tears by the time he got back to his house, and while he was comforted by his mother, his father demanded to know why he had wandered into the pasture and also, why he had left the gate open. *That's how we lose our cattle*, his father told him.

That incident had been the subject of an untold number of nightmares that Jack had suffered. In the dreams, he would be minding his own business and he would then see Ol' Thor running toward him from across the field. He would always think that he would have plenty of time to get away—sometimes he would be in the same field where the initial event happened, but other times, he would be in the yard closest to the house, or even in town. In Jack's dream, the bull would charge at him, but he wouldn't be able to run; it was as if he was running through molasses, as the bull got closer and closer. He could hear Ol' Thor's hoofbeats and could feel his breath on his neck as he tried to run. And then, he would wake up in a cold sweat.

"Jack! Jack! Close the gate, son," Charles barked, shaking Jack from a daze. "When are you going to learn? Wake up, boy! Get back up on that horse, before Ol' Thor sees you're here," he laughed.

Jack climbed up on the horse and the two trotted across the wide field, stepping between the sleeping cows, some of which jumped to their feet and lumbered away. If the old bull had been made aware of their presence, he didn't bother making an appearance as they cut through his dark and grassy kingdom.

After a long day of hunting, as the sun hung over the Rubine River, Charles and Jack paused on the bank to survey the game they had shot. The horses waded into the river and gratefully drank their fill.

"How far are we from home?" Jack asked.

"Why? You have somewhere to be?" Charles said with a tinge of irritation.

"No. Just—don't we need to be getting home? The sun's low. It's getting late."

"I don't know exactly how far we are from the house," Charles said, "Just that it's too far to make it back home tonight. There's only a few hours of daylight left. So, we do need to find a place to camp."

"Camp?" Jack said, suddenly alarmed. "Where? Where we sleepin'?"

"That's what we have to find," Charles said, laughing. He had expected this reaction, once Jack realized they weren't going to be going home that night. He was surprised the boy hadn't figured it out sooner. Charles was pleased that Jack had been so engrossed in their hunting that it hadn't occurred to him to question him about spending the night in the outdoors.

"What about our beds? Where we gonna sleep?" Jack asked.

"Well, let's keep a sharp eye out; maybe someone done come and built themselves an inn on our property. They'd have to let us stay for free."

The thought of staying in an inn excited Jack, but then, when he saw his father's bemused grin, he realized his father was making fun of him.

"There's no inn," Jack said.

"You never know. When was the last time you were here? They could have snuck in here and built one. And we'd get to stay free."

"That wouldn't make any sense."

"Why? It's our land. We get to stay free."

"No, not that. I mean, somebody building an inn on our land," Jack said, disappointedly, though a part of him wanted to believe it was true, especially since he was dreading sleeping out in the elements.

"Right. Our land," Charles said. "It is, indeed, our land. Let me ask you, Jack. Do you happen to know how this came to be 'our land'?"

Jack shook his head "No."

"Do you know why they call this river the Rubine River?"

"Because of Rubineville?"

"Good guess, but actually, 'Rubineville' is named after the Rubine River, not the other way around. My two questions are connected to one another."

"What do you mean?"

"I mean, the Rubine River and the fact that we own this land are tied together in history. Do you know what 'Rubine' means?"

Again, the boy shook his head.

"It's a red. A deep, deep red, like the red of a ruby. A ruby's a jewel. A beautiful deep red jewel."

"I know what a ruby is."

"Well, did you know that a few years ago—well, more than a few, actually—there was a time that this river ran as red as a ruby."

"How? Why?"

"Blood and uniforms."

"What's that supposed to mean?"

"It means the river ran red with blood and uniforms."

"Where did they come from?"

"The uniforms were on the soldiers that wore them. The blood came from the dead soldiers that were still wearing the uniforms. That were floating like bright red logs down the river. That's how it got its name."

Charles could see that the mentioning of blood and soldiers had piqued the boy's interest.

"Let's saddle up," Charles said. "I'll tell you the story while we find a place to put up for the night."

CHAPTER 15
Blood and Uniforms

There was still an hour of daylight left, but the sun was sinking behind a distant hill crest, which was lined by a row of silhouetted trees. In one of the low-hanging branches, a large black crow—the tips of his wings flecked with gold from the setting sun—watched as Charles and Jack made their way on horseback, along the west bank of the river. He voiced his disapproval at their encroachment with loud caws before flying off to another tree, this one taller, on a distant hilltop. Eventually, the two riders came to a fairly large and swift-flowing creek that emptied into the Rubine. It was lined by trees on each bank and was really too large to be a creek, but not large enough to be a river. However, any fisherman could look at it and know that there were fish to be caught within its clear and swift current. The two rode along the side of the creek for a bit, until they came to a waterfall, where the creek plunged over a 20-foot wall of stones and earth.

"See that narrow ditch, there?" Charles said, pointing toward the field beyond the treeline on the eastern bank. "It starts—or ends—here just down from this waterfall, depending on whether you're coming or going, and it goes for several miles, across this pasture and on up onto that ridge. Some of it was dug out and man-made, but some of it is natural. It may have been a creek or stream, and it emptied into this larger creek, which empties into the Rubine River, which ends up in a larger river which eventually ends up in the Atlantic. Or maybe this here creek—with the waterfall—diverted the other one's flow and took all its water. I dunno, I guess we'll never know, for sure. Maybe the Indians that lived here hundreds and hundreds of years ago knew what happened. At any rate, where the dry creek bed quit—or needed some help—shovels took over and did the rest to dig the ditch. Maybe it was some sort of drainage ditch."

"So. What about it? Why am I supposed to be excited about a ditch? And what about the Indians?" Jack asked.

"The Indians are another story. What I'm talking about is the ditch. That's really where the story that I'm telling you starts."

"Fine. It's a ditch. What's a ditch have to do with blood and uniforms in the river?"

"Well, this ditch was the boundary line between the farms of two families, both of which came over from England in the early 1700's. In the beginning, they were good friends with each other, which is a good idea if you're neighbors with one another. If one family needed help building a barn or helping with a sick animal, the other family would gladly lend a hand. Back then, this whole area was governed by England…it was one of England's colonies."

"I do go to school, you know. We do study the history."

"Yes, but this is something that isn't in the books."

"What a surprise. The ditch isn't in the history books."

Charles was a bit annoyed with Jack's impertinence, but he figured the boy's attitude was tempered by the fact that he was still upset about not being able to spend the night in his own bed back at the house. So, he forced himself to be patient.

"It's a little bit of a sensitive point," Charles said, "Depending on who you talk to, England was either a wonderful, kind and benevolent governing force, or a thieving, immoral scourge of the earth. There were those in this area that were loyal to the crown and then, there were those who favored separation from the crown and independence. And unfortunately, these two families—who had once been good friends and neighbors—didn't see eye-to-eye. One family was loyal to the crown; the other felt like America should be free from England's shackles and taxes.

"At first, it was just a difference of opinion. Then the debate became more heated as more and more of the citizens of the state were forced to pick sides. And these neighbors had to do the same thing. The family that chose England had three boys and a girl; the family that chose to be patriots—the one siding *against* England—had two boys. The oldest boy was probably 15 or 16; the youngest was 12 or 13. The England-loyal family's girl was about the same age as the oldest boy in the other family, and them being neighbors, they had basically grown up together. They saw each either in the field when they were working; they were in the same school and so on. And they were sweet on each other."

"What d'ya mean 'sweet?'"

"I mean like romantic. Like boyfriend-girlfriend."

"Oh."

"Well, this actually wadn't that uncommon. Neighbors were always marrying off their sons and daughters to each other, 'specially when they shared a property line. It just made sense to keep the land in the family. 'Course, there's a problem when the neighbors disagree with each other, but their children love each other."

"I think we read a story like that in school."

"Yes. It was probably about Romeo and Juliet. That's the most well-known story. Nobody ever said that this kind of *forbidden* romance was an original idea. There's probably been boys and girls falling in love against the wishes of their families for as long as there have been families and boys and girls. And, I suppose that all through history, there have been fathers who have demanded that their sons stay away from their forbidden girlfriends, and fathers who demanded—*even more emphatically*—that their daughters stay away from their forbidden boyfriends. And, that was the case here. Of course, the two of them still snuck around to see each other, and of course, the fathers eventually found out about it. I think the girl's father would have killed the boy, if he could have gotten his hands on him. But, of course, the girl would always warn her boyfriend about her father, so that her father could never catch him.

"But then, an opportunity arose that gave the girl's daddy an idea. There were redcoats in the area, and the English had a pretty good idea who were traitors to the crown, and who was loyal to the British Empire. One night the girl's family had one of the British officers over for dinner, and legend is that as he was seeing the officer off for the night, he mentioned that his daughter's boyfriend was passing information off to the rebels—*the patriots*—on the whereabouts of the British troops. I don't know what he thought would happen, but whatever he thought, the situation quickly heated up. The next day, the redcoats came riding up to the neighbor's house."

"What do you mean, *redcoats*? You keep saying 'redcoats.'"

"Oh. Right. The British Army's uniforms were red coats. Yes, it didn't really make too much sense…you could see them coming from a mile away. I suppose they thought they were so powerful as an army that they could get away with wearing any color you please, no matter how bright it was. And, mind you, the British army was pretty powerful at the time. They were probably the most powerful army in the world."

"So what happened?"

"See that crest of the hill, way over there, behind that first hill?" Charles pointed to a distant bluff that was covered by a thick treeline. "That's where their house was."

"Whose house?"

Charles sighed, but patiently continued, "The house of the patriots. The house where the boy lived. The one that the girl's father was angry with. Their house was at the crest of that far ridge over there, and the boy's father could see the redcoat soldiers ridin' up, big as you please."

"Because their red coats were so noticeable."

"Yes, and because the house was up on that ridge and he could see all the way down to the treeline on the banks of this creek. So, by the time the soldiers had covered the ground to the house, the father and son—the girl's boyfriend—had their rifles loaded and primed and focused on the British officer. Well, the British officer ordered his men to surround the place, and he yelled up at the house for them to come out and talk. But the boy's father just yelled back for the soldiers to get off their land. 'Your land?' the British officer said, 'You are a subject of the crown!'"

"What's that mean?" Jack asked.

"That means that England thought they were running the show," Charles laughed. "And the shouting got louder, and I'm sure more heated, and someone pulled a trigger—I've heard it both ways—some say it was a nervous soldier, some say it was the boy."

"The girl's boyfriend?"

"Yes, the girl's boyfriend. But to this day, nobody knows for sure. It really don't matter at this point. The only thing for certain is that the officer only had his sword, and not a gun, and that didn't do much good against a musket shot. So somehow, this British officer got shot, and down he goes, off his horse."

"Was he dead?"

"Yessir. Dead. And once he was down and dead, things really got out of control. First of all, the redcoats were angry that one of their own had been killed, especially their commanding officer, and, since they no longer had a commander to keep them in check and under control, they went on a rampage. They managed to set the house and barn on fire, and everyone inside was killed. Some say burned up, others say the soldiers shot them as they escaped."

"That's terrible."

"Yes, it is. So, the neighbor—remember the neighbor? *He was the one who sent the soldiers to arrest his daughter's boyfriend.* He sees the smoke and rides over and realizes what has happened. It was way beyond what he wanted. There's an old saying that sometimes you get what you wish for. I think he may have *thought* he wanted the soldiers to get rid of his daughter's suitor, but in truth, I think he just wanted to rattle the boy's father and get him to keep his boy at home and away from his daughter. But, the real concern for the neighbor is that when he saw the bodies of the family, there was one person missing—and it wasn't his daughter's boyfriend—his body was there in the rubble. But his younger brother was nowhere to be found. The neighbor immediately alerted the junior officer who was then in charge, sayin' that they'd better find him, before he alerts the rebel citizen soldiers—*the patriots.* Because he knew the patriots would seek revenge. They already hated the British army and the idea that the redcoats would massacre their neighbors would light a powder keg. So, these redcoats spread out in all directions. That must have been a sight to see. In fact, most of 'em came right through here, on both sides of the creek, looking for that boy—the younger brother of the one who had been killed."

"The girl's boyfriend?"

"Yes, her sweetheart was dead, but his younger brother had somehow escaped."

"How did he get away?" Jack asked, wide-eyed.

"Funny you should ask," Charles said, "Because that boy had been down here to this creek, fishing. He was actually on the far bank there. He wasn't in the house when the soldiers first showed up. He was right over there, fishing." Charles pointed at the opposite bank.

"Strange, ain't it? Fishin' saved the brother's life. He was just sittin' over there on the bank with his line in the water, when he notices something above the trees. At first, he thinks it's just clouds, but then, he realizes it's smoke and he knows that it is in the direction of his house. Now, most boys would have just run in the direction of the smoke, and if he had done that, he would have run right into the arms of the redcoats. But this boy—the younger brother—he was a smart one. He knew that if there was a big enough fire to cause that much smoke, he wouldn't be able to put it out himself and he would need to get help. And he knew that the family of his older brother's girlfriend would not be the people to go to. So, he crossed the creek and climbed one of the tall trees so that he could see over the ridge. And it's a good thing that he did, because he saw that his house was nearly gone in flames—there wouldn't have been anything anyone could do—and also, he saw several dozen redcoats on horses heading his way, and he knew that if they were willing to burn his house down, they wouldn't think twice about shooting him down, young boy or not. So, he knew he had to hide."

"So, he hid in the ditch!" Jack said, excitedly.

"Now, Jack," Charles said, more patiently than he felt, "Don't you think that at least one of a few dozen well-trained soldiers on horseback would be able to see a boy hiding in a dry creek bed?"

"I dunno," Jack said, "Maybe there were weeds or something."

"Okay, let's say there were weeds in the dry creek bed. But let's also say a few of the redcoats rode their horses down the middle of the creek bed. That wouldn't have been a good hiding place, would it?"

"No sir. I guess you're right," Jack said, embarrassed.

"Well, he knew that at the speed the soldiers were comin' toward him, he only had a few minutes to hide himself. He didn't have time to search for the perfect spot."

"So…since he couldn't find a hiding place, did they catch him?"

"No, Jack. If they had caught him, things would have turned out real different. I said that he didn't have time to *find* the perfect hiding spot. Fact is, *he already knew where there was a perfect hiding place.* And that's what saved his life. Not only did they not find him, once they went back to their camp, he followed them, so he knew exactly where they were. They were camped up on the Rubine. He also knew where the patriot soldiers were. His father had been involved with them, and they were friends of his family. So, that night, he went and found the patriot soldiers. That's really what they were—*patriots and soldiers*—and he told them what they had done to his family's home. And, where their camp was. It only took a few hours for the patriots to get all their men and horses together, and it was just as the redcoats had feared—they were out for revenge, and when you have a bunch of *motivated patriot-farmer-soldiers*, it's really hard to stop 'em. So, just before the sun came up, they swept in like banshees from hell and gave them redcoats no quarter."

"No quarter?"

"No mercy. They took no prisoners. Some of the British put up a fight, some of them ran for their lives. Some took to the river. Funny thing is, most of 'em stopped to put on their red coats. Some got shot while they were putting their coats on. That must have been how they were trained. That's probably why they ended up losin' the war. The Americans—the patriots—kind of made the rules of engagement up as they went. Anyway, that morning, a lot of the British ended up in the Rubine, with their blood and redcoats. That's how the river got its name."

"What was it called before it was called the Rubine?"

"Nobody remembers. It was probably an Indian name."

"So, where did the boy hide? Where was this perfect hiding place?"

"Good question. Um—tell you what. Let's play hide and seek."

"What?"

"You heard me. Let's get these horses tied up. While there's still daylight. And once we do, I want you to hide your eyes and count to a hundred. That's about all the time the boy had to hide. I want to see if you can find me."

They tied the horses up in the shadow of the waterfall over the rocky bluff, and Jack obediently hid his eyes and began counting. When he was finished, he started looking for his father. At first, he rose to the challenge and climbed a nearby tree to scout the surroundings. Then, he started looking in the tall grass. Gradually, as the sun sank lower, he began to panic, and he started screaming desperately for his father. It was then he heard his father laughing. Although he was relieved, he was equally as angry that the game had lasted as long as it did. As he continued to call for his father, his father's laughter only increased. It was an odd feeling—the laughter seemed so close, but yet there was no sign of his father. Finally, in desperation his anger gave way to tears, and he sank down on the side of the creek with his head in his hands.

"Pretty good hiding place, huh?" Jack heard his father say, as he crunched up behind him on the bank where he still sat, his arms around his knees with his face buried. He knew his father had reappeared, but he was too upset and angry to respond. "Tell you what, Jack. Why don't we camp in the hiding place?"

Jack looked up and wiped his eyes. "Where is it?" he asked.

"It's right here," Charles said, "Literally a stone's throw away. Those redcoats rode right by here and were only a few feet away. Come on, follow me. This can be our secret place."

They waded through the creek, and climbing out of the water followed the stream up the edge of the bluff. At the base of the stony wall—totally concealed behind the steady wall of water—was an opening that was wide enough for a full grown man to squeeze through.

"Look, Jack," he said, "It's a door. A natural door in the side of the hill, behind the waterfall. You'd never know it was here."

Jack was still angry, but his curiousity had overcome his anger, and he got to his feet and followed his father through the stream to the waterfall. Once they entered the natural door, a large room opened up and led to a cave, all inside the hill that the waterfall tumbled over.

"This is where he hid?" Jack excitedly asked, once his eyes adjusted to the dark.

"Yes, it is," Charles said, "But you need to keep close to me."

"Why?"

"Because there's a spot toward the back of this chamber that can swallow you up. If you step in it, there ain't nobody that'll ever see you again. Ain't no rope long enough to haul you back up."

"How do you know?"

"Nevermind. I just do."

Charles lit a lantern and held it up so Jack could see the expanse of the room.

"There's no telling how many people have hidden in this cave. See that rock over there? The one that juts out? That's another niche where you can hide. If you go deeper into the cave, over there," Charles held the lantern up higher, revealing a dark tunnel at the far end of the room. "If you go deeper into the cave, there's all sorts of scratchings on the wall. Probably Indian drawings. But you have to be careful. There's also deep, deep crevices that you can slip into."

Jack gasped softly. "How did you find this place?" he asked.

"My grandfather showed it to me when I was about your age. His father or grandfather showed him. And on and on, before that. Probably some Indian showed his great-great-grandfather."

"Who showed the Indian?"

"I don't know, Jack! Maybe the Indian saw an animal disappearing behind the falls."

"Who showed the boy who hid from the redcoats?"

"That's what I'm trying to tell you. My *grandfather* was the boy who hid from the redcoats."

"That was your grandfather?!" Jack said, excitedly.

"Yep. That would make him your *great* grandfather," Charles said.

"My great grandfather?"

"Yessir. Your great grandfather. And to top it off, he married the neighbor's daughter…his older brother's girlfriend. Can you believe it? My grandmother was the daughter of the man who had betrayed our family to the British—and her father died not long after the soldiers burned that house down. After all of her father's betrayal and attempt to gain favor with the British, he died shortly after his neighbors—*my family, the Maddau's*—that he had betrayed. Maybe he died from guilt. I don't know if that's even possible. But I *do* know that his daughter—*the one that he was trying to protect from the Maddau's*—married her boyfriend's younger brother, my grandfather. When her father died, the rest of her family moved up north and she inherited their land, which meant that she and the remaining son of her father's old rival got both farms. So that old ditch no longer mattered. They got all the land. What's more, you got your great-grandfather's looks. With your straight, straw-blonde hair, you look just like him."

"How do you know that?" Jack asked, suddenly skeptical.

"My grandmother told me that story so many times, I couldn't forget it. Remember, she knew him as a boy. They were neighbors. She was very detailed in relaying the story, because it was such an important piece of our family heritage. By then—by the time I was around—she was a Maddau through and through. When I look at you, I somehow see my grandfather."

"Is that why you brought me here to this cave—this hiding place?"

"Sure. That's one reason. But also, I wanted you to know how all of his—this Maddau land—came to be ours. They tried to kill us off, Jack, but we won in the end and we got it all. This is all Maddau land. And that river that this stream flows into—*the Rubine River*—runs right through it."

CHAPTER 16
AIN'T TOO PROUD

They were less than a quarter of a mile from the gated front entrance of Maddau Acres and the local DJ on the oldies station had just finished with the weather report, talking about what a beautiful autumn Sunday it was going to be in beautiful South Carolina. When the first drum beats of the song boomed over the Ford's old radio, instinctively and without thinking, Silas screamed out, "I KNOW YOU WANNA LEAVE ME—" At that moment—also instinctively—Clay hit the handle of the passenger door and was only stopped from ejecting himself from the car by Silas lunging over and grabbing him by his coat and hauling him back into his seat.

"Sorry, sorry, my bad," Silas said, quickly turning down the volume.

"What in the—?" Clay scowled, clearly upset.

"It was the Temps, man! The Temps on the box!"

"So?"

"You know, The Temps? 'Ain't Too Proud to Beg'? 1966? I was raised on that stuff! You gotta sing it, right? Don't you ever hear songs that make you wanna sing?"

"Can't say that I do. I wasn't even alive in 1966, and what kinda name for a band is 'The Temps'? Sounds like a bunch of substitute teachers."

"Watch it now. Don't dis 'The Temps.' 'The Temps!' You know, 'The Temptations'…"

"Right. That clears *everything* up," Clay said, sarcastically.

"Like I said, don't dis 'The Temps.' My daddy—now he was a fine preacher, don't get me wrong. He did everything by the book, and by that, I mean the *Good Book*, but, when he wasn't preaching, he was home chillin' to Motown. 'Specially the Temps."

"Fine. He liked 'The Temps.' I got it. But that don't mean you can scare the crap outta me in your car. We just met, man. For all I know, you were turnin' into a crazy person, like those rednecks in last night's pickup."

Silas laughed, "That's a new one. I never been called a redneck. Oh, there," he pointed, "There's your Maddau Acres."

Clay sighed, "Like I said, no relation. I wish. Nice guardhouse, though. Guess it keeps out the riffraff."

"Wouldn't know," Silas said, "I never been invited there."

"Probably just as well," Clay said, "You'd probably just scare everybody singing 'The Temps' at the top of your lungs."

"Fair enough. Fair enough. Point taken. I guess I had that coming," Silas laughed. "I probably should have been listening to hip hop. Rap. Thas what you're thinkin,' right? Lord knows enough men in my unit listened to that. I just never had the ear for it. 'Course, back then, I was never listenin' to what I was supposed to listen to... or doin' what I was supposed to be doin.' Well, 'least not 'til I got into the service. The Army has a tendency to straighten one out and turn ne'er-do-well's into do-well's."

"I don't know if they straightened me out or made me more crooked. 'Guess the jury's still out on that, as far as my life's concerned," Clay said.

"You don't look the worse for wear," Silas commented.

"Good thing you didn't look at my X-rays."

"Remember, I said, *'Been there, done that'*?"

"Yeah. Right. You served, too."

"I served, yes," Silas said, "But you an' I have more in common than just the military."

"Do you jump outta cars on interstates?"

"Not lately. But I ain't sayin' I never did. The military was not my first choice for a career."

"Yeah? What was?"

"A Cowboy. All my life I dreamed of being a Cowboy."

"Somehow, I can't picture you with a Stetson and a wagon-wheel shirt with fringe."

"No, not that kind of cowboy," Silas said, laughing, "A Dallas Cowboy." He pulled up the sleeve of his yellow polo, revealing a star tattoo. "You got a tiger, I got a star."

"How far d'ya get?"

"Army. That's as far as I got. I was a pretty good high school receiver. All-state my junior and senior years, in fact. Had a bunch of D1 schools sniffin' around. Showin' up at my games. An' at my house. Didn't impress me. Didn't impress my father."

"Why not?"

"I expected it. I thought I was good enough to deserve the attention, so I wasn't surprised that I was bein' sought out."

"What about your father? Did he play?"

"He could have. As a young man, he had the speed and the skills, but he opted for the Lord's team."

"Notre Dame?"

Silas laughed heartily, "No. I mean he was all into the church. He thought I was, too, when I wasn't on the field."

"And?"

"Yeah, I played the game…on the field and in church, but I had some of my own friends. Friends my father didn't know about. I called them my 'fun friends.' You know, as opposed to my 'football friends' and 'church friends.' They were all about fun—an' the different kinds of trouble that runs hand-in-hand wi' that kinda 'fun.'"

"Oops."

"Yeah, oops is right. I'll spare you the sordid details. Let's just say that my 'fun friends' were not always so interested in 'law-abidin' fun.'"

"I got the picture."

"Yeah so did I…and the picture was a mug shot, suitable for framin,' or maybe a post office wall. It was actually pretty serious. I landed in front of a judge."

"Let me guess…white judge."

"Oh, you've heard this story already?"

"It's pretty stereotypical, my man."

"Yeah, he was a white judge, but, for better or worse, he went to our church, and knew me and served on the board with my father."

"Sounds like a conflict of interest."

"Actually, he was very interested in my case. He let me choose my punishment, in fact."

"Let me guess, no stars, just bars, right?"

"Well, he gave me the choice of bars or boot camp, to be more specific."

"Wow. Pressed into service."

"Yeah. Just like the good ol' days."

"What about your father? What did he think?"

"Oh, he was all in agreement with his friend the judge."

"Wow. Signed, sealed and delivered."

"Yep," Silas answered. Then, after a brief pause, he asked, "But, hey, what about you? Were you 'pressed into service,' as well?"

"No sir. I jumped at the chance."

"Oh. One of those. I remember you rah-rah guys."

"Nah. Not really rah-rah. It was just something I wanted to do."

"Let me guess—you grew up with dreams of being a general, right?"

"No, it wasn't that."

"Did you come from a military family?"

"Not so much. I mean, my grandfather was in World War II, but he really didn't talk about it that much."

"Not many from that generation did."

"Yeah, I found out about his military service by accident, actually."

"What? Did you see him in an old newsreel or something?"

"No, now that would have been pretty cool. But, it wasn't quite that dramatic. One summer when I was 10 or 11, my old man had to spend some time on the west coast as part of his job. So, my mother, who had never been to California, decided to go with him. Make a vacation of it. So they left me with my grandparents."

"In Chicago?"

"Illinois countryside...my grandparents had long since gotten out of Chicago. It was a great summer for me. Probably the best summer of my childhood. My grandfather took me fishing and hiking, and we did all kinds of summer projects. He had this workshop that he had built behind their house. It was a good-sized workspace. All kinds of tools. He also had his desk and books and filing cabinets there. Looking back on it, I think it was probably his 'escape place.' Don't get me wrong, Grandma was great, but I think he needed some alone time every now and then. Anyway, one morning I showed up at the workshop after breakfast, and he had left to go to the store or somewhere. I mean, at that point, he'd been up for hours. We'd been working on some sort of project...can't remember exactly what...all I remember is that I needed a tape measure. I looked all over the tabletops and couldn't find it. You know how impatient 10- or 11-year-olds can be. So, I'm going through the drawers on his desk and I find this mysterious 'yearbook.'"

"Yearbook?"

"Yeah, like a high school or college yearbook...or annual. Only it was a military yearbook...a squadron yearbook."

"Hmm."

"Yeah. It was Army green and old and musty and it crackled when I opened it. It had all kinds of cool insignia all over it, and inside, there were pictures of these guys, all together with their crewmates, standing in front of their B-24s."

"Ah. Army Air Corps."

"Correct. South Pacific. 1944. Or '45. I found the picture of my grandfather and his crew, and his plane. It was a fierce-lookin' beast of a plane, but it had a cartoon turtle painted on the side. I wouldn't have recognized him, because he was a young man in the picture, but the name 'Maddau' popped off the page. As you said, it's not exactly an ordinary name."

"Right. So…what happened?"

"Well, I was mesmerized…like in a trance, when I flipped through those pages. I didn't hear my grandfather come in behind me."

"Uh oh. D'yu get in trouble?"

"Actually, no. He was like, 'okay, you discovered my secret.' You know, the cat is out of the bag. So, he spent the rest of the day tellin' me about what he did in the war."

"Wow."

"Wow is right. I mean I had seen millions of World War II movies, but those were all Hollywood stuff. This thing with my grandfather was the real deal. He had been a Chicago kid, obviously street-wise, drafted right outta high school. He qualified for gunnery school and ended up in the South Pacific as a top turret gunner on a B-24. I said, 'Granddad, why are you and your friends standing in front of a plane with a cartoon turtle on it—a cartoon *cowboy* turtle, in fact?'"

"Cowboy turtle? Never heard of a turtle wanting to be a cowboy."

"Shows ya how much you know…it's a common dream of turtles to be a cowboy. Hey…*you* wanted to be *Cowboy*. Don't judge."

"Wow. I can't believe you went there."

"Yeah. Sorry. That was a cheap shot."

"I'll forget about it, if you continue the story."

"Right. The crew was from all over the country, as were most crews. Granddad was from Chicago, the pilot was a Texan, and navigator was from California. In fact, before the war, he had worked in Hollywood on cartoons. Hard to believe, but at that point, animated cartoons had only been around for 15 or 20 years."

"Yeah, and they were pretty zany. Lots of crazy antics."

"That's one way to put it—crazy antics. So, the navigator had worked on a series of animated shorts about this turtle and his *crazy antics*."

"A cowboy turtle."

"Right. A cowboy turtle. *'Git-Along Turtle'* was what they called him. He had a big ol' Stetson and a couple of six guns."

"Doesn't sound familiar. Did you used to watch *Git-Along Turtle* cartoons on Saturday mornings or something?"

"No, the only turtles I ever watched were the teenage mutant ninja kind. The cowboy kind were not even on my radar. I guess ol' Git-Along did most of his gittin' along back in the '30s and '40s. At any rate, he was painted on the side of the B-24. There he was, grinning like an imbecile with a big Stetson and wavin' his six-guns under cartoon lettering that said, in big yellow letters, *'Git-Along Turtle.'*"

"That is a little odd."

"Actually, not so much. The pilot was a Texan, remember?"

"'T' for 'Texas,' 'T' for Tennessee, 'T' for 'Turtle'...they made a soup outa me!"

"Not bad. Not funny, but not bad."

"Come on. You could at least humor me because I'm still hurt over your Cowboy comment."

"Alright we're even."

"I'm even; you're odd."

"Do you want to hear the story?"

"Oh. Yeah. Sorry, continue..."

"So, the pilot was from Texas."

"An, he was a cowboy...?"

"Actually, no. He worked for an oil company. However, his name was Tuttle...Lieutenant Tuttle. Hence the 'turtle.' An' he was from Texas, after all. So, it seemed like a natural leap o' logic. The navigator got in touch with the studios, and, get this, they flew some of the artists over to paint the art on the nose. Both sides, in fact."

"Okay. So your grandfather flew in a B-24 with a cowboy turtle on it."

"Yeah, so day after an early morning bombing raid over Japanese-held Formosa, they were all in formation to return to the base, when all of a sudden, the flak stopped. An' Granddad said that was never a good sign. Sure enough, here they come. A pack o' Zeros. Closin' in fast. An' one of 'im had the *'Git-Along Turtle'* in his sights. He blew apart the tail gunner turret, and was closin' in fast. My grandfather was the only one—at that point—that had a shot at him. He waited as long as he could, and let him have it with his .50 cal Brownings."

"How'd that work out?"

"Pretty well. Granddad said the Zero would have suicide-crashed into the *'Turtle'*, but he'd lost control at that point, and he goes sailin' past their B-24, and the rest of the planes in the formation, in flames."

"Whew."

"Yeah. But here's the point. Granddad said that up until that point, he and the rest of the crew—except for the cartoonist-navigator and Lieutenant Tuttle, the so-called namesake—were not that crazy about a cartoon cowboy turtle on the side of their warbird. Most of the other planes had wild animals, pirates, and other vicious logos that showed they meant business. Something tougher than a cowboy turtle."

"I get it."

"Yeah, I do, too. But, Granddad said, that after that moment, they all loved the logo and their plane."

"What changed their minds?"

"Simple. The look on the face of the pilot of that Japanese Zero as he stared at the cartoon cowboy turtle on the side of their B-24; it was a look of terror mixed with shame and unbelief."

"I guess so. Shot down by a cowboy turtle."

"Exactly—shelled by a shelled turtle."

"I get it. So. Is that why you enlisted? Because of your grandfather?"

"Well, sorta. But, if I was really truthful, I'd have to say it was because of my old man."

"Oh. Was he military, too?"

Clay laughed. "That's a good one," he said, "Actually, far from it. He was one of the original hippies. He hated the military. Got arrested in Chicago in '68 protesting Vietnam at the DNC Convention. You know, 'the whole world's watching' thing? You know, unlike my grandfather who never talked about his service in the war, my old man never shut up about his golden days as a hippie. He lived in San Francisco—Haight-Asbury, even—during the so-called 'Summer of Love,' went to Dead concerts, dropped acid, you know, the whole Woodstock generation stuff. In fact, when he and my mom went to San Francisco—you know, when they dropped me off at my grandparents—he ran into an old hippie girlfriend from those days."

"Uh oh. What did your mother think?"

"Oh, she wasn't there when he ran into her. She was back at the hotel or something. He was having lunch with his business partners or something, and she turned out to be the waitress."

"That was convenient."

"No, I have to believe that it was a coincidence. My old man wasn't smart enough to arrange anything like that."

"So, did they have a chance to talk about the good old hippie days."

"I don't know if they did then or not. Like I said, he was with his business partners. But there was plenty of time later," Clay laughed ruefully.

"Later?"

"Yeah, he and my mom came back to Chicago. They picked me up from my grandparents. I was all jazzed about my grandfather's World War II stuff. Actually, that's beside the point. We got back home. Next thing we knew, he had quit his job and left me and my mother and moved back to San Francisco."

"That's intense."

"You have no idea. The ink wasn't dry on the divorce papers before he and his old hippie girlfriend—she went by 'Electra,' but her real name was Delores—anyway, they were married in some field by the ocean by some kind of cosmic yogi. My mother was devastated. She called his girlfriend 'Neptuna,'" Clay laughed, "Still to this day. 'How's your father?' she'll ask me, 'Is he still with Neptuna?' So, to answer your question, yes, I enlisted in the service to honor my grandfather, but more importantly, the biggest reason I enlisted was to spite my old man."

"Did it work?"

"Absolutely. He was horrified. Disappointed. Very angry. I was so proud of myself."

"I mean…did it work for you?"

"Sure, if you're talking about cutting off your nose to spite your face. It definitely came back to bite me."

"How so?"

"What d'ya mean 'how so'? Weren't you the one who rousted me from underneath an interstate bridge this morning?"

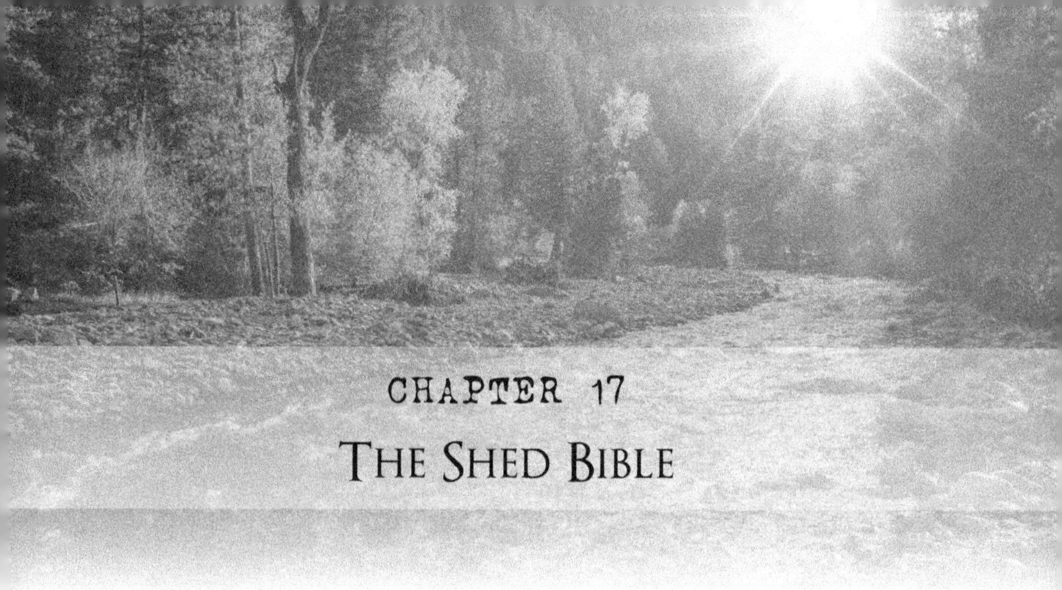

CHAPTER 17

THE SHED BIBLE

Elizabeth slowly turned the finished pot in her hands, searching for defects and irregularities, but there were none. The pot was a slendid specimen, and it shimmered in the late afternoon sunshine that pushed its way into the pottery studio. The brick-and-wooden building had long replaced the old and cramped shed that had served as her first studio when Neemy had begun working with her. As she held the pot up to her face for a closer look, her eye was drawn to Neemy, who was intently working on one of the potter's wheels, shaping and perfecting the clay as it spun between his calloused hands.

"Nehemiah," she said, "You have truly been a blessing these last few years."

Neemy looked up appreciatively and let the wheel slow to a stop.

"Thank you, ma'am," he said.

She gestured toward the big house, as if it represented the whole entity of the plantation. "Of course, the crops and the cattle sell, but the pots have turned into more than a sideline. They've done well, and that's thanks to your help. And, you've turned into quite the little potter. You're a real artist."

"Thank you, ma'am," he repeated, shyly.

"You know, I would have loved for Jack to learn this, but he just doesn't have the inclination. The *willingness* to *learn*. The *desire* to *create*. And that's really what it is, isn't it, Neemy? It's the process and the joy of *creating* something. Something of value, a work of art, right?"

"Yassum." Neemy was flattered by the compliment, but he wasn't exactly sure what Elizabeth was trying to tell him.

"Okay. Look, it's getting late. Your ma is going to be looking for you and Charles—Mr. Maddau—is going to be looking for his supper pretty soon. Hold on, let me light this candle, so we can see what we're doing and not trip over ourselves," she laughed.

She found a candle next to the door and after a few attempts managed to light it and hold it up toward the shed's shelves. "What do you say we pick up where we left off yesterday?"

"Yassum."

"Where was that, Nehemiah?"

"Brother Paul was whippin' the Thesslonites with his words."

"Right. Right. Get the *Shed Bible* down off that shelf, if you would, Neemy."

Elizabeth held the dripping candle up as Neemy retrieved the big, clay-speckled Bible from the shelf in the back of the workroom.

"Here we are," Elizabeth said, flipping through the Bible, once Neemy had retrieved it, "We were reading Second Thessalonians 3. Hmm, right, we stopped at verse 9. Let's pick up there, at verse 10," Elizabeth said, pointing at the words with her finger. "Starting with verse 10— *'For even when we were with you, this we commanded you, that if any would not work, neither should he eat. For we hear that there are some which walk among you disorderly, working not at all, but are busybodies. Now them that are such we command and exhort by our Lord Jesus Christ, that with quietness they work, and eat their own bread. But ye, brethren, be not weary in well doing.'"*

When Elizabeth looked up, Neemy was staring out the workroom's window at the big house. Although he quickly looked back at the open Bible, she knew that he was thinking of her son, Jack, who, at that moment, was up on the big front porch, dozing in the swing as it gently rocked back and forth in the approaching dusk.

"So, Neemy. What do you think?" Elizabeth asked.

"Ma'am?"

"What do you think?"

"I think the Thesslonites better a-listened to Paul."

Elizabeth laughed, "I think you're right. But it's a lesson for all of us, too, don't you think?"

"Yassum."

"You know what, Neemy?" Elizabeth said, closing the Bible, "I think we need to find a new home for the Shed Bible."

"Ma'am?" Neemy said, confused.

"I think this here shed has earned the right to have a brand-new Bible, don't you?"

"Ma'am?"

"I think I'm going to order a new 'Shed Bible' next time I go into town and visit Mr. Klein. In the meantime, why don't you give this trusty old Bible a good home? There's still a lot of life left in it, don't you think?"

Neemy couldn't believe what he was hearing. Looking around the shed, Elizabeth found a big cotton sack and carefully placed the clay-misted Bible into the sack.

"Oh, and here's something else, just for you," she said, handing Neemy a dozen biscuits, carefully wrapped in a kitchen towel, although she knew he would take it home to his mother to be shared with their family, "It's from last night's supper, but I expect they won't be too hard. That's what I'd call food for the body and food for the soul!"

"Oh, Miz Lizbeth!" Neemy said, "Miz Lizbeth! This th' bes' day o' my life, Miz Lizbeth!"

"I'm glad to be a part of it, Neemy," Elizabeth smiled, "Now go on, get yourself home, before your mama comes looking for you!"

With that, Neemy carefully tucked the cotton sack under his arm and scampered down the path through the fields toward their cabin in the light of dusk, eager to share his treasures with his family.

CHAPTER 18
JUDGMENT

It was before dawn on a crisp Sunday morning when Charles Maddau arose to go hunting. He was wearing a red cotton shirt with two button-down pockets. One held some tobacco, the other his old pocket watch. He knew that a red shirt wasn't the wisest choice for the sake of hunting camoflauge, but it was thick and warm, and he figured that his heavy coat would cover and conceal the shirt, anyway.

He went down into the kitchen and the cook was already up. She scrambled a few eggs and fried some bacon in her big, black skillet and slid them off on a plate to go with the hot mug of coffee. She knew he had planned to go hunting and expected a hot breakfast before leaving for the woods. He finished eating just as the first rays of the sunrise came tapping on the kitchen window. As he scooted his chair back from the table, he gulped down the last few swallows of coffee and walked over to touch one of the panes from the kitchen window to gauge the temperature. It was freezing. *Perfect for hunting,* he thought, *but as unpleasant for the humans as it was the animals he would be shooting.*

Maddau had leaned his rifle up against the wall by the front door. His knapsack with his provisions was sitting on the loveseat in the house's foyer. Once he stomped out onto the front porch, he surveyed the front yard and the fields beyond, as they began to be subtly lit by the rising sun. The fields, which had been covered with cotton only a few months before, were again solid white, this time with a late January snow. At the edge of the field, some errant golden stems of grain poked through the snow, and it reminded him of Jack's straw-colored hair, and for a brief moment he thought about going back into the house and waking the boy up to accompany him. He enjoyed Jack's company, but he enjoyed the solitude of the frozen woods at that time of year even more, and he was grateful that he didn't have to weather the boy's whining. The stabbing cold would be enough of a nuisance. He had enough ammunition and food to last all day, but his plans included sending some of his help to fetch whatever game he was able to bring down. He would simply bind the game with some heavy twine and hang it from a nearby tree. He knew the temperature would not be above freezing, and whatever he killed would stay preserved until it could be retrieved.

Sometimes, especially when Jack was with him and they intended to travel a bit of a distance, they would take their horses. That day, however, he liked the feel of the snow crunching under his heavy boots. His land stretched for several miles, all the way to the river, but he doubted that he would have to journey that far. As he reached the first field, he did a mental checklist of what he would need for the hunt. Obviously, his rifle and ammunition, along with enough water and some food to get him through the day. *Did I pack the heavy twine*? he wondered. He stopped and set his knapsack down on a frozen stump and began rummaging through it. When he got to the bottom and found that there was no heavy twine, he cursed himself and his luck. The barn was beyond the house and nearly a half-mile away. He figured that by the time he got to the barn to get the twine and back to where he was then standing, the sun would already be climbing the southern sky. As he trudged through the snow toward the barn, a thought of consolation hit him: *I'll bet Elizabeth has some heavy twine in her pottery shed. That's what she uses to bind those infernal boxes full of her pots she sells to that Jew.*

The shed was in the shadows of the big house, covered in snow, and it looked like a little enchanted dollhouse. For a moment Maddau wondered what their lives would have been like if they had a daughter, rather than a surley son like Jack. He fumbled with the latch, which was frozen, and finally removed one of his gloves, and held it in his teeth while he fished out his large, bone-handled pocketknife. After a few moments of chipping around the latch, it broke free of the ice, and Maddau clomped into the shed. The shelf next to the door held mostly pottery tools and some finished pots, but in the darkened shed, he saw what looked like a spool of the heavy twine on the shelf on the back wall. He didn't want to step on and break any of Elizabeth's pots, so he took a candle from the shelf by the door and lit it to mark his way to the back of the tiny shed. As he grabbed the spool of heavy thread from the shelf, the flickering candle lit up a piece of torn paper that had fallen beneath the shelf, and curious, he bent to retrieve it. He assumed it was one of Elizabeth's lists or recipes that had somehow fallen out of the torn pocket of one of her workshirts. However, as he held the candle up to read it, he immediately saw that it was certainly not Elizabeth's elegant handwriting, but, rather the crude scrawling of a child. In letters big and bold it clearly read: *"Nehemiah sez God is luv."*

As Maddau folded the note, he became more and more angry, and by the time he got up the steps to the house, across the front porch, and threw open the front door, his face was as red as his shirt. He loudly clamoured up the front room's stairs, and made his way down the hall and into the bedroom, where Elizabeth was stirring, having been awakened by his heavy footing upon the front porch.

"Charles?" she asked, sleepily.

"What is this?" he said, thrusting the torn and dirty piece of paper in her face.

"Gracious," she said, "I have no idea—even if I could see it."

Maddau crossed over to the east side of the bedroom and ripped the drapes down from the window, letting in the morning sun. Elizabeth stared at him for a moment, still bewildered, and then glacnced down at the paper. Maddau watched as a look of recognition crossed her face.

"What is this?" he repeated. "Actually, save your breath. I know what it is."

"Charles—" Elizabeth began.

"I thought we had an understanding. I was fine with you teachin' that boy how to make pots, but I think I was pretty clear in telling you—*not asking you—telling* you that you were not to be teaching him reading and writing. Not only is it against the law. It's flat out dangerous. An' I was very specific in tellin' you not to teach him to 'make his letters.'"

"Charles, I didn't teach him."

"Well, he sure enough knows enough to write his name and 'God is love.' How do you explain that? Did he absorb that learning through you teaching him to make those silly pots?"

"I didn't know—"

"You didn't know that you were teaching that boy how to read and write? Can you hear yourself? What kind of a fool do you take me for? I can't believe that all this time—"

"Charles—"

"There is only one thing we can do now. You have forced my hand on this."

"What does that mean, Charles?"

"That means he can't stay here. I'm going to have to sell or trade him."

"You can't be serious."

"I am dead serious, and there's no discussion, here. This is all on you."

"You can't do that!"

"Of course I can. Watch me."

"You know you can't!"

"And why can't I?"

"You know quite well why you can't."

"I can and I will."

"What about his mother?"

"As far as I'm concerned, she can go with him. I will make that concession. She can be sold or traded along with the boy."

"Get rid of Belle?"

"You're the one that asked about the boy's mother."

"So that's her punishment then? For being Nehemiah's mother? What about her husband and the boy's brother?"

"They'll have to stay. They're much too valuable as workers. Palmer certainly won't mind the boy being gone, and I can convince him of the woman, but I can hear him now on the other two."

"This is so unfair. They are a family."

"As I said, you created this situation. And, you've ruined my hunting day."

"*Your hunting day?!*" Elizabeth said, angrily, "I am so sorry that I've ruined your *hunting day*, while at the same time, you have just matter-of-factly issued an *edict* that will devastate a family and affect every one of them for as long as they live."

"Well, you should have thought about that before you disobeyed me," Maddau replied, "It's not just my—what, *edict*, as you say—it's against the law. And, it happens to be a law that I agree with. And you should, too. You should be ashamed of yourself. I honestly don't know what you were thinking."

"I was thinking that I would share the Word of God with Neemy, who has been a wonderful help to me. That's what I was thinking!"

"Well, you should have thought it out more carefully. Besides, it doesn't matter now, anyway, whatever your intent was. All that matters is that I'll be back tonight, and you need to tell the boy today. You can blame it all on me, if that makes you feel less guilty. I'll tell Palmer when I get back tonight, or maybe tomorrow. But, either way the boy will need to be gone this week. With or without his mother." Maddau sighed. "If you really need help—with your pot things—I'll get Palmer to find someone else that he can spare."

"But Charles—"

"It's decided," Charles said, holding up his hand, "It was decided when I found that boy's writing on the floor of your little shed. So you go ahead and tell them today. And don't think by *not* telling them, and hoping I'll change my mind that somehow this will all be forgotten and forgiven. I've already made my final decision. I made it the minute I found that scrap of writing. All I'm doing now is giving you the chance to tell your little helper, before we come and get him. You should be thanking me for that. I hope you'll *think* before you do anything like this again."

With that, Maddau turned and stomped out of the bedroom, down the stairs and out the door on his way through the snow to the fields. He was nearly a mile from the house when he came to one of his larger fields that held a portion of his cattle. By this time, his trudging through the snow, along with the early morning's freezing temperature had cooled his anger. When he reached the pasture inhabited by Ol' Thor, Maddau reflected on how the old bull always frightened Jack. As he chuckled at the thought of his son's fear, the bull meandered through the snow to check him out.

"Well, look who's here," Maddau called out to the bull, "As I live and breathe, it's Ol' Thor, the king of the snowy pasture."

The old bull slowed down on his way to where the man stood, and Maddau could see the twin plumes of frosty steam coming from the bull's nose. *He sure fits the bill of a dangerous bull,* he thought, but he brushed away a warning twinge which urged him toward caution.

"So now, I'm supposed to be afraid of you?" he shouted at the bull. "Why is everbody all of a sudden trying to tell me how to run things? This is my property. That's my house back there. This is my place. This is my pasture. You—you are only standing in my pasture at my pleasure. You think you're gonna scare me? I ain't Jack. See this gun, Mr. Thor? I could end your very existence in a split second. You gonna try me, you old bull? Well? Well?"

With that, Maddau opened up his heavy jacket to let the bull see that he was wearing a red cotton shirt. He laughed derisively when he thought of how frightened Jack would have been at his action of showing red to the bull, and he continued making his way through the heavy snow and walking among the cattle. The bull followed him cautiously from a distance—to his side—as Maddau crossed the field. As they neared the gate at the outer most edge of the field, the old bull scampered forward, his breath still blowing twin plumes of steam and stood between Maddau and the gate.

"Well, well," Maddau said, "So now, you're 'Old Thor the Gatekeeper.' Who gave you a promotion, you old fool? And although I could go around you, I don't much feel like it today."

The bull stood still, staring at the man and his red shirt. Maddau paused for a moment, staring back at the bull. "This is what my life has come to," Maddau said out loud, "Arguing with a bull. It's not enough that I'm being questioned by negroes and women. Now, I'm in high-level negotiations with a 2200-pound steak."

Maddau dropped his knapsack and got a firm grip on his rifle, and moved slowly toward the bull with his jacket wide open, his red shirt plainly visible against the vast whiteness of the field. "Git!" he finally shouted at the bull.

Ol' Thor suddenly jerked his head back and moved aside, bellowing loudly as he moved through the snow out of the man's path. Maddau turned to retrieve his knapsack, and again thought of how the scene would have played out had Jack been there with him. The image in his head made him again laugh derisively. "I'm surrounded by people and animals who all think they're smarter than me!" he yelled. "Well, how did that work out for you, Ol' Thor? Well?" The bull seemed to be more puzzled than frightened at the man's shouts and actions, but he chose to move on away, just in case the man posed an actual threat. And that only fueled Maddau's tirade.

"What about you, Elizabeth?! My dear wife?! How did that work out for you?!" he screamed in the direction of the big house, although it was much too far away for his loudest screams to be heard. Suddenly an intense pain shot up his arm and into his chest, and he dropped his rifle and ammo bag and fell to his knees, clutching his chest. As he fell, he could see the bright red fabric of his shirt between his clutched fingers, as if his heart had exploded into a million pieces. A second later, he was face down in the heavy snow. A few of the cattle came over to inspect, but Ol' Thor had already forgotten about the interaction and was moving toward the far end of the snowy field.

By mid-day, it had begun snowing again and by nightfall, Maddau's body had been totally covered, as had his footprints leading up to—and *into*—the field.

Back in the big house, Elizabeth built a hearty fire in the parlor and pondered the morning's argument and conclusion. For an hour or so, she poked at the fire and brought in some more logs from the back porch. When the afternoon rolled around, she hesitantly wrapped up to begin the trek to Belle's cabin to deliver the unwelcome news. However, as she stepped from the porch, she noticed the snow falling in big puffy pieces, ironically, closely resembling the cotton they picked. As she made her way through the accumulating snowdrifts, she neared the area where the quarters stood. From a distance, she could see some of the children playing in the snow. At the center of the activity was Nehemiah and Jonathan. They were barefoot and dressed in the thread-bare clothes that they wore year-round, but they seemed oblivious to the cold, focusing solely on the joy that only an all-encompassing snowfall can bring to the young.

"No," she said out loud, "I'm not going to do it. There simply *has* to be another option." With that she turned and made her way back to the big house and her seat in front of the fireplace in the parlor. After a few hours, the cook summoned her to the dining room, where she had laid out that night's dinner, fried chicken, potatoes, green beans, tea and apple pie for dessert. Elizabeth picked at her food and reminded the cook to save some for Charles.

"When he be here?" the cook asked.

"That's a good question. But the important thing is to have it ready for him as soon as he walks in the door."

The sun had long been down, but Elizabeth surmised that it wasn't all that unusual for Charles to return from a hunt after dark, especially because of the day's snow…and the morning' argument. Actually, it wasn't that unusual for Charles to stomp off to the hunt after one of their arguments, only to return as if everything was normal. However, she feared that the morning's argument would be different from the norm. But, when midnight arrived and he had still not returned, she summoned Palmer and they organized a search party. Palmer sent for all the workers and servants, both men and women, and they went out into the snowy night with lanterns. They owned a huge property, and

Charles could have gone in any direction to hunt. The cold, darkness, and snow made the task at finding him even more extreme. By dawn, they all had returned to the front porch of the big house, and after a quick breakfast and a summary of the areas that had been searched, they once again went out into the fields and forests on the Maddau's property. Jack led one of the search teams, and on a hunch, he directed them into the pasture where the cattle where still huddled together.

"Watch out for Ol' Thor," he yelled to the others, "Watch out for the bull!" About an hour into the search in the pasture, one of the workers searched near the far gate and tripped on Charles' rifle buried in the snow and called for Jack. They found Maddau, still face down and buried in the snow, a few feet away. Jack, rifle in hand, leaned over the body, and upon glancing up, caught sight of Ol' Thor, who was milling around with a few of the other cattle. Without a second thought, he leveled his father's rifle and fired a single shot into the old bull's head.

CHAPTER 19

MOTOR CITY / MUSIC CITY

"Wow, look at the time," Silas said as he gunned the Ford down the straightaway toward the Rubineville Community.

"Are we late for something?" Clay asked.

"Nope. Right on schedule."

As they flew by a classic two-story house with a wrap-around porch draped with a collection of flags, Clay shook his head.

"What?" Silas asked.

"I don't think I'll ever get used to all these rebel flags," Clay said. You'd think South Carolina won the war.

"Oh, well that place back there has an excuse—it's a Civil War Museum. Sherman's boys came through this area in the last months of the war."

"Really? I understand he was pretty careless with matches."

"Yeah, well that's why you won't see a lot of 'anti-bellum' structures. Plenty of 'post-bellum' houses."

"I guess we can learn a lot from South Carolina."

"How so?"

"Plans don't always work out the way you think they should."

"It sounds like a personal statement."

"You're right. But something tells me you can relate."

"Again, how so?"

"Well, for instance, your plans for football. From what you told me—or didn't tell me—I'm guessing your football dream never became reality."

"You got it, man."

"No college? No football?"

"No football. I got some college…during and after I got out of the Army. They paid for it. I still had a lot of anger, though. The Army wasn't a magic bullet."

"Yeah, but did it cure you from the Temps?"

"That would never happen. Wait a minute…didn't you hear me singin'?"

"Oh. So that's what that was."

"Come on, now. Don't be mean."

"Just bustin' your chops, man."

"What about your music? What's your pleasure? What'd y'all play in your downtime over there?"

"Con-tree music!" he said.

"Okay. I had Motown, you had Nashville. I get it."

"It took some doing. It was definitely an 'acquired' taste. These Chicago ears didn't really know how to process banjos and pedal steels." Clay reflected for a second and then smiled a sad smile, "My best bud, Beau, was a hardcore Southern boy. I mean, you don't get more Southern for a name than Beau…as in Beauregard."

"Was that his full name? Beauregard?"

"Nah, just Beau. Sometimes I'd call 'im Beauregard just to tick 'im off. It's funny—when I was growin' up—you know, *up north*—we used to think all Southerners were a bunch of inbred redneck cavemen. Man, I woulda been quick to tell you that, too. We watched too many TV shows about hillbillies, I guess."

"Oh, so you believe in hillbillies," Silas said.

"Oh yeah. They do exist, indeed."

"So your friend Beau was a hillbilly?"

"Nah. Well, maybe. Well, I don't know. He was just different from the guys I had known all my life," Clay said, "'Course I'd never met anybody from Alabama before him."

"There are some hardcore Alabama people."

"Oh yeah. Roll Tide. Right? That was the first thing out of his mouth. Bama this, Bama that. But even if he wadn't spoutin' off at the mouth, there was no doubt to his loyalties. We were still in our civvies on the bus, and there he was with his 'Big A' sweatshirt, and you can imagine what I thought that Big A was..."

"Uh...the 'Scarlet Letter?'"

Clay laughed. "That's one explanation!"

"But not what you were thinking, right?"

"Yeah. But kudos for the literary reference."

"Noted."

"But here's the thing. You know I said we were best buds? What's so funny about me and Beau...we really banged heads—and I do mean *literally*—the first week of basic. Man, you'da thought they woulda run us so ragged we wouldn'ta had time for extracurriculars, right? But ol' Beau, he was always poppin' his head up to see if the sergeant was around. I guess he musta had something he didn't want to get caught with. Picture of his girl back in Alabama, maybe. I don't know. Never found out. Anyway, he was always popping his head up, quick, like a prairie dog. So, I called him 'Beau Peeps.' I always was a little bit of a smart aleck, and I thought I was being funny—actually, it got a big laugh from everybody. Well, not everybody. Beau was not amused. In fact, that little remark got me a quick uppercut to my jaw, and man it was on!"

"So, y'all somehow became friends?" Silas asked.

"Yeah, that. The sergeant came in right in the middle of our tussle an' he said something to the effect of 'since you girls are so intent on dancin' with each other, well let me just see if I can score some tickets to the ball for the both of ya.' The 'KP Ball.' What that turned out to be was 20-mile-runs, obstacle courses, *and do it all again*. You name it, anything unpleasant you can think of, that old sergeant made us do.

Man, we were handcuffed—*figuratively*—to each other for the next week or two. At some point, we forgot we didn't like each other."

"Thas the way it works, brother."

"I guess. Well, anyway, we ended up together in the sandbox. I don't know if they thought they were rewarding us or punishing us when they left us together. But, at any rate, when we were out on point, he ran the tunes…to get back to your question. So, it was country this, country that. He loved Garth Brooks. Kenny Chesney, you know the Nashville guys. But, he especially loved 'Lynyrd Skynyrd'," Clay laughed softly, "He knew they were from somewhere down in Florida, but *'Sweet Home Alabama'* was like his theme song. I used to tell him, if I have to listen to one more song about tractors or Alabama, I'm gonna turn into a boll weevil."

"Ouch!"

"Yeah. Funny thing is, I didn't even know what a boll weevil was!"

Silas laughed, "Y'all get out at the same time? You keep in touch?"

"Nah."

"He stay in?"

"Actually, the truth is," Clay said, taking a deep breath, "Beau and Baker and Kincaid and Wharton and everybody else in the Humvee got blown into a million pieces. 'Cept me. Of course. Last man sittin'."

"Sorry, man."

"Yeah, me, too. Other than not being able to hear for a while, I pretty much got off lucky. Medics got there quick. 'Course I couldn't hear what they were sayin'. I saw the horror in their eyes and saw them movin' their jaws at me, but it jus' came out as 'Wha, wha, wha, wha.' Remember how the grownups talked on the 'Peanuts' TV specials? 'Wha, wha, wha?' Anyway as they took me away, I got a look at what used to be the Humvee. An' what used to be my friends ridin' with me. An' man, I swear I heard *'Sweet Home Alabama'* playin' on that busted box. I couldn't hear anything else. The medics were still going, 'Wha, wha, wha,' but somehow, cuttin' through all the…*cacophony*… came *'Sweet Home Alabama.'* To this day, I don't know if that was real or imagined, or if I was in shock and hallucinating. But the upshot is that I can't hear that song anymore without dropping back into that nightmare. Usually, it's on the radio, and I can just shut it off. Even if I'm in someone else's car, I have to shut it off. Even if I'm in the backseat."

"It's a wonder your friends in the pickup didn't play it on their radio."

"You have a valid point there. It would have been nice if it would have come on the radio before we finished that cheap liquor…it may have saved me a roll under the bridge."

"Yeah, but you wouldn't be on your way to a hot breakfast this morning."

"I suppose you're right. The problem is, sometimes, some jackass just has to play it on some hole-in-the-wall jukebox, and that's when the trouble starts. Someone who would drop a dime—or a dollar—in the box to play it usually don't take kindly to someone like me unpluggin' the machine. That has typically been a sore point in my past dealings with some citizens and some lawmen. Maybe we can compare mugshots sometime."

"Uh, think I'll pass on that, brother."

CHAPTER 20

JACOB'S LADDER

The singing drifted through the trees in beautiful, but quiet—*almost whispered*—harmony, and the notes hung in the wind and blended with the soft summer breeze. It was deep into a July night and equally as deep into the thick, dark forest at the edge of the Maddau property, just over the ridge from the Rubine River. It was also a secret gathering, hence the softness of the music. When the song was finished, Neemy's Uncle Jobe, limped over to a stump of a tree that had fallen in a thunderstorm the previous summer.

"Boys, y'all come on up here, now," Jobe said, leaning on his lion-head cane and directing his gaze toward the back of the group where Neemy, Jonathan, Belle, and Gabe stood. Jonathan looked over at his mother, and she smiled and nodded her head. He and Neemy made their way up to the front to stand by their uncle.

"Tonight, we gon' talk 'bout Jacob," Jobe said, "Jonathan, boy, what do you know 'bout Jacob?"

"His ladder."

"Watchu say?"

"Ladder. He got a ladder."

"Yessir. Dat Jacob gots hisself a ladder. What he gonna do wi' dat ladder, Jonathan?"

"Climb."

"Yessir. He gonna climb it. Now, Jonathan. Is it a song about Jacob an' dat ladder?"

"Yessir."

"You gonna sing an' lead us wi' dat song?"

"Yessir."

"Well, then sing it, boy!"

"We are…climbin'…Jacob's…Ladder," Jonathan began singing with a clear and beautiful voice, *"We are…climbin'…Jacob's…Ladder, We are…climbin'…Jacob's… Ladder, Soldiers…of the…Cross."*

And as he began the next round, the group joyfully joined in and the rich harmony surrounded and cloaked them with a blissful presence. *"Every…rung goes…higher…higher…"*

After the song was sung, Jonathan scrambled back to where Belle and Gabe stood in the back of the group, but Neemy stayed beside his uncle.

"Jacob an' his ladder. I loves dat song!" Jobe said as the worshippers settled onto their blankets and quilts spread out in the clearing.

"Yas!" someone shouted.

"Das a marvelous song!"

"Yas!"

"I love dat story!"

"Yas!"

"I heard th' story from the time I wuz little. But I had to just trust that it wuz truth. Mama tol' it to me. She tol' me 'bout Adam and Eve. She tol' me 'bout Moses and Abraham. She tol' me 'bout Goliath, that big ol' giant fightin' David and his lil' ol' slingshot, heh, heh, heh.

"She tol' me 'bout Daniel in they lion's den. Don't git me started bout lions, heh, heh, heh," he laughed, "I got me some personal experience wi' they lions. Heh, heh. But my mama also tol' me 'bout Jacob an' his ladder, and that's whut we's talkin' 'bout tonight. But, it ain't jus' a story that my mama made up. Lissen now. You don't have to trust th' word of ol' Jobe and his mama."

With that, Jobe leaned down, and with the help of some of the elders, picked up a large cotton bag, which he had placed beside the stump. As one of the elders held a flickering candle high, Jobe withdrew the large black, clay-speckled Bible from the sack. "But you can trust th' Word of God's Holy Book. Now I cants read his story. Jacob's story. But we gots us someone here who can."

"Yas!"

"It's a blessin', I tell you! We gots someone who can read it from God's Holy Word! Neemy, bless you, boy. Reads this for us."

Jobe had asked Neemy to bookmark the passage before the meeting began, so as Jobe and one of the other men held the big Bible, lit by the candle above the boy's head, Neemy began to read: "This is from Gen-sis. The first book of the Ol' Test-ment. The first book of the Bible. Readin' from Gen-sis 28:10: *'An' Jacob went out from Beersheba, an' went toward Haran. And he lighted 'pon a certain place, an' tarried dere all night, 'cause th' sun was set; an' he took of th' stones o' that place, an' put 'em for his pillas, an' lay down in th' place to sleep. An' he dream, an' behol' a ladder set up on th' earth, and th' top of it reached t' heaven; and behol' th' angels of God ascendin' an' de-scendin' on it. And, behol', th' Lord stood 'bove it, and say, "I am th' Lord God of Abraham thy father, and th' God of Isaac; th' land whereon thou liest, to thee will I give it, an' to thy seed; And thy seed shall be as th' dust of th' earth, an' thou shalt spread abroad to th' west, and to th' east, and to th' north, and to th' south; and in thee and in thy seed shall all the families of th' earth be blessed. And, b'hold, I am wi' thee, and will keep thee in all places whither thou goest, and will bring thee again into this land; for I will not leave thee, 'til I have done that which I have spoken to thee of." And Jacob awaked out of his sleep, an' he said, "Surely th' Lord is in this place; and I knew it not."'*"

Neemy paused for a moment and looked out over the crowd, all sihouetted in the darkness of the thick woods. Although he couldn't make out their faces in the dark, he knew them all, and he knew some of them would have their eyes closed as they listened. Some would have their heads bowed. Some would be gazing into stars dotting the vast, deep-ocean-blue of the nighttime summer sky. And, he knew that some of them had never heard the reading of the actual words from an actual Bible. The candle flickered above him, and he saw his shadow dancing on the pages of the open Bible.

"Thank you, boy," Jobe's eyes were closed. "Thank you, Nehemiah. You's a blessin', boy. You gots a gift from God. Now go on over there with you brother."

Jobe waited until Neemy had made his way back to his parents and Jonathan, and then he said, "What I tell you 'bout that song? 'Bout that story? I din make it up. Jacob lays hisself down an' uses a rock fo' th' pilla. Now, dat makes my head hurt jest thinkin' 'bout it."

The congregated people chuckled at that, and Jobe continued. "So, ol' Jacob done dreams hisself up a ladder that goes all th' way to Heaven. But they ain't no hayloft, an' they ain't no hay at de top o' dat ladder!"

"No!" someone says.

"Ain't no cotton dere!"

"No!"

"Brothers an' sisters, this ain't no usual ladder. I jes' wants to tell you 'bout this ladder. We been singin' 'bout it tonight. We been singin' 'bout fo' as long as I can 'member. So, there must be somethin' special 'bout this ladder fo' someones to make up a song 'bout it, an' we be singin' it all these years. This ol' ladder ain't like what we use fo' th' paintin' th' house or puttin' the hay up in th' barn. This ladder goes straight up into th' sky. An' I'm gwine-a tell you sumpin' I'm gwine-a tell you what it is at de top o' dat ladder."

"Tell it!"

"The voice o' de Almighty God!! An' He wuz a-talkin' to Jacob. Now, let me tell you sumpin 'bout this Jacob. He wuz a vexing man. He didn't deserve to be loved by God. But none of us is. Jacob wuz a crafty man. Smart like a fox. But that ain't always a good thing. Fact is, ol' Jacob din always do right. He did some real badness. But God still love Jacob, even though he had his moments of meanness. Why, ol' Jacob even trick his poor ol' daddy, Isaac."

"No!"

"Yes, that's true. Now Jacob's daddy is th' same Isaac that wuz th' boy on the altar. Isaac's daddy, Abraham took 'im up to de altar for to be a sacrifice. But God send down an' angel an' say, you leave dat boy be, Abraham! But dat took faith. Abraham had th' faith for to be willin' to sacrifice his only boy. Isaac."

"Yes."

"Jest like God sacrificed his only Boy!"

"Uh huh!" two others joined in.

"So Isaac lived, and he had hisself two boys."

"Tell it!"

"He had him Jacob. 'Member we talkin' 'bout Jacob."

"Yessir!"

"Now, Jacob weren't fustborn. That wuz his brother, E-saw. Like I tol' you, Jacob was full-a tricks. He trick his older brother, E-saw. He trick his daddy, Isaac, too. Dat's a whole 'nuther story fo' a 'nuther time. We's talkin' 'bout ol' Jacob. I guess ol' Jacob gits to thinkin' he can trick mos' anybody. But din, ol' Jacob meets someun' he can't trick. Yessir, ol' Jacob meets a angel, and he figgers out real soon that he's no match fo' de angel!"

"Yes, brother!"

"Genesis 32 tells us dat de angel, he fights wid Jacob."

"Yes!"

"He fights wid him all night long!"

"Tell it, brother!"

"He hasta fight dat angel all night long. He gits hisself a limp outta dat ordeal but he also gits hisself a blessin.' Childern, I knows how it feel t'git a limp and a blessin' at th' same time. You jest gotta dwell on th' blessin' an' not th' limp. An' ol' Jacob gits sumpin' else—he gits hisself a new name. He becomes a new new nation. Wid a new people. He is no more a Jacob. He is a Is-rel. The daddy of a par-ful people. A par-ful nation!"

"Yes! Yes! Yes!"

"An' his childern an' their childern an' their chilldern an' their childern spread out all over the world. Like dese stars!" Neemy stretched out his arm with his palm open. Above them were stars, hundreds, thousands, *millions* of stars covering the Southern sky. "Jes' look atem, brothers and sisters."

"Yes! Amen!"

"But ol' Jacob Is-rel always seemed to be trickin' somebody. Or lookin' up at a ladder. Or fightin' a angel. Yessir, he hadda fight dat angel 'fore he gets dem childern. So, brothers. Sisters. Are you ready for da fight?"

"Yes!"

"'Cause deres a fight dats a-comin' if you wants a blessin.' Jes' like Jacob's fight."

"Tell it!"

"Deres a fight dats a-comin'!"

"Yes!"

"Deres a fight dats a-comin' an' it ain't wid a angel we gwine be fightin'."

"Yes!"

"An' we may haf to trick some people! An' we may haf to fights some people!"

"Yes!"

"But we's going to gets ourselves a new name. An' a new nation!"

"Yes, brother, yes, brother, yes, brother, yes!"

"This life here ain't fo-ever. Praise God. This ain't Heaven."

"Yes!"

"Other day, a sister ast me a question. I ain't gonna tell you who it wuz, cause she sittin' here tonight an' that'll most like 'barrass her. She wuz comin' outta they field an' she say, 'Brother Jobe, you figger dere's gwine-a be cotton in Heaven?' 'Cotton in Heaven?' I sez. 'Well, Sister Inez—oops. 'Scuse me, Sister, I done tol' on you!'"

A light chuckle went up through the crowd sitting there in the darkness.

"Heh, heh," Jobe said, "Sister Inez, fo-give me for dat 'un. So, she ast me, 'Brother Jobe, there gwine-a be cotton in Heaven?' and I sez to her, 'cause this is the Lord's truth. 'I don't know. But what I *do* know, is that if they is, you an' me an everbody sittin' here t'night ain't gwine-a be pickin' it.'"

"Amen!"

"The Bible sez dat those who's fust gwine-a be last and those who's last gwine-a be fust. This misery we gots here is jus' a blink of a eye, compared to what's waitin' fo' his childern. Think on that, people. It's just a blink of a eye. Think on dat t'morrow when you out in they hot sun. Think on dat when you thinks you jes' can't go nomore..."

"Horse and rider!" The words were spoken in a loud whisper, and it came from outside the clearing. It was the designated sentry. Immediately, there was a quick flurry of movement in the clearing among the worshippers. Jobe and the men standing beside him quickly scooped up the big Bible and extinguished the candles. Meanwhile the group quietly scurried away in all directions, disappearing into the dark forest. There was no panic, and no words were spoken, but within a matter of seconds, the clearing was dark and empty. The rider was Mr. Palmer, and when he drove his horse into the clearing, he raised his lantern and swung it around it all directions as his horse pranced around, but it was as if no soul had ever set foot there.

CHAPTER 21
TINY FLOWERS

Late in the night, hours before sunup, Neemy was awakened from a deep sleep by someone shouting his name and holding a lantern in his face. The cabin door was wide open and both the lantern and the voice belonged to Palmer, the overseer, and he was shaking the boy by the shoulder to wake him. Mr. Palmer was frantic, and he had no intention of leaving the cabin without Neemy.

"Wake up, boy! Wake up!" he shouted. "Miz Maddau needs you in the big house!"

As he threw on his clothes, Neemy saw his family, all wide-eyed, huddled in the corner of the cabin. Apparently, he was the last one to be awakened. However, as frantic as Palmer was, he waited patiently for Neemy to get dressed and hurriedly escorted him out of the cabin and across the field and up the path that led to the front lawn and the big house. Neemy knew that there would have been a time, in years gone by, that Palmer would have been beating and kicking him all along the way up to the house with the pretense of having him hurry. Sublety was not one of Palmer's chief qualities. As they hurried along the path, in the glow of the lantern that Palmer carried, Neemy noticed that what he had first thought was a since of urgency on the old man's face was, in fact, a look of semi-controlled panic.

"What's happnin' in da big house?" Neemy asked.

"Just hurry," Palmer replied, quickening his steps.

Once inside, the two were met with a gathering of people in the parlor. When they entered, the conversations suddenly stopped and the crowd parted to let them through, and they continued on up the stairs. Neemy was ushered into Elizabeth's bedroom, where another group of people—including Jack and the doctor from town, Dr. Adams—were standing around her, on both sides of the bed.

Neemy looked around the bedroom as he cautiously entered. There were lanterns and candles placed strategically around the room, and they cast dancing shadows on the walls. The room's walls were decorated by yellow-ocre wallpaper, odorned by a garden of tiny blue flowers. The shadows on the wall made it appear that the garden of flowers was teeming with life. In the center of the wall was an ornately-framed portrait of a young man with straight, blonde hair. The oval golden frame circled the image with overlapping tarnished, but delicately engraved leaves. His first impression was that it was a picture of Jack, who stood beside him, but at a second glance, he saw that it was of an older man, possibly in his mid- to late-30s. The man glared out from the frame, as if daring anyone to approach the portrait. *He certainly has the same look and attitude as Jack,* Neemy thought, but as he pondered this, his attention was suddenly directed to Elizabeth, who lay silently in her bed.

His first impression was that Elizabeth had passed away in the middle of the night. Her eyes were closed and her rosy complexion had been replaced by a pale, ghostly white. Her dark hair—tinged by more grey than Neemy had remembered—had been carefully brushed, and her hands were stretched out on top of the quilt that covered her. Palms up, her pale and marbled wrists revealed delicate traces of blue veins as they lay in stark contrast on top of the colorful quilt.

"She asked for you," Jack said, breaking the silence and nodding at Neemy. His eyes were red and he smelled like liquor.

Elizabeth's eyes slowly opened. They were a beautiful pale blue, but with a sad hue; not the bright and flashing blue eyes that Neemy was used to. "Hello, Nehemiah," she said, softly. And then, to the others in the room, she spoke in a halting voice, breathing heavily between words, "Could I…have a moment alone…with Neemy?"

"Mother. I'm not so sure that's a—" Jack began.

"Please," Elizabeth sighed with a whisper, "Just…a moment. Jack. Do this. For me."

Reluctantly, the others slowly eased out of the room and, with an exasperated glance back at Neemy, Jack closed the door behind them.

"Neemy," she said, weakly motioning to the table beside the bed, "Open up…this Bible…for me."

"Yassum," Neemy said, taking the large, black Bible off the table, the flame in the bedside lamp quivering. "Where do I open it?"

"You choose, Neemy," Elizabeth said with a sad smile.

Neemy placed the big Bible on the side of the bed and slowly opened it with apprehension.

"Read me…something."

"Ma'am?"

"Go ahead. No…one…is watching."

Looking back over his shoulder toward the door, Neemy quickly thumbed through the pages of the Bible. It was the same size as the one from the shed, but it was newer, and pages were crisp. They made a soft crackling sound as he thumbed through them, searching for a passage to read. As he looked through the big Bible, he flashed back to the late afternoon when Elizabeth had presented him with the *Shed Bible*, and he remembered they had been reading from Thessalonians. He found what he was looking for and put his finger on the verse. "Dis is from th' 'possel Paul, writin' to they Thess-lonians," he said. "*'Fo' our conversation is in Heav'n, from whence also we look fo' th' Saviour, th' Lord Jesus Christ…'*"

Looking again back at the door, he paused for a brief moment, and then, silently praying that no one would be immediately entering, he continued, "*'Who shall change our vile body, dat it may be fashion' like unto his glor-us body, 'cording to the workin' whereby he is able even to sub-due all things unto hisself.'*"

"That's good...Neemy. That's right. That was...perfect. Don't you think?" Elizabeth said, weakly.

As soon as he finished the verse, he heard someone shuffling outside the door and fumbling with the doorknob, so he quickly closed the Bible and turned it toward Elizabeth, as if she had been reading it. When the door opened, it was Jack and he was ushering in an older man. The man looked strangely familiar to Neemy, and in the flickering light of the candles and lantern, he struggled to place a name with the face. However, once the man spoke, he recognized him as Rev. Barre, and he remembered meeting him in Mr. Klein's General Store in town, all those years ago—as they discussed Elizabeth's pottery.

"Mrs. Maddau," Rev. Barre said, brushing past Neemy and leaning over the bed, "I'm so sorry to hear about your spell."

Neemy froze and wondered if the minister had heard their conversation from the other side of the door. He studied the man's face, but he didn't discern any expression on the minister's face that would indicate he had heard him reading to her from the Bible.

How sad it is that anyone would have to worry about such things, Neemy thought in a fleeting moment of irritation, but he quickly waved it away. *The very idea that I could be punished over an act of kindness... reading from the Bible.*

"Reverend...Barre," Elizabeth said in a whisper, "Thank you. So much. For coming at this...late—*or is it early?*—hour. But...I'm afraid...it was a touch more...than a...*spell.* Doctor has...been here... says it's my heart...just like Charles. Mr. Maddau. And I don't..." she sighed.

"Save your strength, Mrs. Maddau," the minister said, grasping her hand.

"I don't know...what my son plans to do...for...with...the estate..." she wheezed.

"It's alright, Mrs. Maddau. Please save your strength."

"No. No...listen. Nehemiah. Neemy...come over here."

"Yassum," Neemy said, rising to stand beside the bed.

"Reverend...you...take...Nehemiah...Take him with you. To help. Your church."

"What?! Mother, please!" Jack had come into the room and was standing just behind the minister. Then, to the minister, "Sorry, Reverend. She's confused. It's the fever talking—"

"No. Jack. I am anything...but confused. That's... all...I... want...Jack...I want...Reverend...take...Nehemiah..."

In a flash, Jack was at the door, yelling out into the hall, "Doctor! Doctor!" Doctor Adams had been at the foot of the stairs speaking to some of the neighbors, and when he heard Jack, he bounded up the stairs, and missing the top step, he almost tripped as he hurried toward Elizabeth's room.

"Quickly, Doctor," Jack said, desperation in his voice, but when the two men rushed into the room, Neemy was on his knees at the side of the bed weeping softly. While the doctor pushed Neemy aside to attend to Elizabeth, Jack looked up at Rev. Barre. "I'm sorry, Jack," he said, "I'm so sorry."

CHAPTER 22

The Cost of Freedom

The sun was just coming over the bluff east of the big house, when Doctor Adams, Rev. Barre and Neemy eased out of the house, and onto the front porch. The large front lawn was filled with the servants and various neighbors who had heard the news in the night of Elizabeth's impending death.

"Thank you for coming—on such short notice," the doctor said to the minister, "I know you're not the family's regular clergy."

"Yes, he must have been unavailable," Rev. Barre replied, "But I was happy to fill in."

"Actually, she asked for you, specifically," the doctor said, with a sidelong glance at Neemy.

"Oh?"

"She wanted to tell you in person about her intentions regarding the boy."

"The boy?"

"Him," the doctor said, nodding at Neemy, who stood off to the side curiously listening to the conversation.

"Doctor," Rev. Barre began, "Although you and I are in different professions, we are both dedicated to saving people. Yes? You are focused on their outer body—their physical needs; me, I am focused on their inner soul—their spiritual needs. That dedication has no doubt brought us both to numerous bedsides of those who are on the verge of leaving this world for the next."

"That is true, indeed, Reverend. What is your point?"

"My point is, that no doubt, you must have—as I have—heard and witnessed all sorts of deathbed regrets, promises and requests."

"Also true."

"So, whatever Mrs. Maddau was saying in her last moments here on earth, I feel that they must be tempered and taken under the dire circumstances in which they were spoken."

"Sir, if you are thinking that this was some sort of fevered, last-minute decision, you are mistaken. I honestly believe she had a premonition about her death. She spoke about it more than a few times. Always without dread or fear. And, over the last few months, as her health declined, she had mentioned this to me numerous times—I mean about the boy. Nehemiah. She had also told me that it is in her will. And, as I said, that was why she summoned you. It was not for any 'deathbed confession,' I assure you."

Rev. Barre glanced at Neemy and then turned back to the doctor. "Doctor Adams," he said, "I know that you and I are only casually acquainted, but do you not understand that my family has never been involved in that institution? By that, I mean the owning of another human being. As a Southerner—and even as a Southern *minister*—I realize that is an unpopular stand here in the South, but it is abhorrent to me...and my ministry."

"Yes, I can see that, simply from your reaction. And, I believe that is precisely *why* Elizabeth—*Mrs. Maddau*—made her decision. I truly believe that it is because of that very stance that she wanted you to take the boy." The doctor gestured toward Neemy, who had been standing off to the side.

"So, actually—" the minister said, looking back and forth between Neemy and the doctor, "What you're really suggesting is for me to add another adolescent to the two I already have...who, by the way are constantly at war with one another, as it is..."

The doctor sighed and rubbed his forehead. "I do understand that this was not something you were expecting."

"To say the least."

"Let's look at this under a different light. A different perspective, if you will. You, of course, are not bound by law to agree to this arrangement."

"I would think not!"

"So, let us consider this young man's situation, should you not agree to this arrangement."

"With all due respect, Doctor, this young man's situation is really none of my concern. I don't even know him…"

As a reply, the doctor stared silently at the minister, as if waiting for the last sentence to rise above the two as an echo and fall back down, like a light rain shower. At that moment, Rev. Barre realized the impact and implication of what he had just spoken.

"My apologies, Doctor, that may have sounded a little cold," he said, clearly embarrassed, "It's just a lot to consider. It's a big responsibility."

"Yes, it is, Reverend. I understand," the doctor said, smiling sadly and turning to head across the lawn to his parked carriage, "I'm sure the Lord is pleased with your compassion and dedication to come out on such a cold evening as last night, and I trust that He will continue to bless you and your family, and your church."

The minister gently grabbed the doctor's arm as he turned to leave. "Wait up," he said, "Are you entirely certain that Mrs. Maddau set this up correctly?"

"If you mean, *legally*, then the answer is *absolutely yes.*"

"What about her family? Her son? Are they going to stand by and let me take off with one of their…uh, workers?"

"You mean, one of their *slaves*?" the doctor said, suddenly serious. "Her son is the only family she has left. And look at him," the doctor nodding at Jack, who was sitting on the porch behind them with his head in his hands, his dirty blonde hair cascading around and through his fingers. "He's in shock, and he's inebriated, and he is in no state to make any kind of decision or to protest any sort of decision that has been made, legal or otherwise."

Rev. Barre sighed with resignation and motioned for Neemy, who was still listening in the shadows, to follow him.

"What about the boy's family? What about the others?" the minister asked.

"I do not know the answer to that." The doctor was about to say, *or as you so aptly put it, it is none of our concern*, but he knew that he had already made his point and the minster was grudgingly taking the boy, and to belabor the point could only turn the minister's contrition into a guilty anger and possibly reverse his decision.

As the doctor climbed up into his carriage, he turned in time to see Neemy and the minister astride the minister's horse, trotting toward the gate that opened out onto the road through the fields and into town.

CHAPTER 23
A Brand-New Home

It had been a long and life-changing night, and Rev. Barre hadn't known exactly what sort of reception he would receive from his sons when he came home that morning with Neemy. He guessed that both boys would be amenable to the arrangement, but for different reasons. He figured that his oldest, Curtis, would favor the addition of a "servant" to the household, because he would naturally assume that Neemy would handle his chores, but Rev. Barre had no intention of imposing this role on the boy. The minister hoped that his younger son, Andrew, would have a more positive and productive attitude about Neemy's arrival; Andrew was an avid outdoorsman, something that was not shared by his older brother. And, with his various responsibilities at the church, he seldom had the time to accompany Andrew on his hunting or camping trips. Rev. Barre hoped that Neemy would possibly be willing to fill this role as a companion to Andrew.

The parsonage was a modest, two-story house, and it was adjacent to the church on the main street of Rubineville, on the north end of the town. Rev. Barre figured that he could put Neemy in the large storage room toward the back of the house, and thought that once he put down a makeshift bed on the floor, it would give the boy privacy of his own room. The morning sun was already high by the time the two got to the parsonage. The minister knew that both of his sons would still be asleep, but he also knew that they would want to know what was going on as soon as they woke up and saw that there was a stranger in the house.

Neemy helped Rev. Barre to unsaddle his horse and to get him secured in the barn. He assumed that the minister would ask him to stay and sleep in the barn, as well. "Let's get on up to the house and get you settled in," the minister told him, "And then we can talk about your role here."

Although Neemy was pleasantly surprised that he would be allowed to sleep in the parsonage, he assumed that his "role" would be more of the kind of work he had performed at the Maddau plantation—minus the pottery. *Still a slave*, Neemy thought to himself, *Always a slave.*

Rev. Barre saw the cloud that came over the boy's face and read his thoughts. "Listen, son—Neemy—" he said, pausing at the door of the barn, "I know what you're thinking. But we all have our role here in this house and parish. I was hoping that you could help me here in the house and in the church."

"I can sweep a church same as a house, same as a barn," Neemy said.

"You're not a slave. You're not even an indentured servant."

"Don't feel like I'm free."

"What do you think would have happened to you if you hadn't come home with me?"

"Probly same as my family."

"Which is…?"

"Probly sold or worked to death or both. I heard Miz 'Lizbeth's boy—Jack— talkin.' He gonna sell everthing. All the workers. My mama. My papa. My brother." Neemy smiled a rueful smile, "Can't sell Unca Jobe, though."

"Was your uncle able to buy his freedom?"

"Nossuh. Unca Jobe never have da money fo' dat. The angels done come an' free 'im. Two weeks back. Ain't no slaves an' ain't no plantation in Heav'n."

"Listen. Neemy. I want you to understand—you are free to go. Anytime. But what do you think will happen if you leave here? How far do you think you'd get…?"

Neemy stared back at the reverend in silence.

"At least here, you can…*feel like* you're free," Rev. Barre said.

"You jes' don't know."

"Don't know what?"

"You don't know what it's like to *not* be free an' your ma and pa not be free. An' their ma an' pa 'fore that and 'fore that and 'fore that…"

"All the way back to across the ocean?"

"Yassuh. All the way back 'cross they ocean."

"You're correct that I don't know—*myself*—what it's like to *not* be free. But, you're wrong when it comes to my family and our heritage—we haven't always been free."

"They wuz brought 'cross the ocean in chains?" Neemy realized that he must have sounded sarcastic, but he was tired and his weariness had diminished his manners.

"No, but there's different kinds of slavery, Neemy," the minister said patiently, "There's people enslaved and there's people oppressed, for a number of different reasons. But, they all have one thing in common—they *dream of* and *yearn* and *live for freedom*. That dream—*that basic human desire*—unites every man, woman, and child who has ever been oppressed, enslaved or imprisoned."

Neemy thought for a few seconds and then slowly said, "What if you has to pretend? Ain't dat a differt kind of free as you?"

The minister drew in a breath and hesitated for a second. "I understand what you're feeling," he said, "I know how it looks. But again, you're free to leave anytime."

"Yas. Free 'til I walks out da door."

"That's right. That's my point. At least you'll be free here under this roof. And someday, hopefully, even outside this house. I have to believe that things are going to change. Some states no longer allow slavery."

"Dis ain't one."

"Yes. Not yet. But the time will come."

"What makes you sure? Whad if I has to preten' to be free fo' the rest o' my life? Dat makes it more din one kind of freedom. You wuz born free. An' so wuz your pa. An' his pa, an' his pa."

"But that's where it stops, Neemy."

"How you figger dat? You say you granddaddy's pa wuz a slave?"

"He wasn't a slave, but he wasn't free, either. My family hasn't always lived on this side of the Atlantic."

"You from Africa?"

"No. No. We came to America from Ireland. My family has always been involved in the church. But the Church, as we know it, has gone through a lot of transition over the years, and not all of it has been peaceful."

"Did da Church have slaves?"

"No, well, not exactly. Actually, I don't know. That's a good question. Again, that depends on your definition of slavery."

"I means folks like me."

"I'm not trying to dodge your question, but as I said, slavery comes in many forms. Once upon a time—*not so very long ago in the scope of history*—the Church was run by a group of religious leaders, and they were sanctioned by the various governments of the countries where their congregations were. It wasn't like our town, where there's a choice of churches, one on each side of town. You had to be a member of this one Church. Also, if you were just an ordinary citizen, you would have to depend on the Church leaders to tell you what was in the Bible…you couldn't read the Bible for yourself."

"I knows 'zactly what das like and how it feels."

"I realize that. I just wanted you to understand that our society today—South Carolina, or America, even—didn't invent that form of oppression. There's always been one group of people who feel like they have God's ear. The irony is that back after Jesus walked the earth and His followers began forming churches, the leaders and the governments killed and tortured the early Christians. The funny thing is, the more they came down on the Christians, the more the church grew. The Church gave the early Christians something to *live…and die* for. And then, over the years, the Church became so prevalent that the leaders and governments had to tolerate them, and then, they had to yield to the power and the sheer numbers of Christians. Then, after centuries, the Christians had the power. I guess the devil didn't like that."

"Yep. They's always ol' Nick in the bushes."

"Indeed. And the devil loves religion. So, my family was a fairly well-to-do French family."

"Thought you say I-land."

"I said they came to America from Ireland. They started out in France. They were Huguenots, and I don't really know where the name came from. All I know for sure is the king of France—*that would have been Louis XIV*—made sure they lost their political and military privileges. They lost everything. Does that sound familiar? And the thing is, he wasn't even the first to persecute them. Before he came along, there were massacres here and there, and thousands were killed. Maybe even tens of thousands. Some were killed, some re-converted and swore allegiance to the existing government-sanctioned Church. So, there were people—like my family—that escaped and got out of France. That's how we ended up in Ireland. But even in Ireland, they were still the minority religion."

The minister looked up to see if Neemy had followed all of that, and sensing the boy's interest, he continued. "There was the status quo," he said, "That just means they were the sanctioned, uh, *official and legal,* Church at the time. The one in power. Then came Protestants that were 'protesting' the hold that the government church at the time had on the body of believers. I mean, unfortunately, their idea of 'the Church' was different than the government's idea of the Church, and that got many of them killed."

"Kild fo' goin' to th' church?"

"Kind of ironic, isn't it? Christians killing other Christians over Christianity, or their particular form of it. Not exactly biblical in principal. Christians getting hunted down."

"I know all 'bout worshippin' in secret. 'Least we wudn't kilt if we's caught. Whupped maybe."

"Yes. That's unfortunate."

"They hunt yo' folks down?"

"Not so much, at least not in Ireland. My grandfather's father's people were experts in weaving and lace-making and glove-making. So, they were pretty much accepted in Ireland. Sometimes the worth of a people is determined by what talent they have or what they can offer their society as a skill."

"So, why theys leave I-land?"

"Because America was a land of freedom. A new start."

"Maybe fo' some it wuz freedom. Not fo' all wi' they new start. An' maybe not everbody wants to come to America."

Rev. Barre pondered this for a second. "Again, you do have a point, Neemy. You would think that since they clawed their way to the New World looking for freedom that they would have wanted to help everybody achieve freedom. But, believe it or not, there are some of us that do see things that way."

"Maybe so. But, I guess theys keep theys thinkin' secret, 'cuz th' way I sees it, it sound like everbody who gits kicked 'round, once they gits the freedom an' da power, theys lookin' for someun to takes they place. Someun' theys can kick 'round."

"Well, Neemy, you're not wrong on that matter. And believe me, I'm not going to sit here and defend oppression. All I can say is the human is a flawed animal, and this ain't Heaven."

"That's fo' sho. Not yet, anyway."

"I'm not sure what Heaven is going to look like, but I do know it's not going to ever look like Rubineville."

"Maybe a shiny-clean Rubaville," Neemy said.

The minister bristled at the remark. He had meant to be supportive, but Neemy's remark seemed to sidestep his intent. "Don't be blasphemous, Neemy," he said.

"Don't know whut blast-mus is."

"I mean, it just sounded like you were getting close to belittling the promises of God. Specifically, the promise of the glories of Heaven. I don't mind taking you in, Neemy, but there are some rules that you will have to abide by."

"Don't talk 'bout Heav'n. Thas one o' da rules, I 'spose."

"No, no, no. We—you—can talk about Heaven, but let's keep it in reverential terms. Not comparing it to Rubineville."

"Guess we thinks different on Heav'n, then."

The minister sighed with a deep breath. It had been a long night and, because it was nearly mid-morning, his patience was beginning to grow thin, especially in light of the circumstances of Nehemiah returning home with him.

"Guess you can thinks of it yo' way, an' I can thinks of it my way," Neemy said.

"Fine," Rev. Barre said.

"Bible say Heav'n gwine be comin' down, and dis' is gwine-a be th' new Heaven, and here we is in Rubaville." Neemy said.

Rev. Barre bristled. He was beyond tired and his patience was totally gone. "So, tell me," he said irritatedly, "What was the name of the seminary where you studied and where you were ordained?"

Neemy could tell that he had crossed some sort of theological line, or somehow offended the minister, but he didn't know why or how, so he continued. "Only cemeteries I know is up on the field 'bove the big house where they puts Unca Jobe. An' there's that nice one over dere by yo' church dat we passes on da way to dis house jus now."

"No, not *cemeteries*. Oh, nevermind," Rev. Barre said. He was already regretting rebuking Neemy, but he was too tired to either apologize or argue about it. "I'm just saying that there are some spiritual doctrines that are...infallible," he finally said.

"Like Heav'n?"

"Yes. Regarding Heaven. Good. You understand."

"What I think I understan'—an' maybe I don't understan' at all, but I thought that when ol' John wuz on th' Isle-a-Patmos, he writes down all deze things 'bout Heav'n."

"What?" Rev. Barre said, blinking. He was too tired to engage in that kind of a theological debate.

"I sez ol' John, in th' Rev-lation twenty-one, after he's dreamin' on Patmos I-land writes: *'An' I saw de new Heav'n an' new earth: fo' de firs' Heav'n an' de firs' earth was passed away; an' dere was no mo' sea.'"*

"What?" the minister repeated.

"An ol' John, down in the tenth verse of th' Rev-lation is writin' 'bout what an angel tol' 'em to put down: *'An' he carry me away in de spirit to a great and high mountin', and sho me dat great city, the holy Druse-lem, de-scendin"*—purty sho dat means comin' down—*out o' Heav'n from God...'* Th' way I reads it, dis angel shows John a picture of the ol' Druse-lem bein' gone—Preacher, has you seen th' pictures of Druse-lem?"

"Well. Obviously, I've seen paintings from biblical times. And there's certainly engravings in my Bibles."

"Nosah. I'se talkin' bout real pictures from now. Today. Not paintin's. Camera pitchers. I seen 'im. Jus like th' Bible sez. I'm sayin' dere is a Druse-lem over dere, right now, today, it's jus' up da way from Africa. Ain't no Is'rel—th' childern of Is-rel went an' lost they home. But theys a Druse-lem over dere now, today, as we stan' here. But ol' John is tellin' us it goes away, an' here's th' thing—a new un'—fresh an' clean, all shinin' and bright—come on down from 'bove. Th' angel shows John from da mountain dis new Druse-lem comin' down—an' it has to have a place to be put. An' dat place is th' new earth. Thas jes' th' way I sees it. Heav'n ain't no fancy cloud to sit on playin' th' harps. An' if deres a shiny new Druse-lem, 'cross th' ocean, why can'ts they be a new Rubaville over here?"

"You've taken this way out of context."

"You sed it fust—you says this ain't Heav'n. You's right. But I think its gonna be th' new Heav'n."

"You really think Rubineville is going to be part of the new Heaven? I'm sure I've never seen that in the Bible—Old or New Testament. There' no Rubineville in the Bible!"

"Preacher, dis ol' worl' has good an' it has bad. For those o' us that's a chile o' God, th' bad things o' dis world are th' only Hell we'll ever see, an' that's just for a snap o' th' fingers compared to the fo-ever of the New Heav'n. An' the good things of dis world are th' only good things people who go to Hell will ever see. Again, it's jus' a snap o' good, an' a fo-ever of fire. Dis life here only matters what you do to gits ready fo' the next one. Dis life is only th' snap, whether you is a slave o' a free man. Slave can't hep bein' a slave. It ain't a sin on his part. Even if yous live to a hunnerd, slave o' not, its just a snap o' th' fingers in the big picture. Iffen I's had my choice, I's gladly be a slave for a finger snap jes' to be able to spen' fo-ever in th' new Heaven."

"Where are you getting this?!"

"Ain't from no cemetery, Preacher."

CHAPTER 24

FROM WEST POINT TO RUBINEVILLE

April 22, 1861
West Point, New York

Father,

It was with both joy and disappointment that I read your recent post, and I hastened to share it with Martha. We were both relieved and gratified to hear the news of your parish and of the other happenings in Rubineville, and that everyone is striving to maintain an air of normalcy.

However, I must admit that both Martha and I were extremely disappointed to learn that you will not be able to attend our impending wedding ceremony, but given the circumstances, we do understand your decision. From your vantage point, it must seem that it was spur-of-the-moment, but I can assure you that both Martha and I have put a great deal of thought and prayer into the matter, and that our decision to wed and to have the ceremony immediately after my graduation from the Academy is anything but irresponsible and impractical. For that matter, if there is anyone that might be branded irresponsible, (and responsible for our somewhat hasty wedding plans) it should be Beauregard, who ordered the unfortunate firing on Fort Sumter—that action has obviously changed the lives and plans of not only us as cadets, but also, literally everyone in the nation, North and South.

Some of us here at the Academy are still mystified about his decision to take up arms against the Union, especially in light of his graduation from here and his previous service with distinction.

Father, does it also seem to you that our very world and existence has been forever altered and upended? I wish that I could tell you that my friends and fellow cadets are standing united, but there has been an ominous line drawn separating the North and South, even here at the Academy. Even among some of my closest friends there are arguments and disagreements, in many cases, spear-headed by my brothers-in-arms hailing from Virginia.

Last September, a month before the national presidential election, some of the cadets here held a mock election—I suppose to try and ferret out the loyalists from the "states-rights" fellows. It was not sanctioned by the administration—in fact, I'm sure they would have frowned on it, and rightfully so. Of the nearly 280 cadets, 214 voted. Just under a hundred of them voted for Breckinridge; just under 50 voted for Douglas, Constitutional Union candidate Bell got a few over 40 votes, and Lincoln only received 24. My Southern brothers were jubilant, but the cadets from the Northern states were furious.

It was as if the Academy had been dealt a slash with a sabre, and over time, the wound would fester. Two of my close friends, who had once been friends themselves, found themselves at opposite sides of the argument. As I am told (I was not there), it started as a simple, friendly disagreement, but escalated, both in rhetoric and in volume. They did not come to blows, but rather, found themselves in a fiery debate. After a "cooling off" period, they shook hands and issued apologies, but, unfortunately, as is oft the case in similar exchanges of passion, some of the accusations and insults they hurled at each other can never be "unsaid," no matter the handshakes or flowery and profuse apologies.

Then, in November, our friend from Laurens, Cadet (Henry) Farley left the academy a full month before the state left the Union. With his flaming red hair, he had literally stood out on campus as a self-described "fire-eater" from our state. Prior to this academic year, we had often engaged in lively discussions, as to what direction this national debate about slavery and states' rights would take. As a fellow Carolinian, he would often say to me, "Barre, there is swiftly coming a time in which you and I will be obliged to put our loyalty and honor on the line. I would strongly advise you to weigh and consider, as I have, all of the consequences and repercussions of that decision, for it shall be one that we will be forced to live with in this life and possibly, the next one, as well."

I remember the first time he said this to me, and, I confess, I was more amused than moved, thinking that he certainly had a flare for the dramatic. I regret that I took his advice (and admonition?) so lightly at the time, since the subsequent years have proved him to be painfully accurate in his charge and prediction. To underscore that point, after Farley left the Academy, he was followed by another South Carolinian, Cadet Hamilton four days later. The rest of the cadets hailing from that state left the following month (Merry Christmas!), along with several Mississippians and Alabamians. Since then, there has been a steady stream of our Southern brothers-in-arms resigning and exiting from the Academy. When they leave, it is nearly always with a heavy heart. Those of us remaining (especially us Southerners from the deep South) are not angry to see them leave, but rather, saddened by their decision and departure.

And, although those of us remaining had felt that we had been suitably hardened and conditioned to the exits of our Southern comrades, we were, to a man, shocked when Fort Sumter was fired upon. What's worse, my afore-mentioned former fellow cadet, Henry Farley—now a Lieutenant in the 1st South Carolina Artillery, was credited as being the first to fire on the fort! Though we had all often talked about fame and about achieving glory and honor on the battlefield, what a bitter pill to swallow it was, to learn that Farley had succeeded in this on behalf of our sworn enemies. I say this without any twinge of hatred, nor jealousy. On the contrary, it is with the utmost respect that I view his accomplishments. However, in my heart, I believe that path to loyalty and honor that I have chosen is the only one that was acceptable to the very core of my being, and I hope that you and Curtis will understand and support my decision.

In your last letter, you had indicated that Curtis had still not joined the state's guard, nor had he been pressed into service. I spoke with one of my instructors, and he assured me that if he can arrive here within the next month that there will most assuredly be a place for him on a roster. Due to the issues he and I have had in the past, I would be surprised if he took me up on this offer, and frankly, I am hesitant to totally vouch for him. However, I am doing this for you, because I do know how it would pain you if something were to happen to him.

I hope to hear from you soon. In the meantime, Martha sends her love, as does her family. Also, please extend my best wishes and salutation to my former faithful companion, Nehemiah. Tell him I think of him often and hope to see him in the near not-so-distant future.

Your devoted son,
Andrew

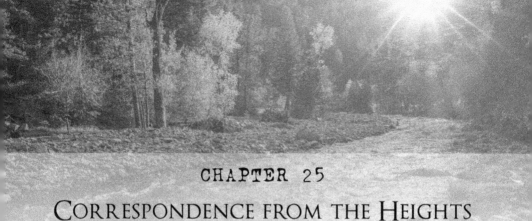

CHAPTER 25
CORRESPONDENCE FROM THE HEIGHTS

December 10, 1864

Dearest Andrew,

What a joy it was to have received the letter from you! Husband, I could almost hear your sweet voice reciting the words as I savored the lines on the parchment. I was very happy to hear that you have recovered from the illness, although, I must admit that I would not have been sad had they sent you home for your recovery!

We have watched with much anticipation General Sherman's success in the Georgia campaign, and we are all so very much encouraged over the success that he has had in an effort to bring this horrible war to a successful conclusion. You and your men must be very proud to be a part of his army and the history that it is making.

We are all well here. Mother and Father asked that I send you their love, and little Willy misses his father! I am sure that once he begins forming his words (he is walking now, if only a step or two) he will express his own desire (alongside mine) for your safe return from this horrible war.

We have been steadily busying ourselves with the preparations for Christmas and, though I am anxious to see the look on Willy's face when he sees what "Santa Claus" has delivered (yes, Mother has been filling his head with stories and pictures!), I am equally burdened by the emptiness of our home that only your presence can remedy.

I continue to be amazed at the influence and effect and, at the same time, the *lack of effect* that this war has visited upon the people, both here in Brooklyn Heights and over in Manhattan, as well. This was especially apparent when we celebrated Thanksgiving a few weeks ago. Although this "celebration" was strongly encouraged by President Lincoln, there are so many families that have more reasons for sorrow than for giving thanks. We had a delicious meal and several of Mother's relatives came over to Brooklyn to help us celebrate, but there was still an empty seat at the table, Andrew, that only you can fill. I could not keep from thinking about how fortunate and comfortable we were, while at the same time, the deprivations you no doubt are forced to suffer on a far-away southern battlefield.

Mother obviously noticed my melancholy behavior and she must have been concerned, because she awoke me the following morning, strictly instructing me to "get dressed for the city." She then whisked me by carriage to the ferry and over to Manhattan under the pretense of visiting her aunt (who had not attended our Thanksgiving meal) and possibly getting some shopping done. However, as we took our lunch in the city, she surprised me with tickets to a play at the Winter Garden Theater. It had to be premeditated, because the play featured the brothers Booth (a first for all three to appear together on stage) in Shakespeare's "Julius Caesar." John was Mark Anthony, Edwin was Brutus and Junius (Junior) was Cassius. It was "packed to the rafters" in the theater, and there were a number of dignitaries in attendance, so I have no idea how Mother was able to secure such sought-after tickets (yes, I asked—several times, in fact—and she would just smile conspiratorially and change the subject!).

The event was billed as a "Booth Benefit for the Shakespeare Statue Fund." The Booths' father was famous as a Shakespearean actor, and I assume that is what brought the brothers together (although I understand that there is a good deal of friction between Edwin and John over the same issues that our nation is facing!). Also, the following day, *The Times* stated that the brothers' mother, Mrs. Booth, was also in attendance that evening (that may very well be why the three of them got along so well for the performance!).

Oh, the play was splendid—world class, in fact—and I must admit that for a fleeting moment, all of the cares of our little world were forgotten, as we found ourselves intrigued by that sad tale of ancient Roman assassination. Mother and I stayed over in the city, since it was so late and neither of us wanted to suffer through a cold, winter night ferry back to Brooklyn. We had also arranged for Anita to attend to Willy (and to Father!), so we were not desperate to return home (she had agreed to stay over, should we not return Fri. night).

The Booth brothers' performance certainly measured up to their lofty reputation(s) as thesbians. And, it is certainly refreshing (and morale-boosting) to know that, in this time of war, entertainers such as these fine performers (John notwithstanding) can "soldier on" to provide us with a small taste of normalcy. That is not to say that they are limited to the stage in the efforts on this behalf! On the week following that dramatic and eventful weekend (I will elaborate on that directly), *The Times* carried an interesting story about how Edwin Booth happened to be traveling either to or from the city and was on an over-crowded train platform across the river in Jersey City. In the hubbub of boarding the train, a young man somehow either lost his footing or was pushed by the onset of the crowd—at any rate, he ended up falling in the narrow space between the platform and the train, as the train began to exit the station. Fortunately, our Mr. Edwin Booth was, at that moment, on the same platform, and thinking quickly (as befitting a world-class actor!), he grabbed the young man by his coat and hauled him up out of harm's way before he could be injured! If that wasn't enough, dear husband, here is the most amazing thing: *the young man was Robert Todd Lincoln, our President's son!* He was traveling from school (at Harvard) to Washington. Mr. Booth certainly was in the right place for the moment, and I'm sure the Lincoln family will be eternally grateful to Mr. Booth!

I implied that our weekend in the city was not without drama (other than onstage!), and I only mention this because you may have been privy to the news of this event. And, by this, I am referring to the fiendish fires that were set throughout the city by rebel sympathizers. It seems that, at the same time we were enjoying the talents of the Brothers Booth, there was a plot afoot throughout the city to create chaos and destruction among the populace. I realize that newspapers throughout the nation have carried the story, and lest you worry, I wanted you to know that we were *mostly* unaffected by them. In fact, it is our understanding that all of the fires were quickly extinguished and no lives were lost; it was yet another failed coup on the part of the rebels. And though we were unaffected by the blazes, that is not to say that we were not caught up in the general terror that was spread throughout the city.

The paper reported that the fires were set in at least 13 hotels throughout the city, as well as in Barnum's splendid museum, in a (fortunately failed) attempt to create terror and apparently to soften the resolve of our city (and nation) to continue to press onward to victory in the war. The paper also went on to say that all of the perpetrators—*save one*—escaped. And, it was from this lone captured assailant that the officials received the information about the motive for the fires. In addition to the terror that the Confederate agents hoped it would create, there was also the element of revenge for the fall and burning of Atlanta. As it turned out, one of the hotels that was set afire was just a block down from where Mother and I chose to stay the night. *It was almost as if the arsonist(s) realized that the wife and mother-in-law of one of the officers advancing on and helping to destroy Atlanta was in the immediate vicinity!* Of course, I didn't realize that until after the details about the attack were made public.

At any rate, it was quite a commotion, both with the anxious citizenry and the brave men extinguishing the fire. With all the tumult and the fire wagons constantly rumbling past our hotel, we were unable to sleep until the wee hours of the night, when everything quieted down. I would, however, have to admit that it was a bit unsettling to retire for the evening after taking in such an enjoyable performance at the theater, only to have the mood shattered by the dastardly acts of the desperate rebels and their firebombs. I can only imagine what the

Booths must have thought of our city! It's one thing to bring to life a tragedy of Roman assassination; it's quite another to be threatened by real bodily harm in our modern time. I would assume that all of the Booth brothers stayed the evening. I know for a fact that Edwin stayed, since he performed in "Hamlet" the following night.

I wish that I could tell you that Saturday morning's sunrise erased the aftertaste of the unfortunate events of the previous evening. But alas, upon awakening, I found myself even more melancholy with thoughts of you and the war (thanks no doubt to the previous evening's blazes), and even the Christmas decorations that had cheerily been put up throughout the city could not ease me from my darkened mood. I was cheered somewhat, once we got home to Brooklyn, by seeing Willy's sweet smile and happy face, as he celebrated our return.

It was then that I realized that, as difficult as it has been for us to be apart these last few years, we are so much more fortunate than many of those around us. In our church alone, there are too many families to count that have lost a son, husband, or father, and yet, there are those (even on our block) who live their lives and still go off to their work at their businesses everyday as if nothing has happened—or will ever happen—to intrude upon their existence. I have seen both men and women walking haughtily down the sidewalk, and in their wake, passing those poor souls clothed in black and draped in sorrow, no doubt in response to some dreadful news from the war.

And the bad news does not always come from the battlefields. Do you remember the Patrignos? Matthew and Jane? She was Jane Bridgefield before she married—as in the "Brooklyn Bridgefields." But you wouldn't know it by talking to her. She is so sweet and humble. You'd never know she came from money. Their place is on the corner, and we had a delightful dinner with them in the courtyard behind their brownstone, just before you left. If you recall, it was a few months before Willy arrived, and the two of them talked constantly about children and wanting to have as many as possible. I remember Matthew saying "at least 10!" and Jane pretending to be horrified. Matthew had just gotten his commission as a captain, and you and he shared some mutual acquaintances from the Academy. I believe he had already graduated before you arrived there. At any rate, he is safe and has had a good deal of success on the western front with General Grant and has already received several promotions, some of them even in the battlefield. However, here at the "home front," things are not so cheery; Jane has contracted consumption, and she has been confined to her bed since the Spring. The doctors (and they have retained the very best in the city) fear that she shall not last through the year, and it is even doubtful that she will be with us to celebrate this Christmas. It's the worst news possible. Her parents have moved up (from Pennsylvania?) and have been staying with her since this past Summer. Her mother told me that they have tried to get word to Matthew, so that he can take a furlough to come home and be with her. We are desperately hoping that he will arrive soon! Oh, my heart aches for them! Jane will soon be free from the sickness and the evils and wars of this world, but it is for those of us left behind—such as Matthew—who must endure the awful pains of loss and the bittersweet sorrow of having only the cherished memories with which to live.

My dearest Andrew, I sometimes wonder if you have spared me the horrors of what you have witnessed on the battlefield! Father has assured me that this awful war will be over soon (Pres. Lincoln has publicly said as much). Hopefully, we will only have this one more Christmas to endure your absence before your blessed return, and we shall all be together next Christmas. Of course, I am hoping for it to be even sooner! I miss you dreadfully, and Willy asks about you constantly and will not be calmed until I fetch the tintype with your handsome face and gallant uniform. He is so proud of his papa! *But his mama is even more proud of his papa!*

We are praying for your safe and timely return. What a joyous occasion that will be! Until then, please know that you are in our hearts and prayers.

Your loving wife,
Martha

CHAPTER 26

ANDREW'S SWORD

As the rain and sleet mixture popped on the roof of his tent, Andrew gathered up the sheaths of paper bearing the news from his wife. It reminded him of July 4th fireworks from what seemed to be at least a lifetime before. He smiled sadly at the recollection and comparison; that night was anything but a celebration. He had read and re-read Martha's letter so often that some of the edges of the pages were rough and torn. He put the pages in order and placed them in a leather satchel, that also contained a small pouch which held clippings of hair—Martha's chestnut brown curls and the light wispy strands of his son, William's straight, dark brown hair, which was so similar to his own when he was a young boy. Also, inside the leather satchel, there was a small tintype of Martha.

Just outside, Corporal Daniel Richards slogged through the sleet and mud to the tent. He carried a lantern in one hand, and in the other, he clutched a brown satchel—similar to Andrew's—with fresh dispatches from the field headquarters. Although he had the slight carriage of a boy, Richards had actually just turned 20, and he walked with the gait and determination of someone who had seen more than their share of the war and its horrors. The icy rain pooled on the brim of his cap and plastered strands of his wet hair to his forehead, before dripping down onto his army-issued slicker. When he arrived at the tent, he saw that the flap was already open and Andrew was stuffing the letter from his wife into the satchel. The satchel was laying on top of a field map, which had been spread open on his small table and lit by his own lantern.

"Excuse me, Captain," Richards said, before entering the tent.

After no response from the man inside, he cleared his throat and spoke louder, so that he could be heard above the sound of sleet on the tent. "Captain? Excuse me, Captain Barre?"

"Oh," Andrew said, as if emerging from a cloud of thought, "Yes, please enter. Sorry, Corporal. Please come in. Dry off. Nasty night."

"Yessir. Dispatches from headquarters."

Andrew sighed. "Yes, of course. Thank you. Sit down, Danny."

The relationship of the two was more than one of a captain and corporal. Together, they had endured a series of long and bloody campaigns and those experiences had forged a friendship between the two. Consequently, the corporal instinctively knew when news that he brought troubled the captain. As Andrew pored over the dispatch, the corporal quickly surmised that was the case at hand.

"We've been ordered to branch off and to move north," Andrew said.

"Yessir? And—?" the corporal asked.

"And—" Andrew said, after a moment's pause, "...and that takes us by the Rubine River up through Rubaville."

The corporal looked puzzled. "The Rubine River?" he said, "I know I've heard of it, but I can't place it. However, from my experience, it seems that the more famous or well-known the river is, the harder it is to cross. I've come to appreciate the rivers that I ain't heard of. Rivers that ain't so prominent on the map."

"Yes, but the Rubine River runs beside Rubaville," Andrew said. "And, that's where I grew up. That's where my father's church is."

"Right. That's where I heard of it. You have mentioned that in the past."

"It's alright Corporal—Danny. I realize that it's a prickly point, at least with some of my superiors. I'm a Southerner, trying to save the Union. But somehow, this order flies in the face of that. It's almost like they're continually wanting me to prove my loyalty, as if I haven't done that since this war began. As for this dispatch—it's ordering us to destroy all military targets."

"Sir? Is that a problem? After all, military targets are marked that way, because they are helping the enemy prolong this war."

"I understand that. And, I don't have a problem destroying military targets. But you know, as well as I do, that lately, when our army has moved through a town, *everything* somehow gets burned to the ground. Not just the cotton warehouses and munitions factories and the uniform factories, but also the shops, the citizens' homes, the schools—*even the churches*—they all seem to also get caught up in crossfire of the blazes."

"To my knowledge, the order doesn't include the destruction of schools and churches," the corporal said.

"It doesn't matter," Andrew scoffed, "You know very well that they become collateral damage. Our soldiers aren't so concerned about keeping things all within the proper lines. And some of our good soldiers are hell-bent on punishing every living creature in the state of Carolina. And these people in Rubaville are people I know. My father. My friends. These are people I love. And, as I said, it is where my father's church is."

"Surely, you could appeal to General Sherman…to go around the town."

"The problem is that there *is* a cotton factory there. That's a prime military target—although, ironically, we are seeing less and less of any sort of semblance of uniforms on the enemy these days. And though, that is the only target, I'm afraid that would be the fuse, the kindling, as it were," Andrew said.

"But, Captain, sir, isn't there some way the collateral destruction can be contained? Don't you think the general will listen to reason? As I recall, there was a town outside Atlanta that he left mostly unscathed because of a similar appeal."

"Madison. Madison, Georgia."

"Yes. Madison. It's been said that ol' Uncle Billy—er, General Sherman—had a sweetheart there in the town," the corporate said with a sly grin.

"Yes, that has been said, and I'm sure Uncle Billy got around, but the truth is that it was more likely a political decision. That was Georgia and this is Carolina. There are still Georgians in Washington. They are not the most popular, but those that are there are still loyal to the Union and some of them still have the president's ear. However, I'm not so sure that there is a single South Carolinian left in Washington," Andrew said with a grimaced smile. Most of them got out of Washington once their state's soldiers fired on Sumter.

"Still. My point is that it wouldn't hurt to appeal and suggest a slight deviation in our unit's path to the north. Or, at least to make sure the town is spared when the cotton plant is destroyed."

"I'd like to believe that's possible. I know some of the workers in that factory—I grew up with some of them—and that factory is a major part of Rubaville's livelihood, but I'm afraid that its destruction is not up for debate."

"Do you suppose that the factory will be heavily-defended?"

"I doubt it very seriously."

"Well, then, if the town or factory won't be defended, maybe we could send a small group—a select unit of handpicked soldiers to take care of the factory, to put it out of commission; hopefully, with a minimal amount of damage beyond it and its property. And, maybe that would insure that the rest of the town is spared."

"Thank you, Danny. That's a splendid idea! It's at least worth a try. And, as for your suggestion about going *around the town*, I could send that request to the general...*if this intolerable rain ever lets up...*"

"Yessir. Rain, sleet or snow, I would be most happy to personally deliver it."

"I hate to ask you to do that, but frankly, you're the only one I can count on to make sure it gets safely delivered. I'll draft it now and have it ready before dawn. Hopefully, by then, the weather will be a little more agreeable. Also, I'd prefer to keep this between us."

"Yessir."

"There are still some men here, both enlisted and officers, that don't trust me and never will. It's like they can't believe that there are

Southerners who didn't take the oath to defend the 'homeland.' There's no sense in adding more fuel to the fire."

The corporate nodded.

Andrew sighed, "And I mean literally adding more fuel to the fire to burn down everything in this state. And, for the record, I *did* take the oath to defend the homeland—*America*. That's the homeland; not some bastard country cobbled together by ignorance."

"Yessir."

"Thanks, Corporal. Check back with me at dawn. Oh, and here—"

"Sir?"

Andrew leaned over his cot and grabbed his sword and after carefully re-sheathing it, handed it to the corporal. "Here, Danny," he said, "Take this."

"Sir?"

"For luck. For protection. And, just in case any of our sentries try to slow you down."

"Sir? I don't know if I could ever assault one of our sentries with sword, pistol or rifle."

Andrew was taken aback. "No, no, Danny!" he said in protest, "Not use the sword on them! I meant to show them my sword—it has my name engraved on it. It would hopefully speed and legitimize your mission."

But then, Andrew noticed Danny was grinning back at him as he held the sword, the water from his slicker dripping on its shiny blade, and he realized the corporal was anything but serious.

"So, that's how it is, eh?" Andrew said, mustering a smile at being the target of a jest. "Corporal, please feel free to freely wield it against any of the rebel sentries…or officers, for that matter!"

"Thank you, sir. Will do!"

"Thank you, Danny. But seriously, be careful. There are still reb stragglers and pockets of resistance."

"Yessir. Thank you, sir. I'll stop back by, directly. It's not too long before sunup."

And with that, he was off.

CHAPTER 27

The Frozen Swamp

When the rain finally let up, Curtis and his spotter, a Private Simmons, found a tall tree and began climbing it to survey the area beyond the swamp. The January weather had been miserable, and the elements of the swamp had only added to the unpleasantness. It was an ugly landscape filled with frozen black swamp water and bare, sharp trees jutting out like dark and rotten fangs.

"I wish the skies would decide whether to rain or snow," Curtis said, "It's too cold for rain, but I guess not quite cold enough for snow."

"It's cold 'nuff for the swamp to freeze over," Simmons said, as he climbed in the branches above Curtis.

"Yes, but not thick enough to walk on," Curtis said.

"You are sho nuff right 'bout that," Simmons said, peering down at Curtis as he scooted up the tree, "I ventured out yesterday and stepped right through. I first thought I's snakebit. It was like a hunnerd teeth bit into my feet. Then, thinks I, ain't no snake fool enough to be in this frozen mess. They serpents be smarter than we's human bein's. Guess that's one good thing about all this misery—the varmits have hightailed it out to warmer quarters. Nosir, I eventually figgers all they's icy teeth in my feet wuz that dadblamed swamp icewater. Oowee, my pore ol' feet wuz froze through and through and it shore 'nuff made for a bad night tryin' to dry 'em out. But, hey, maybe it's a good thing. I'm thinkin' it's in our favor it's like that. 'Cause if its bad fo' us, it's gotta be equal bad for those Yanks. It's not like Sherman and his boys could just skate on over. You know?"

This guy talks too much, Curtis thought, but he simply said, "I hope you're right, but I learned not to assume anything."

After checking a few sturdy-looking branches, they found a couple at the top of the tree that they hoped would safely support their weight. Curtis took a torn rag out of his pocket and, drying off the Whitworth's scope and placing it to his eye, he scanned the horizon. In the distance, he saw the black smoke from a dozen fires staining the grey sky. He knew that they weren't campfires, but rather, the evidence of towns and homes being burnt to the ground by the invaders. It was a painfully familiar site for Curtis; it had become more and more common as he and his Carolina unit had been chased out of Georgia. However, now Sherman and his men were bringing the war and its all-encompassing destruction to Carolina…with a new and even more aggressive vengeance.

As Curtis scanned the southern horizon, he saw the first lines of Union blue, and their unexpected audacity caused him to involuntarily gasp. A few branches above him, Simmons, armed with a spyglass, verified his discovery.

"Great stars!" Simmons said, suddenly with alarm, "They comin'! They less than a mile off, right cross the swamp. Froze o' not froze. So much fer th' swamp stoppin' 'em. Ain't nothin' stoppin' 'em. Nothin'!"

It's almost as if all the devastation they caused with their march through Georgia energized them and made them indestructible, Curtis thought. *Like they're actually feedin' off the destruction. Like wild animals.*

Simmons was correct—it seemed as if nothing could stop them. Since Sherman's victory over and destruction of Atlanta, he and his army had mastered the art of slash and burn. They were "living off the land" and burning everything in their path that they couldn't loot or eat. And, rivers and swamps may have slowed them, but only briefly; Sherman's engineers would quickly rebuild the bridges the rebels torched to stop them. Or, they would build their own. Or, they would simply corduroy a path across, using the surrounding logs from trees they would fell or from houses they would demolish.

But, the soldiers that Curtis spotted through the scope of his Whitworth weren't waiting for a bridge to be built or for the engineers to corduroy a path across the swamp; they were wading into the icy muck with grit and determination. For a minute or two, Curtis watched them as they approached. The winter wind was blowing harder in the upper reaches of the tree and the branches—with Curtis and Simmons astride—swayed in the breeze. Curtis made a mental note to factor in his branch's movements as he searched for his targets. There were hundreds of bluecoats, all half-emerged in the swamp's black icy waters, most of them waist-deep with their rifles held over their heads. It was as if some unknown entity had poured blue dye into the water, and it was seeping around the trees jutting out of the water and oozing blue toward them.

At least they can't drag their cannons into the swamp, Curtis thought. A bullet from the Whitworth could travel three-quarters of mile. The accuracy of a shot from that distance was not guaranteed, but if there were at least a dozen men, side-by-side, it was more than likely that it could hit at least one of them. Curtis gauged their distance and took aim at the ones at the front of the encroaching tide. He figured he could take out a number of them before he, himself was in range, especially if they insisted on wading into the water shoulder-to-shoulder. He figured their tactics were intentional, in case one of them tripped on a submerged root in the murky water. Or, maybe they thought it would be warmer if they waded in as a group.

His first shot missed, but his second was true, and, through his scope, he saw the soldier drop into the water and disappear. Because of the distance, he knew the man never heard the sharp report from his rifle. He also saw the fallen soldier's comrade on his right drop his own rifle to dive down below the freezing black water to fish him out.

"Gotcha," Curtis said, smiling grimly, "Fare thee well, blue belly."

After Curtis' next few shots, he didn't bother to see if they had found their mark; it became more routine—load, aim, shoot, load, aim, shoot. He still couldn't believe that the icy swamp hadn't halted them. As he fired, he grudgingly admired the approaching soldiers' tenacity and courage to brave and overcome the elements as they trudged through the sharp-biting, icy swamp waters. *That still won't keep me from shootin' 'em,* he thought as he reloaded the Whitworth. However, as he scanned the swamp through the scope, a puff of white smoke from a distant tree caught his eye.

"Simmons, can you see if there's someone in that distant—" he began, but before he could finish, the younger man dropped from the branch above him. He didn't immediately fall to the ground, but instead, snagged by the branch between his former spot and where Curtis perched, hung there briefly, his head upside down, but eye-to-eye with Curtis. The bullet had torn through Simmons' forehead, but as he swung from the limb, he seemed to stare wide-eyed and accusingly with his mouth open in violent protest. *He's got nearly all his teeth,* Curtis thought, absent-mindedly. *What a shame.* Before Curtis could regain his senses and secure the Whitworth, so he could catch Simmons, the younger man fell from branch to branch, careening to the bottom of the tree like a ragged puppet. His body broke the ice below the tree and then sank into the frozen black water. It was only then that Curtis heard the familiar crack of his enemy's own rifle wafting across and over the icy swamp. He didn't wait for another shot; clearly, the Union sharpshooter had skills that matched his own.

As he slid down the tree to rejoin his unit, he noticed a flurry of activity to his right, which was accompanied by rifle and cannon fire in the distance. The enemy had apparently breached their right flank, on his side of the swamp. They were a half-mile away and closing fast. He grabbed his haversack and rifle and ran toward where he thought his unit would be, but they had apparently seen the impending breach in their flank and had retreated to a more defendable position.

The dull zip and thud of Minié balls as they struck the tree beside him alerted Curtis to the nearness of the approaching force. Once he scampered over the embankment where his unit had previously been entrenched, he noticed his commander officer's grey, riderless horse among the confusion and chaos that had ensued with the breaching of the right flank. Without thinking, he threw his haversack over the saddle of the horse and, Whitworth in hand, climbed up and galloped off toward the grassy area that bordered the area above the swamp. He was vaguely aware of men from his unit calling to him, and others shooting and, in turn, being shot, but it all seemed to blend into a loud cacophony of sound of orders, screams, and artillery. It seemed everywhere he looked was death and destruction, so without thinking, he kicked his boots into the sides of the horse and galloped through the confusion. *Gotta think—gotta think—gotta think! Where do I set up? Where do I regroup? Where do I set up? Where do I regroup? Gotta think—gotta think—gotta think!*

As he rode off—away from the noise, it seemed fewer bullets whizzed by his head, and he continued riding until all of the familiar sounds of battle ceased. In fact, nothing seemed familiar; not the rain, nor the countryside, nor the very essense of his being. He kept riding, impervious to his surroundings or even the time of day. He didn't know how long he had been riding or where he was. *Nothing was familiar.* It was as if he had entered into a foreign world, where all of the natural laws had been suspended. When he finally calmed down and came to his senses—he had never panicked in battle before—it was dark, and he was hopelessly lost. He figured he was somewhere in South Carolina, but he wasn't sure if it was out of harm's reach or in the middle of the advancing front of Sherman's army. It had begun to rain again, so he found a densely covered bluff, at the foot of which offered a shelter of sorts, so he dismounted and tied up the officer's horse and crouched beneath an overhang of branches to plot out his next move. He knew that, with a horse, he could travel further and faster, but he also knew that it would be harder to remain hidden with a horse if the Union forces overtook him. Also, he surmised, it would be hard to explain what he was doing on an officer's horse in the heat of a battle. So, he untied the horse and slapped its flank, sending it fleeing into the rainy darkness. He pulled a ragged blanket from his haversack and dug in beside the bluff to try and get some sleep. He had become accustomed to sleeping in the pouring icy January rain, so in a matter of minutes, he had drifted into a fitful sleep. In the minutes before dawn, he was awakened by the presence of a silhouetted soldier a few yards from where he had been sleeping.

Where's my rifle? he wondered, as he quickly sat up.

"D'you lose your Whitworth, boy?" the soldier asked with a grim laugh. The rising sun was at the shadowy soldier's back, and Curtis could see the man's form backlit like a sort of *body halo,* looming over him menacingly with a large rifle in his hands.

"I am not going to a Yankee prison," Curtis said.

The soldier replied with a derisive laugh, "Really?"

CHAPTER 28

The Road From Richmond

Rev. Barre and his two sons, Curtis and Andrew, first arrived in Rubineville a little less than a decade before the war, and they had all hoped for a new start. Their exit from Richmond had been abrupt and unpleasant. The minister's sermons in his Richmond pulpit had been fairly bold, as he denounced slavery and called for the abolishment of the institution. He realized—albeit much too late—that he had misjudged his congregation, and instead of the Christian encouragement and support he expected, he began receiving bricks through his windows in the middle of the night. However, the bricks were eventually replaced late one evening by tar-capped torches, and he found himself packing up his two boys and whatever belongings and books he could save and escaping the flames in the depth of the night. The boys were young, but old enough to be terrified by the experience, and the memories of that night would scar them and dictate their destinies.

With his rickety wagon loaded with all that he could rescue, Rev. Barre made his way to the North Carolina mountain home of a good friend of his from his seminary days. For a while, he helped his friend and family with the heavy jobs around their home and occasionally preached at several mountain churches. Then, after a couple of years of correspondence and inquiries to a number of churches, asking them if they would be willing to have him pilot their pulpit, he received an offer from the church in Rubineville; their minister had abruptly died and, whereas their church had been growing, they didn't want to lose what they called their "redemptive momentum." And, if the offer of a new start wasn't enough, included in the correspondence was a detailed engraving of their beautiful stained-glass window. Rev. Barre was overcome with relief and gratitude, and the following day, he rode over the mountain and into Asheville, where he was able to send a telegraph to the church, saying he would gladly accept their kind offer and would be there within a fortnight, fully prepared with a sermon on the first Sunday of the month. Although his conscience nagged him, he resolved to not make the same choice of subject matter for his subsequent sermons that had wrecked his tenure at the Richmond church.

Rubineville was everything the minister could have hoped for. It was a small, but friendly community, a pleasant little village, a beautiful church building, and—most important for his sons—a one-room, but well-respected town school that was run by an experienced and well-educated schoolmarm. The two boys, Curtis and Andrew, were only a little over a year apart, and both were a little smaller in stature than their rural counterparts. Curtis was the older of the two, and their mother had died giving birth to Andrew. Although he was too young to remember his brother's birth and subsequent mother's death, he kept a tintype picture of his mother in his bedroom and was able to save it from their torched house when they fled Richmond. Although his father doubted it, Andrew claimed to remember his mother. Rev. Barre assumed it was because he had often heard stories about his mother from various family members.

Once the two boys started at the one-room school in Rubineville, they discovered the true nature of the reality of small town schoolyards. The king of the schoolyard was Jack Maddau, a two-fisted bruiser of a bully. As the only son of one of the area's well-known planters and estate-owners, Charles Maddau, many of the townspeople felt that the apple hadn't fallen far from the tree. Jack was the same age as the older Barre boy, but because he was larger than most boys his age and Curtis was slightly smaller, there was a noticeable size difference. Curtis became painfully aware of this on the first day.

At recess, within the first five minutes, he was tripped by Jack's muddy boot and he found himself face down in the dirt and relieved of his lunch pail. As Curtis looked incredulously at his tormenter, Jack smiled and said, "Hey preacher's boy, din you ever hear about sharin' loaves and fishies?" This had never happened in Richmond, so the treatment took both of the Barre boys by surprise. Curtis responded by taking Andrew's lunch. By the end of the week, they discovered that the treatment at the hands of Jack Maddau would be a daily affair.

"That's it, preacher's boy," Jack would say, "Turn the other cheek and let me smack that 'un, too."

"He can't lick us both," Andrew said after the third or fourth day.

"I don't need your help," was Curtis' response.

Andrew began taking two lunches and hiding one in the woods leading up to the schoolhouse. Finally, he had enough, and during one recess episode, he jumped on the back of Jack who had pinned Curtis to the ground and was feeding him pieces of grass from the schoolyard "for payment of his fine lunch." The rescue had mixed results—whereas it effectively stopped Jack from pounding Curtis on a daily basis in the schoolyard, it incited Jack to turn his attention to the smaller Andrew. Not only was Andrew easier prey, Curtis would stand by—finally able to eat his own lunch—and watch as his younger brother took a beating. It wasn't that Andrew didn't fight back; he tried in vain to give as good as he got, however Jack Maddau was older, bigger and stronger.

Andrew knew better than to hope for Jack to be absent—the teacher had already complimented Jack on his perfect attendance. That afternoon after school, Andrew paused at the door and saw Jack waiting for him in the schoolyard. He turned and asked the teacher if he could help her with some chores, and Curtis walked home alone. The teacher was impressed and delighted. After a half hour, from a window in the schoolhouse, he saw that Jack had finally lost interest in waiting for him to emerge and had decided to head home. Andrew acted as if he had suddenly remembered a chore his father had asked him to do and politely excused himself from the schoolroom. However, instead of returning home, he followed in the direction that Jack had headed, careful to stay out of the older boy's view. Jack's trek home took him through a thick forest, full of undergrowth and vines, along a well-worn path. After a quarter mile or so, Jack came to the edge of a fenced-in cow pasture, but instead of crossing the field, he followed the fenceline until he was out of sight. Andrew debated on whether or not to continue following Jack, but after a glance at the quickly-setting sun, he instead turned and made his way home. On his way back through the woods, he carefully surveyed the trees and the surrounding elements. It was dark when he finally got home to the parsonage, but his father was engrossed in writing the following Sunday's sermon, so nothing was said.

For the remainder of the week, the tormenting continued, and Andrew fought back the best he could, while his bemused brother watched from the picnic tables. However, on the following Saturday, Andrew found an old rug that had been stored away in their attic, and he borrowed a shovel and some buckets from their barn behind the house and made his way into the thick woods. At the point in the woods that he gauged to be midway, he found a large tree about ten feet off the path. He tied a rope to the trunk and began digging a hole in the soft earth at the foot of the tree, just under a large branch which jutted out in the direction of the worn footpath. Then, when he finished, the hole was about three feet by three feet and deep enough that he had to use the rope to climb out. He then took his buckets and shovel to the edge of the pasture where he had seen Jack stop, and he slipped between the fence's slats. There, along the inside of the fenceline, were a number of fresh cowpies, which he quickly shoveled into the buckets, and, after topping them off, made his way back to the hole. After dumping the contents of the buckets into the hole, he threw the rug over the hole, and then covered it with the clumps of bushes, sticks, and downed saplings that he found in the underbrush. Finally, he removed the rope from the tree and tied a bright yellow sign that he had painted at home earlier that morning to the branch which hung over the covered-up hole. The sign faced the path that Jack would be taking on his way to school the following morning. In black letters it read: "Jack Maddau." However, "Maddau" had been painted through in red, and above it written, "Mad Cow."

The following Monday, Andrew was the only one in the class not surprised when Jack's perfect attendance record came to a close. The teacher even waited a few extra minutes before starting the lesson, expecting him to show up at any second. The following day, as Jack returned, Andrew handed him a bright yellow note with wording matching the lettering of the sign in the forest: "Jack MadCow." To the teacher's horror and surprise, Jack pounced on the younger boy and began pummeling him until the teacher, with the help of several of the other boys, pulled him off.

"Beat me if you will," Andrew said through his busted lips, "But I will always get my revenge...*Mad Cow*."

"He...he...he called me *Mad Cow*!" Jack said, but the response was a school room full of loud and raucous laughter and his immediate suspension from the school. After he returned the following week, he turned his attention back to Curtis, until after a few days, Andrew cornered him, telling him that bullying Curtis would be treated similarly and that "revenge will be swift and will match the assault." Jack wasn't totally sure about what *"the assault"* meant, but as luck would have it, Herbert Butts, a barber from somewhere up north, opened a new shop across the street from Klein's General Store that very week. Herbert had three daughters and a skinny son, Harold, who was the same age as Jack and Curtis. Jack eagerly turned his attention to tormenting the newcomer, whom he called Harry. Jack's reign of terror and bullying came to an end the following school year, when Harry returned to school after getting a growth spurt during the summer and working with the town's blacksmith. He was 30 pounds heavier and a head taller than Jack and during recess the first day of school, he insisted on demonstrating to the other students how he learned to shoe horses over the summer, using Jack as a "blonde gelding."

That summer was also when Andrew first read about West Point. He spoke with a local politician (who attended his father's church) about the admission process and, together, they began writing letters to solicit recommendations on his behalf. In the meantime, Curtis was given a long rifle by a recently widowed woman, also in their father's congregation. Her husband had used the rifle in target competitions, and she thought it would be a suitable present for Curtis. The gun was a painful reminder of her husband, but she didn't have the heart to sell it, and Rev. Barre had been extrememly supportive during her husband's illness and death, so she elected to give it to his oldest son. Curtis began shooting targets at the beginning of the summer. By September, he could hit a bullseye at a hundred yards.

CHAPTER 29
BROTHERS IN ARMS

Curtis immediately recognized his mistake and his perilous predicament when he reached for the Whitworth and found an indentation in the grass where he had placed it the night before. Although the sun had not yet come up, it was light enough to see the soldier standing over him, holding the Whitworth. He figured he was doomed either way—if it was a Yankee, he would be shipped to a northern prison, but if it was a rebel soldier, he could be considered a deserter and shot on the spot. Or, he would be taken back to camp and shot or hanged.

"You lookin' for this Whitworth, boy?" the soldier said with a hoarse laugh, "You a lil' bit careless with your rifle, ain't ya?"

The soldier was still in silhouette, but there was something familiar about his voice.

"Well? Speak up, fool!" the soldier said.

"I tol' you, I ain't goin' to a Yankee prison."

"Well then, you'd better get a move on, because they whol' Yankee army ain't but a couple-a miles from here. They on hosses, an' they's closin' fast." He leaned over, his face close enough for Curtis to smell his foul breath.

"Mad Cow!" Curtis said, rubbing his eyes.

"Well, I will be dipped. As I live and breathe," Jack said, "If it ain't the preacher's boy."

As Jack and Curtis made their way toward the Rubine River, the winter rain returned with a vengeance. Along the way, they had seen a rabbit caught in a snare. It had apparently been set by one of the local residents—food was scarce throughout the state and region—but the two had no qualms about stuffing the trapped rabbit into Jack's haversack.

"Where are we goin'?" Curtis asked, "Or do you even know?"

"You worry about how we gonna cook that rabbit," Jack said.

They had been careful to stay off the main roads, and to parallel the roads at a distance, so as not to be surprised by any troops, Union or Confederate. At one point, the road they were shadowing hugged the crest of a hill covered with stones and boulders and smothered by a thick covering of overgrowth. They elected to climb the hill, through the brush and over the stones, rather than to stay close to the road. Although it was more time-consuming, they surmised that it was a safer plan. As they crouched at the crest of the hill, hiding behind a thicket, they saw an approaching rider on the road below, a half-mile away, on a light brown mare. Observing him through the Whitworth's scope, Curtis could see that he was alone, and in a hurry.

"That's not a good sign," Curtis said, "He's coming from someplace up north and heading south. That means there's Yankees to the north."

"Not necessarily," Jack said, "There's a crossroads up about a mile. He may have come from the east."

"*North*east," Curtis said.

"They're targeting Columbia—the capital—not us. But, it would be nice to know what they have in mind. Maybe we should ask our friend."

"Are you insane? They'd hear a shot from this Whitworth for miles around."

"I know that—I ain't no fool! I got a better idea. Let's head down this side of this hill."

The road below the bluff had been built to go around the hill, rather than over it, and it hugged and wrapped around the base of the bluff. The two scampered through the brush and down the side of the hill, where there was a huge boulder that had apparently rolled down the side of the bluff and nestled up to the side of the road.

"Now I know why they went around this hill," Curtis said, "It's made up of big rocks."

"Yeah, well, I'm gonna use this big rock to hide," Jack said, "You gonna play the part of a wounded Reb. Here, gimme that rifle. You lay down in the middle-a th' road, like you're dead or sick."

"What if he rides on over me?"

"Then, I'll bandage you up! Somehow though, I don't think he will. I never met a Yankee that wadn't as curious as a housecat. Now, hurry, git over there."

Just as Curtis rolled into position on the road, as if he were dead or wounded, Corporal Daniel Richards rounded the curve and pulled up to a stop just short of where Curtis lay.

"You!" he ordered, "Get up!"

When Curtis didn't move, Richards cautiously dismounted— with pistol in hand— and stood over Curtis, prodding him with his boot.

"Get up, Reb, I said!"

As he cautiously leaned over to take a closer look, Jack sprang from behind the rock, and swinging the Whitworth like a club, knocked the corporal to the ground with a sickening thud, and the pistol went sailing out of his lifeless fingers as he tumbled to the ground. Curtis grabbed the pistol and he and Jack stood over the fallen corporal.

"Now it's our turn to give the orders," Jack said, "To your feet, Yank!"

Curtis bent over the fallen soldier. "You killed him," he said, "You smashed in his head. Look at that. You done caved it in."

"Look at his uniform—he's a corporal. Like I said, curiousity killed the corporal," Jack laughed, wiping his nose with the back of his hand.

"You didn't have to kill him."

"Maybe I hit 'im a little too hard, but there is a war on, you know," Jack said, "Better t' be safe than sorry. 'Sides, he'd a done the same to us, if he'd got the drop on us, 'stead of us gettin' the drop on him, so don't be goin' all soft on me, now. Check his pockets, and I'll go through his saddlebags. Maybe he's got some food or provisions. Oh, and get his sword. And hurry. He may not be alone."

"There wadn't anyone with him when we spotted him."

"These Yanks travel quick, though. So, hurry. We need to get him off the road into the brush here. Hurry, it's startin' to rain again. But maybe that's a good thing. Look at that sword he has."

"I don't believe it!" Curtis said, as he examined the sword.

"What?"

"This is my brother's sword!"

"Is this your brother?"

"No. Unfortunately, it ain't that traitor," Curtis huffed, "That's wishful thinkin.' But it's definitely his sword. Look, here's his name, plain as day, engraved here on the handle. Wonder how he got his hands on my brother's sword?"

"So, your little brother's a blue belly? Guess that shouldn't surprise me. He still digging holes for people to fall in?"

Curtis had forgotten about that incident, and he chose to ignore Jack's comment. He wanted to laugh about it, but he figured that it would have been a sore point with Jack. He also hoped that Jack wouldn't decide to get some sort of revenge for something that had happened more than a decade before. Still, he made a mental note to not drop his guard.

"We gotta rid of his body," Curtis finally said. As he dragged the corporal's body into the heavy brush, Jack went through the saddlebags on the horse. There was a half-full canteen and the sealed message from Andrew, but no food.

Jack opened the paper and slowly read the order.

"They're gonna be going to Rubaville," he said, "Hey, speaking of your brother, is he an officer? A captain?"

"Yeah, I think so. Weren't not exactly on speaking terms these days. Why you askin'?"

"I think I know the answer to your question about your brother's sword. This is a message from him. Signed and sealed. I'm thinkin' the sword was to authenticate the message. Or maybe it was for protection. If that's the case, it didn't work so good. 'Least not as good as your Whitworth worked. Now, that's one lethal weapon."

"I don't think it was designed to be used as a club."

"It worked, didn't it? Let's ask our friend how good it worked. Hey, Corporal, how you like Curtis' Whitworth? How's your head?" Jack laughed.

"Actually, let's get him hidden before they come lookin' for him," Curtis said.

"Do you have any idea where we're going?" Curtis asked. The rain was still pouring down and the woods were growing darker by the minute. As miserable as the weather was, Curtis was greatful to be out of the frozen swamp—and close to home.

"You just hang onto your rifle and your brother's sword, and let me do the navigating," Jack sniffed, "We're almost there."

"Where is 'there'?"

"You'll see."

It was dark by the time they finally reached the hidden cave behind the waterfall that Jack's father had shown him all those years before—a lifetime before, actually. The cold temperature had slowed the waterfall, but there was still enough water rushing over the rocks at the top to keep it from freezing and to keep the cave opening hidden from view. The bluff that the waterfall plunged from was a sheer wall of rock, ice and various trees.

"What in the world?" Curtis said, "What is this?"

"Old family secret," Jack said. Confident the driving rain had covered up any trace of their trek, Jack led Curtis to the edge of the bluff, and feeling his way in the dark, found the opening to the hidden cave. Once they crawled through the hole, and were safely inside, they built a small fire to dry off, warm up and to roast the wet rabbit they had poached from the snare. Jack felt fairly sure that the heavy rain would smother any smoke—and even the smell of smoke—that may seep out from behind the waterfall. It had been several days since either of them had eaten, and they had almost forgotten how hungry they were.

The fire lit their faces and made jumping shadows on the cave wall behind them. The previous weeks and months of war had not been kind to either man. Their muddy clothes hung in rags off their lean bodies and their hair and beards were matted. The flickering firelight added an animated, ghostly quality to their facial figures. They roasted the rabbit and divided it in half. Neither of them waited until their portion had cooled; rather, they tore into the meat like wild animals. There would be nothing left but scorched bones when the two were finished.

"Best rabbit I ever ate," Curtis said.

"Yep. Sure beats eatin' our boots," Jack said.

"'Least we got boots to eat," Curtis replied, "That's more'n some of 'em in my unit had. Glorified sandals and goin' barefoot was the normal footwear."

"Yep. Same with mine. But they wuz careful to make sure all the officers—and *sharpshooters*—were well shoed."

Curtis bristled at the implication. "Hmm," he said, "Maddau, you're wearin' boots. Are you an officer or a sharpshooter?"

"Oh, you know, Barre. I ain't smart enough to be an officer an' I ain't dumb enough to be a sharpshooter, sittin' up there on a birdy branch, just to be picked off by a Yankee sharpshooter on th' other side. Nossir, a dead Yankee gave me his boots. He said he didn't need 'em where he was going." Jack said, laughing at his own remark.

"So...did you check his pockets for anything else?" Curtis said, brushing off the sharpshooter remark.

"What? Like another message from your brother?" Jack said.

"No. I mean, like money."

"Oh, you mean, am I holdin' out on you, right? No, Barre, I don't got no Yankee dollars that I'm keepin' from you. But then, I didn't bother to check his pockets. I had my eye on his boots."

"So you really didn't check his pockets?"

"I said no, but here, see for yourself!" Jack stood up and pulled his pockets out from his ragged pants. A single round wooden object fell out and rolled over to where Curtis sat.

"Gimme that!" Jack said, leaning over with his hand out. "I forgot about that."

"Here," Curtis said, but as he offered it back to Jack, he noticed a detailed carving of a tiger on the makeshift wooden coin, the linework shimmering in the dancing firelight. "What's that? A tiger coin?"

"It's my lucky tiger head. An ol' boy in my unit carved it. Met him early in the war. He saved my life, actually."

"Really?"

"Yep. We were in a tight spot. It was pretty much hand-t'-hand. Rifle-t'-rifle, rather. I was tryin' to reload, and I look up an' there's this Yankee barrel pointed right at my head. I just closed my eyes and waited for the shot. He already had a bead on me an' I knew I couldn't git my fool rifle loaded an' aimed by the time he could squeeze his trigger. Figured it would be the last thing this side of hell that I'd hear and feel. I heard the shot, an' thought, 'Am I dead? If not, how in the world did he miss? He was only a dozen feet away. It was an easy shot."

"Lemme guess. It was your friend takin' the shot."

"Yep. My friend, the carver. He was quite the artist. *He drew his rifle just in time!*" Jack laughed.

"Humorous. I get it."

"Yep, he was a good man. He and his partner, both. They was from New Orleans. They march to a different beat down there. My friend learned how to carve from his time in a traveling circus, and came back home to New Orleans and opened a signmaking shop with his woodcarvin' and paintin' partner. When the war broke out, he and his partner closed their shop to enlist. They were both Irish boys. Joined up with the 6th Louisiana Volunteers. Called 'em the Confederate

Tigers. Don't know why. Didn't know they had tigers down in the Louisiana swamps. Or in Ireland, for that matter. Anyway. He was th' best artist—an' carver—I ever met. An' a deadly fighter. You don't think of a artist being a fighter, but he was. Maybe all that carvin' and paintin' makes you good at aimin' a rifle. I don't know. But he got hisself kild fightin' with Lee in the Second Battle of Manassas. Both him an' his partner got kild. Within a few minutes o' each other." Jack smirked. "That was a victory for us, remember. Hurray for the Confederacy."

"Yep."

"He and his partner didn't git to celebrate. I keep this tiger head to remind me."

"Of what?"

"I don't know—whatever. Manassas. The Confederacy. Louisiana. Ireland. Tigers. The futility of life. My friend, the signmaker. Whatever," Jack said. Then, suddenly irritated, he said, "Does that answer your nosy questions?"

"How long you think we can stay in this cave?" Curtis asked, changing the subject.

"Don't know. Far as I know I'm the only one still alive that knows about it. And as long as we don't do something stupid like send up smoke signals or get spotted by a scout, we could stay here indefinitely."

"We gotta eat."

"Yep. We gotta eat. But there's fresh water and there's even fish, if we can figger out how to snag 'em without bein' seen. In a couple-a months it'll be warm again, and this war can't possibly go much longer."

"Yeah? An' then what?"

"Well, I don't know about you, but I'm getting out of the South. Probably head west. They got gold out there just for the digging."

"Why leave the South? Ain't this home?"

"Home? You an' me—we don't have a home or country anymore. If the Yankees catch us, they'll still most likely send us up to some northern prison. An' it'll be worse if we get caught by our own people, seein' that we're deserters an' all."

"Speak for yourself. I ain't no deserter."

"You just keep right on trying to convince yourself of that. You said yourself that you hightailed it off the field of battle on the back of an officer's horse. Try explainin' that while they're stringin' you up."

Curtis pondered the thought, and he realized that there was truth in what Jack was saying.

"Let me ask you something, Barre. Does your daddy have any money stored up? It ain't so far to Rubaville."

"I don't know. He always talked about his treasure, but he never showed it to me," Curtis scoffed.

"Treasure? Hmm. I like the sound o' that. Was it real?"

"He talked like it was real. But then again, he was always buildin' his lofty sermons."

"Maybe he was skimmin' from the collection plate. They passed the plate, didn't they? Maybe he was hidin' some away every Sunday. That'd add up over the years."

"I guess that's possible, but that wasn't really his character. Besides, even if he had something that he stored up, that don't mean he'd share it with me," Curtis said, "If it was shared with anybody, it would be with my little brother. The Yankee captain. In the eyes of my father, he was the golden boy, not me. But, hey, what about your money, Maddau? You were the one in the big house. I heard you had yerself a big wedding and got yerself all married up and all. What about your fortune? You leave it with your wife?"

Jack scoffed and threw a stone into the fire, "Right. Ain't no fortune, that's fo' sure. There's nothing left. My high-and-mighty wife up and left—with my boy—long before the war even started up good. Went on up to her sister's in Chicago. Talk about a head-strong woman. Married up, you say? Her old man like to make people think they wuz all that, but they didn't have nothing. Thas the joke—both of us—me and her—thought we wuz marrying rich people. Joke wuz on both of us."

"What happened to your land? Your big house? You used to be rich."

"I don't know that we were ever rich. Land rich, maybe, but you can't put dirt in the bank. An' once my father died, things started slippin' and when my mother died, everthing else went up in smoke. By the time I married, most of the land had been sold off. So, there's nothing left for me here. An' there sure ain't anything for me up there in Chicago. It was mostly gone before I left, and I'd bet there'll be even less once Sherman and his boys get finished. 'Sides, the house and most of the property were sold and most the slaves were all sold off...except the one, of course, that my mother gave your father. I almost forgot about that. How'd that work out, Curtis? What'd y'all do with him?"

"Ah yes, Nehemiah. Good ol' Neemy. My father couldn't figure out if he wuz a slave or a preacher. You'd haf to ask my brother. He was the one that was all best friends with that slave boy."

"Speakin' of your baby brother..." Jack pulled the paper they had taken off the corporal and threw it in the dwindling fire. "We need to git rid o' that. That's the last thing we need to be caught with. They'd hang us on the spot as spies."

Curtis laughed ruefully. "If they find that dead corporal, they'll hang us anyway. Actually, I don't think they'd waste the rope. They'd shoot us on the spot."

"Anyway. We don't need the parchment evidence. 'Sides, we know the orders now. Your brother's been ordered to Rubaville, his hometown. Our hometown. And he don't want it to get all burned up. Bless his heart. He's thinkin' of your pa and his church."

"That sounds like him. Always the hero. You know, I've lived in his shadow all my life. An' I was the older one. Shoulda been the other way 'round. When he went up north, I thought good riddance. But now. Now, this war has brought him right back. Right back here," Curtis laughed.

"What's so funny?" Jack asked.

"I was just thinkin' about what my brother would do if he wuz to get his hands on us..."

"We'd have Union neckties..."

"No, my brother plays by the rules," Curtis said, "We'd be on a train to a prison somewhere up north. I think you're probably right about what would happen if we got caught...most likely, my brother and the Yankees would treat us better than the boys in our old units would treat us if they were to ever catch up with us."

"I said that before we met our corporal friend. I don't think the blue bellies will be so gentle with us if they find his body."

"You're probably right. I keep forgettin' about that corporal."

"So. Why do you have it in for your little brother? I seem to recall you two never got along, even back when we were in school together. Even before he turned Yankee. I remember you not carin' so much when I pummeled him."

"Right...Mad Cow."

"Yeah. Mad Cow. I'm startin' to remember why he was so unlikeable. As I recall, he made a pretty big fool outta me."

"Yeah, but I've got a better reason to hate him," Curtis said. "I know you lost your mother to an illness."

"It was her heart give out."

"Right. But in mother's case, she didn't have to die so young. My little brother killed her."

"What? How do you mean?"

"By being born." Curtis said. "He lived, she died. I had a mother until he came along."

"No wonder you hate him. And especially if you think he'll get your old man's treasure."

"Like I said, I never saw any treasure...I just heard about treasure all the time."

"So, help me understand," Jack said, "Was your family in favor of the war or against it?"

"My father loved this land." Curtis made a wide sweeping motion with his hand in the darkness of the cave. "Our town. Our people in it. So, if that's the Confederacy, then that's what he loved. But, he has always hated the idea of one man owning another."

"So that's why he needed his own slave," Jack said, smirking.

"That wasn't his idea. You know that, and I'll thank you to stop saying that."

Jack smiled. "My apologies, Barre. I believe that was—*is*—a sore point for both us. Sounds like your family has some disagreements. You say your daddy loves the Confederacy, but that he'll probably leave all his money—his *treasure*—to your *younger* brother who is a *Yankee* officer. Sounds confusin'."

"Yeah. Confusin'. And that's not even talkin' about the religion aspect."

"Yeah, that *is* confusin'," Jack said. "You got a man of God with two sons; one is a Rebel sharpshooter who kills men from a distance of a half mile, and you got the other one that kills Rebels—or at least orders the killing of Rebels, and I'm guessing that includes sharpshooters."

"Yeah. Like you said, *confusin'*. I never said my family made any sense."

"I'm wonderin'," Jack said, "How you think things'll fall out if something happens to your brother?"

"What d'ya mean?"

"I mean, let's think about this. Apparently, he's the officer in charge, at least in this area. At least, the fact that he's sending out messages like the one we confiscated shows that he has a good deal of authority. At least when it comes to Rubaville."

"So?"

"So, I say, cut off the head-a the snake. Come on Curtis, you're the sharpshooter. You're the one with the Whitworth and scope."

Curtis quietly pondered Jack's comment. "That *would* settle a few scores between us," he said after a minute, "Settle 'em in spades, actually. Once and for all. But as tempting of a thought as that is, I don't think that would change the strategy of the Union Army. Not when they're bein' driven by Sherman. We both have seen enough of the war to know that it don't matter if you shoot one Yankee officer. They just put another one in his place."

"All I'm sayin' is maybe losing one of their officers could slow things down long enough for you to see your old man and get what's yours," Jack finally said, "It don't make no nevermind to me. But it seems like it would be the perfect way to square things with your little brother...and get what's rightfully yours from your father at the same time. Take care of your brother, get your money an' all we gotta do is get into the mountains. Yanks won't follow us there, an' most o' the mountain folks didn't want this war in the first place. They ain't so excited 'bout being Confederates. We'd have a clear path to the mountains, 'specially if we had a day's start on the Yanks." Jack added some sticks to the dwindling fire and let his last comment sink in.

"Again...I don't know that there is any money," Curtis finally said, "But, you're right about settling an old score."

"How close do you have to be to make the shot?" Jack asked.

"Do you remember Turner's Knob?" Curtis asked.

"Sure. I know it well."

"'Course it's been years since I've been there, but as I recall, there's a big old oak tree square on top of it. It's about a half mile from the turnpike that runs down by the main channel of the river...the bluecoats'd have to take that route to Rubaville, and I probably could make the shot from there. I'd only get one shot, and we'd have to get away quick...those boys could cover a half mile pretty smartly. Do you know how to get there from here? And back here, quickly?"

"Sure do."

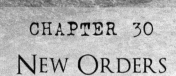

CHAPTER 30
NEW ORDERS

It was an hour or so before sun-up when the riders galloped into the camp and, after dismounting, the ranking officer among them, Lieutenant Franklin Cheswick, was directed to Andrew's tent. One of the enlisted men on duty outside the tent, saluted and peeked into the tent, and, seeing Andrew asleep said, "Sir, Captain Barre is asleep."

"Step aside, Private."

The commotion immediately awoke Andrew, and he sat up in his cot. "Enter!" he yelled from inside the tent. The lieutenant pushed past the sentry and threw open the tent flap.

Andrew looked up from his cot and frowned. "Oh," he said, "I was expecting my corporal."

"Lieutenant Cheswick," the lieutenant said, saluting, "I've got a message from the general."

"Here, Lieutenant," Andrew said, motioning to a stool in the corner of the tent, "Have a seat. I must admit that I'm also a bit surprised that they would send an officer to deliver a message. Did you come alone?" He held out his hand to receive the message.

"There is no written message," the lieutenant said, waving off the offer to sit, "I am the message. And, no, I didn't travel alone. There are seven of us."

"I see," Andrew said, eyeing the lieutenant, "In that case, proceed."

"Your orders are to leave—*immediately*—and move on to the town of Rubineville and destroy the cotton mill on the south end of the town."

"Understood. But, I don't think it will take the whole company to destroy a single factory. It isn't guarded."

"If I may ask, why would you not want to use the entire unit?"

"For several reasons. First, we've been marching the men pretty hard, and I believe they would appreciate an extra day to rest."

The lieutenant didn't speak, so Andrew continued. "But frankly, I've been disappointed at the lack of…*restraint* that some of the men have had when it comes to these small Carolina towns, not to mention the private homes. I'm not so sure it was General Sherman's orders to burn down all of South Carolina."

"Sir. He hasn't specifically ordered it. It's just that…"

"Yes. Continue, Lieutenant…"

"Yessir. It's just that I don't think the general is that upset if a few fires get started. After all, this is where the whole war began. Right here in South Carolina. The so-called *Cradle of the Confederacy*. So I suspect that some of our men get a little careless with matches."

"Yes, but the private homes…"

"Yessir, but many of these houses that have been, uh…"

"Destroyed."

"Yes, destroyed. Many of these homes happen to belong to the planters and the slaveholders. The genteel and wealthy, upper class of the South. And many of my men feel that this war was started and perpetuated with the likes of them. In fact, I, myself can't seem to understand why some of these poor threadbare farmers around here fought for the rights of the rich men. Most of these poor fools have never had slaves, and will never hope to be able to afford to. Why would they fight to the death? For someone else's riches and way of life?"

"I suppose if you were to ask them, they would say 'for honor.'"

"Ah yes, *honor*."

"And because we're here. We're the invaders."

"We didn't start this war, sir."

"Yes, but look at what we're talking about…we're burning this state to the ground."

"Yessir. But that's not my orders. My orders—*our orders*—are to destroy the cotton mill in Rubineville."

"Yes. The mill. Not the town."

The lieutenant smiled silently. "Yessir."

"And Lieutenant, to that end, I think we can get the job done with a few dozen riders. In fact, I had dispatched my corporal to headquarters to propose just that. And to concentrate on the mill, rather than the town." Andrew paused. "Speaking of which…to your knowledge, perchance, did my corporal deliver a message to your camp? To the general?"

"No sir. Not to my knowledge. However, I do know that the general is not happy, and I am sure that he wants your undivided attention to this order and to see that it is executed…uh…post haste. As for how you execute the order and the number of troops you feel is necessary, I'm sure the general has every confidence in your leadership and discretion. However, I would suggest at least 40 or 50 riders, and I got the impression that was around the number of troops the general was *expecting* you to take with you."

"Thank you, Lieutenant," Andrew said. He scrutinized the younger officer's demeanor to judge if he was being sarcastic, but his nagging concern for his corporal tempered his response. "One last thing, Lieutenant—what road did you take to get to our camp?"

"The south turnpike, sir."

"Did you happen to meet my corporal on the turnpike, say, close to your camp? On a light brown mare?"

"No sir. But it's odd that you would ask that."

"How so, Lieutenant?"

"We did encounter a pale horse a little ways down the turnpike, but it was still dark, and even with the full moon, we couldn't see whether it was brown or grey. It was on the other side of the fence row.

Seemed spooked. In the moonlight it was just light enough to make it out as a horse."

Anticipating the next question, the lieutenant added, "No rider. Couldn't make out whether the horse had a saddle or not. But again, we weren't really focusing on it. Our concern was that it was a rebel scout...or worse, a patrol."

"Thank you, Lieutenant. That will be all."

"Sir?"

"Yes?"

"My orders were to make sure you understood the general's direction."

"Yes, you've made that crystal clear."

"Yessir, but—I was also ordered to stay and help you carry it out."

Ah, a nursemaid, Andrew thought to himself, but instead, he said, "I understand. Let me assemble the men who we will be taking on the mission."

After the lieutenant left to gather up the men who had ridden into the camp with him, Andrew grudgingly emerged from the tent and gave the order for one of the junior officers to select 40 riders for the raid on the Rubineville Cotton Mill. He also knew that he would have to maintain discipline and total control, if he was to keep the destruction of the Rubineville Cotton Mill from spreading to the rest of the town. As upsetting as the order was and the implication that he had ignored the first one to destroy the mill, Andrew found himself much more troubled that Corporal Richards had disappeared. What's worse, the young corporal had disappeared while trying to deliver a message from him.

CHAPTER 31

A Long Shot

It was afternoon before Andrew and his raiding party rounded the bend on the turnpike above the rushing creek that made its way into the Rubine River. Beside him rode Lieutenant Franklin Cheswick. They had been riding in silence, but as they crossed the creek, Lieutenant Cheswick spoke.

"I understand you were raised in these parts, Captain."

Andrew stiffened, bristling at what he perceived as being a recurring type of insinuation, questioning his loyalties.

"Lieutenant, why didn't you mention that during our discussion in my tent when you first arrived? Did you know that before you brought me the order, or has one of my men shared this with you?"

"Sir—" the lieutenant stammered, blushing with being called out.

"Where did you receive your commission, Lieutenant? Were you at the Academy?"

"No sir, I attended a little—"

"Well Lieutenant," Andrew interrupted, his voice rising, "I *did* receive my commission at the Academy, and I assure you that my *raising* and my *background* have nothing to do with the allegiance and dedication I have to our flag and country. That was instilled in the very marrow of my character during my education and training at *the Academy*. And my service record and my successes in battle will testify to that."

"Yes sir, sorry, sir," the lieutenant said, suddenly sitting straight up in the saddle, "I certainly didn't intend to impugn your service or dedication. I merely meant to suggest that you may be familiar with this area—its terrain and possibly, the most suitable vantage point and direction from which to approach the town and the mill."

"I see," Andrew said, gazing around at the area as the last of the riders splashed out of the creek, and halting the troop. He grudgingly admitted to himself that the lieutenant had a good point, whether or not he was being facetious. *Was I overreacting,* he thought to himself, *or was he really baiting me?*

As the company gathered around Andrew, he said, "Men. Listen carefully. The cotton mill is on the south side of the town, and that is our target." He paused for effect, "This cotton mill—*the Rubineville Cotton Mill*—is our *only* target. We are to destroy it *quickly* and *efficiently* and return to our camp. We are to leave the rest of the town intact. Am I clear?"

As the "yessirs" sounded out through the ranks in waves, Andrew continued.

"As I stated, the mill is on the south end of the town. It is on the river—and the river is fairly deep at that juncture, so it would be difficult—if not impossible—to reach and breach from the east. Obviously, the river serves as a natural defense. And the road that approaches the town from the south is straight and visible from the mill. I'm not worried about anyone putting up a fight from the town or the mill—I don't believe there's much fight left in most of the civilians in these parts—but still, I would like to think we have the element of surprise. And yes, Joe Wheeler is still at large and has a nasty habit of popping up and bedeviling us, but I don't have any reports of him being in the vicinity of Rubaville. The Rebs have bigger fish to fry than Rubaville."

"Like protecting Columbia," Cheswick offered.

"Thank you, Lieutenant," Andrew said, eyeing the lieutenant. "Yes, like protecting Columbia. Columbia *is* the capital, and it *is* a prize. An' it's a target for what's left of the rebs in these parts to try and protect, even though it's only a matter of time and numbers—and we have *both* on our side—before it falls...an' goes the way of Atlanta. So, we'll leave Columbia to whoever Uncle Billy decides is worthy to burn it down. Meanwhile, we have the distinct *honor* of goin' after the *smaller fish*, the Rubineville Cotton Mill. And this is how we are going to proceed. We're going to approach the town from the south, but before we can be spotted—if anyone is even there to look for us—we're going to get off of the turnpike a mile south of the town, and we're going to continue west and then move to the north and then swoop down on them from west of town. That will give us the element of surprise and hopefully will minimize our losses or civilian losses, if the mill is defended."

"What about coverage? Are there any woods or is it just open space?" The question came from the sergeant who had ridden in with Lieutenant Cheswick.

"Not only is it wooded," Andrew answered, "But there is a hill that edges up to the side of the road. As I said, from the mill, you can see at least a half mile down the road to the south, but you can't see over the hill. And, it's highly unlikely that they would have any lookouts posted on that hill. The cotton mill may be a military target, but it's run by civilians...regular townspeople. Again, there most likely won't be any resistance; they won't put up a fight."

"What about the livestock, sir?" a private asked.

"Thank you, Private, but I don't believe the livestock will put up much of a fight, either," Andrew said, evenly. There was a moment of silence, but then the entire troop burst out into laughter.

"Sir? I only meant—"

"No, Private, you are not to set fire to the livestock, either." Again, the troops reeled into laughter. Sergeant Jenkins, whose face was normally ruddy and red, was the color of an apple, tears streaming down his face.

In the middle of the laughter, however, Andrew was distracted by a tiny flash of a reflection from a treeline atop a distant bluff to the south. As he squinted toward the distant bluff, his gloved hand instinctively reached down to the side of his saddle, extracting his field glasses.

"Sir?" the lieutenant queried, trying to follow his gaze.

"Hold on, Lieutenant," Andrew said, bringing the binoculars up to his eyes with one hand and pointing to the treeline with the other. "Men!—" But before he could issue an order, he suddenly violently jerked up, as his field glasses dropped to the ground. Andrew slowly looked down at his chest with a grimace of pain to see the blossoming of a red rose of blood on the faded greatcoat over his heart. He then turned to the shocked lieutenant with a quizzical expression before slumping off the horse. When Andrew's body hit the frozen ground beside the binoculars with a heavy thud, there came the distant clap of a rifle shot from the direction of the treeline on Turner's Bluff.

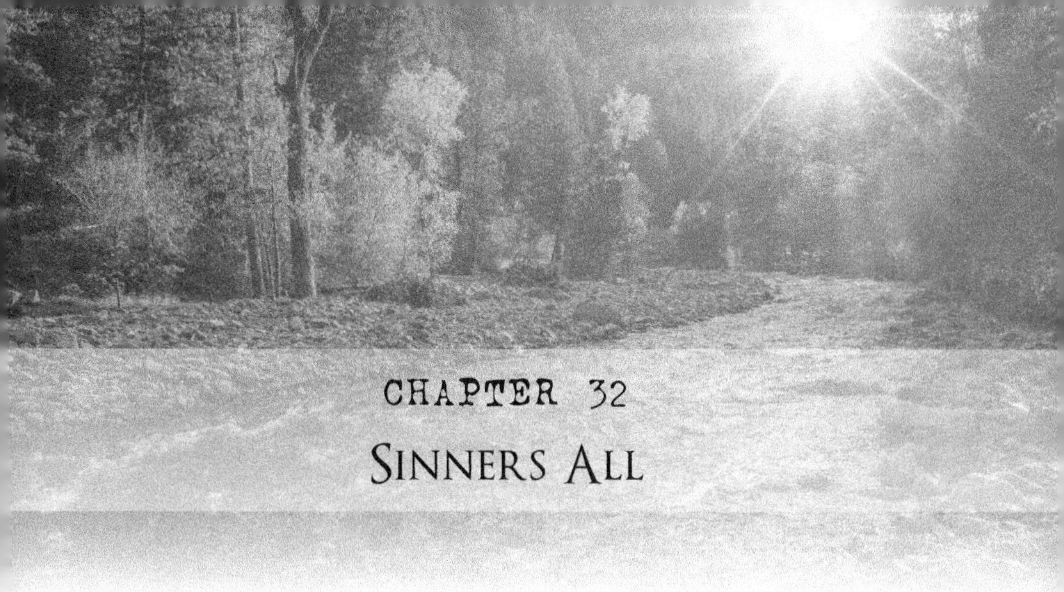

CHAPTER 32
SINNERS ALL

As soon as the bullet left his rifle and he saw the result through the scope, Curtis took his finger off the trigger and quickly lowered the Whitworth by the frayed rope tied to the strap down to Jack, who was waiting at the base of the tree.

"Well?" Jack said, looking up and shielding his eyes.

"Well, we better get outta here." Curtis was already halfway down the tree. He had done this enough that it came as second nature.

"I mean, did you get 'im?"

"Yes. But it ain't no time to celebrate. Once his bluecoat friends figger out what happened and where it came from, they'll be on us like fleas on a mangy dog. As I tol' you, it don't take much time to cover a half mile with a fresh Yankee horse."

Jack was holding the Whitworth in his left hand and reaching inside his tattered coat with his right hand as Curtis slid down the bottom part of the trunk of the large oak, hugging the tree to slow his descent.

"Hurry up, Curtis," Jack called up at him, "Go ahead and drop—it's only 20 feet to the bottom."

"I don't wanna break my fool leg! I at least wanna make it hard for 'em to catch us."

"Come on, it's only a 15-foot drop. We gotta git!"

"You're settin' my leg if I break it," Curtis said, loosening his grip slightly on the icy tree trunk and quickly sliding earthward.

At about six feet from the ground, he pushed back from the tree to free fall, but, to his surprise, Jack was immediately below him, stopping his fall. As his worn boots hit the frozen ground below the tree, a sharp and sickening pain hit his back and spread through his body and extremities. Rolling over, to his surprise, he saw that blood was beginning to soak his shirt and ragged coat, and looked up to see Jack standing over him, holding Andrew's sword.

"What the—?" Curtis gasped.

"Sorry it had to be this way, Barre, but do you really blame me? You acted like you wadn't interested in your daddy's fortune—*treasure*—and I can sure use some getaway money. Even a little bit'l go a long way in the mountains. Or even out west." He knelt beside Curtis and wiped the blood off the sword using the sleeve on Curtis's torn coat.

"I'm guessin' you shore stirred up a Yankee hornet's nest with that shot. Nice shootin', by the way."

"What—?" Curtis tried to say, but no sound came. *Can't breathe*, he thought.

"Yessir, those blue bellies gonna be mad now, an' I'm thinkin' they ain't gonna stop at torchin' that old cotton factory…I figger that shot just signed our old town's death warrant. But it may as well go the way of the rest of this state. Ain't gonna be nothing left nowhere, anyway. Sherman's decided to burn everthing down to the ground. And good riddance, I say. I also figger that since your old man's church is on the far side-a town, he'll have plenty of time to hide any valuables. He'd be a fool to let anything of value burn with his church. But, maybe they won't burn his church, after all. Maybe your brother told 'em it was his father's church and to leave it be. But…then again, you did shoot him, so who knows how it'll play out."

Jack turned the sword over and fingered its engraved name, "An…'least your brother was kind enough to loan me his sword. Thanks to his little brother, he sure ain't gonna need it anymore."

Curtis stared back in shocked resignation and watched as Jack picked up the Whitworth that had landed beside the tall tree. He immediately flashed back to when Jack had stood over him when he had first fled from the scene of battle. *That had probably been an omen,* he thought grimly, *one that I should have paid more attention to.* The terrible pain in his back had begun to subside, but he couldn't move and the sharp stabbing of the cold was gradually replaced by a warmth spreading up from his feet. It had begun to pour again, and he noticed how the stark trickle of blood was slowing and mixing with the freezing rain, creating patterns meandering down the hill.

As he felt his life—his spirit—seeping out, he felt his anger leaving, as well. It was slowly being replaced by an overwhelming and calming sense of forgiveness mixed with remorse. He thought of his father and how the deaths of both of his sons would affect him. *We are all sinners,* his father used to tell him and Andrew. *We are all sinners, but we also can be forgiven. And if we are forgiven, we must forgive.*

He then had thoughts of his brother's wife—whom he had never met—and their young son. He had only a tintype of the three of them as a reference. Andrew had sent it to his father soon after the baby was born. *Why didn't I think of that before I pulled that trigger?*

"Forgive me, Brother," he tried to say, though, still, no words would come, "Forgive me, Father." He then realized—*to his surprise*—that he was unable to conjure up any sort of malice toward Jack, and somehow that brought him a huge degree of comfort. He began to chuckle at the irony and gradually started laughing, soft at first, and then getting louder. *I can't breathe, but I can still laugh,* he thought.

By then, Jack had picked up the sword and rifle to head down the bluff, but Curtis's laughter stopped him in his tracks, and he whirled around to investigate. Noticeably unsettled, he lunged at Curtis, putting his hand over his mouth, to no avail. Curtis only laughed harder.

"We are all sinners, Maddau," he said in a gaspy voice, "And I forgive you. What do you think of that?"

Panicked, Jack quickly glanced in the direction of the advancing Union soldiers and just as quickly, he slammed the butt of the Whitworth against Curtis's forehead and scampered down the muddy hill.

Satisfied that he had put an end to the laughter, Jack made his way down to the icy creek, pausing at the edge to secure the sword under his belt. The rain was deafening and the sound of it beating on the creekbank sounded almost like laughter. *Was that laughter?* he thought.

"I must be hearing things—or going mad," he shuttered. He stomped into the icy creek and carefully crossed to the other side and up the hill. At the top of the hill, there was a cliff that jutted out above a fork of the creek. It would have been an easy jump into the creek, but instead, Jack backed down the hill, carefully cradling the Whitworth and making sure to step back into the footprints that he had made in the mud as he climbed up. At the bottom of the hill, he stepped back down in the frozen creek and followed it upstream for a quarter mile, then stepped out on a rocky bank. He then climbed over the bank and using the larger rocks as stepping stones made his way to the edge of the woods.

"The fool's probly still laughin'," he said to himself. But he also knew that whatever footprints they could find would be most likely washed away in the rain before they traced them through the creek and then to the top of the hill. Soon, he was at his trusted secret hideout, and with a quick glance over his shoulder, he disappeared behind the waterfall into the cave. As he crawled into the cave, dragging the sword and Whitworth beside him, his relief at being safely hidden was overshadowed by a dark and ominous thought—*If that sword and that Whitworth rifle butt didn't take care of Barre, he'll lead them straight to this cave.*

It took less than a half hour for Lieutenant Cheswick's two scouts to find where Curtis landed at the foot of the big tree. One of them, Private Brannon, immediately began tracking Jack's footprints in the frozen mud, while the other, Sergeant Hatch, cautiously prodded Curtis's body with his rifle, and satisfied that he indeed was dead, draped the body over his horse and returned to the main group of riders.

"Is that the shooter? What in the blazes happened to him?" Lieutenant Cheswick asked the sergeant as he returned with Curtis's body. "Did he fall out of the tree he shot from?"

"He's the shooter, alright, but somehow I doubt that he fell out of the tree. Someone with the skill to take the sort of shot he took has been in more than his share of tree branches. And, if the branch he was on had broken, we would have found it under the body," Hatch replied.

Cheswick dismounted and pulled Curtis's body off the horse. "This man was slashed by a sword or longknife," he said, examining the gash running the length of Curtis's back.

"Yessir," Sergeant Hatch said, "That's what we were thinking."

"What's more, see that indentation on the side of his head?" Lieutenant Cheswick asked. "It appears as if it was created by the butt of a rifle. Look at the clean shape. Look there, see that round spot?" he said running his finger down the indentation, "That's where the bottom screw in the butt made its mark."

Cheswick stood up and looked back toward where the shot had been fired. "Where's Brannon?" he asked.

"In pursuit of the man—or men—who did this," Hatch said, "Unless this poor wretch somehow managed to slash himself in the back. And slam his head with a rifle butt."

"Are you totally certain this man was the shooter?" Cheswick said, "Maybe he tried to stop the shooter and was killed for his trouble..."

"I found these in his pocket," the sergeant said as he held out his open palm, displaying a handful of hexagonal soft lead bullets. "These are for a *Whitworth Sharpshooter*, and one of those can have a barrel length of anywhere from 33 to 39 inches. Long enough and accurate enough to make the shot that killed the captain. Also, look at the redness under his eye, as if it's getting ready to bruise. My guess is that it was made by the same rifle butt that hit him on the side of his head. A Whitworth has a nasty recoil, bad enough to give the shooter a black eye iffen he ain't careful. But a Whitworth don't recoil bad enough to make that kind of indention, and it wouldn't make it on the side of his head. No, he had some help with that indention."

"Makes sense. Did you find the Whitworth? Or the sword?"

"No sir. Just this dead man."

"Take a few men and see if you can catch up with Brannon and find the killer or killers. See if he's friend or foe. I'm guessing foe. I also suspect you'll be looking for someone with a sword and a Whitworth. See if you can find 'im and bring 'im back to me...alive. I got some serious questions that can only be answered by a man who ain't dead."

"Yessir!"

"In the meantime...we've got work to do. Let's move!"

With that, Lieutenant Cheswick led the unit down the turnpike toward Rubineville.

CHAPTER 33
THE SWORD AND THE WHITWORTH

By the time the unit reached the outskirts of town, Jack was still hidden inside the cave under the waterfall. He could hear the searchers on both sides of the creek, and although he knew that the cave was not visible from either side of the waterfall, he also knew that if they got to Curtis while he still had a breath in his body—*forgiveness or not*—he would have told them about the hidden cave behind the waterfall. He kept the Whitworth loaded, and he sat quietly in the darkness at the far end of the entry room. By then, the rain had stopped, and in the small gorge in which the creek ran, sounds—*especially voices*—tended to be amplified. After listening intently, Jack guessed that there were three or four searchers, all on horseback.

"Brannon! Yo, Brannon! It's a dead end. Unless you're a jumpin' fish and can swim up the waterfall. Let's get on back, before they send someone to look for us."

"Go on ahead," Brannon called, "I'll catch up with you. Since it's stopped raining, I just wanna look up on this bluff for tracks…if they haven't been all washed away, that is."

"Suit yourself."

"Tell the lieutenant I'll be there directly."

Private Josiah Brannon was a coarse and generally unpleasant man with a checkered past. Plus, he had a personal vendetta against the South and, in particular, that part of South Carolina. He had been born a few towns (and counties) away from Rubineville, so he was vaguely familiar with the area. His father was a drunken ne'er-do-well who, along with his immediate family, had been chased out of the state when the young Brannon was 13.

After their hasty departure, his father decided to take his family to California in the early 1850's, so he could join in the gold rush and strike it rich. However, he left his wife and Brannon's siblings in St. Louis, so that he could "get set up" in California and send for them. They never heard from him nor saw him again. When Brannon's mother died a few years later, young Josiah had to fend for himself at a fairly young age. Although they had left relatives in South Carolina, Bannon refused to go back and beg for help or work. He refused to give them the satisfaction of proving them right with their negative predictions about his father and the rest of his immediate family.

Before the war, Brannon had been a mostly unsuccessful *jack-of-all-trades*, including working as a small-town blacksmith's hapless apprentice in a small Missouri riverfront town and serving on the crew of a Mississippi riverboat. While working the latter job, he was unfortunately prone to falling overboard, which prompted the captain to dismiss and eject him at the boat's southern destination, New Orleans.

Brannon found a job with a French Quarter tailor who had become a victim of his own success and was desperate to find employees who could help him with his overflow of orders. Before she died, Brannon's mother had taught him a little about sewing, and he thought that he could get by with that *threadbare knowledge*. Although he had worked there for only a few months, Brannon was eager to impress the tailor, so one afternoon when his boss was out of the shop on business, Brannon struck a deal with the two owners of a nearby sign-making business; he agreed to custom-make a suit for each of them in exchange for a new sign, which would be carved, painted and installed above the tailor's shop window. The following week, the sign was delivered and installed and the suits were picked up, but the suits were promptly returned the next day by the furious signmakers. Not only did the suits not fit, the two men claimed that when they tried to put them on to wear, the coats and pants actually made their limbs cramp up, making them actually look somewhat deformed. At any rate, the two claimed, they certainly couldn't wear the suits in public. The two then donned the coats to illustrate the matter, which made Brannon laugh uncontrollably, much like a drunken donkey. That was obviously not the proper response. Their demands for the return of the signage only made Brannon laugh that much harder—to the point of tears.

Finally, the two left the shop, but they were determined to make Brannon pay, one way or the other. The opportunity came late one Saturday night as the two worked on signage for a new hotel going up in the Quarter. They happened to see Brannon stumbling by their shop, no doubt on his way home after a night of tavern-hopping. The two quickly gathered up some supplies and followed Brannon at a safe distance, until he approached a deserted and unlit area of town, at which point they easily overpowered him, dragging him into a dark, out-of-the-way alley.

The next morning, a bright and sunny Sunday, Brannon awoke and realized that he had been relieved of all of his clothing—save the bottom part of his long underwear. What he didn't realize at the time, as he embarrassingly made his way home, was that on his back was multi-colored, beautifully-styled lettering with the inscription, *"Caution: Unfit!"* carefully brushed in weather-resistant, oil-based paint. The tailor, who had initially been very pleased by his new sign, soon found out about the incident when the signmakers retrieved the sign over his shop. By that time, the previous sign (that the new one had replaced) was long gone, as was Brannon. He slunk out of town and secured passage upriver on a riverboat owned and operated by his previous employer, who still refused to let him have his old job back.

However, once he was back in Missouri, he was quite surprised to discover—actually, by accident—that he had a legitimate—if hidden—skill as an overland scout and guide. Whereas the misshapened horseshoes he had forged and the asymmetrical suits he sewed in New Orleans rarely fit their intended customers or end-users, the frontier-bound settlers that he helped guide to the wild west's *promised land* never ceased to sing his praises. He often boasted that his success at this occupation found him, rather than the other way around. What's more, his unpleasant and gruff demeanor actually served him well in his new profession, especially in the wilderness while tending to and leading vulnerable pilgrims.

A year into his new-found success, the war broke out, and he felt obliged to lend his talents and services to maintain and preserve the union. To anyone that would listen, he would claim that he felt it was his duty to apply his gifts to the best of his ability in order to help bring the war to an end. The truth was, however, he really felt that the sooner the war was over, the sooner he could get back to making money by helping settlers find their way west. As for his passion for finding the captain's assassin, the real reason fueling his desire for that objective was most likely his deep-seated thirst for revenge. *For all I know,* he thought, *the man that pulled the trigger this morning could be kin to the people that ran us out of the state all those years ago.*

As it turned out, he had about given up on the creek as an escape route for the assassin's accomplice. Actually, as a youth of 10 or 11, he had fished on the banks of the creek—mostly unsuccessfully—so he vaguely remembered the surrounding area, but he didn't recall the waterfall. *Shoulda fished here,* he thought, *'stead of wasting all my time downstream.* For that reason, before turning back, as a last-ditch effort, he decided to check out the crest of the hill beside the waterfall, so he tied his horse to a tree on the edge of the icy creek to begin the climb. Although it had quit raining, the bank was slick with a pelt of mud and ice, and he struggled to pull himself up to the top. However, before he made it to the crest of the hill, a brief flurry of wings caught his eye at the edge of the waterfall, and he felt the surge of adrenalin.

Why is there a bird coming out from behind a waterfall? he asked himself. *That's a little more than curious, ain't it?*

Brannon surmised that there could possibly be some sort of opening behind the waterfall, but he knew that he would have to go through the icy water, and the idea of it being just a hunch made him hesitate. *I'll either be a freezing fool or a freezing hero,* he thought, but still, *freezing* figured into both scenarios. Brannon figured it couldn't be any worse than wading into the icy swamp, as he and his unit had been doing for the past month. He stood for a minute or two on the bank, the icy mist from the waterfall splashing his face. Then, he clinched his teeth and plunged under the flow into a solid and frozen wall of stone. Instinctively, he stretched both arms out to find some sort of hold, a root or crevice, perhaps to grab onto, and with his right hand, he felt emptiness. It was an opening of some sort. He dropped to his knees and with the icy water pouring on his head, he was able to crawl through the opening of the hidden cave. The discovery energized him to the point of not even feeling the icy water.

Inside the cave, when Jack heard Brannon enter the cave, he knew he was dealing with a very motivated and determined man; he knew a tenacious man like that could be extremely dangerous. A hunter like that would typically never give up the hunt until his prey was in hand. Jack knew that he could easily dispatch the hunter with the Whitworth—he was far enough back in the darkness not to be seen. However, he wasn't sure whether or not the other trackers were still on the banks. *Maybe they sent a single scout into the cave to see whether or not it was empty.* If that were the case, they would easily hear the shot from the rife echoing inside and outside the cave, and there would be no escape.

There was a niche in the left wall at the back of the main chamber of the cave, and it was there that Jack chose to wait with the Whitworth. Afternoons were always the brightest in the cave, even if there was no sun. The narrow opening allowed a thin shaft of light—refracted by the waterfall—to spill across the cave floor. To the right of the shaft of light, there was a deep and dangerous crevice. It was only a few feet wide, not quite wide enough for a full grown man to fall into, but certainly wide enough for a small animal or child, as Jack's father had warned him so many years ago, but Jack had never been able to gauge the distance to the bottom.

As Brannon eased himself into the room of the cave, it took a few seconds for his eyes to adjust to the dark. However, the strip of light that extended from the opening to the far end of the cave's entry room illuminated a shiny object protruding from the darkness. Brannon pulled his Colt revolver from his belt and slowly pulled himself to his feet. He paused briefly to see if he was alone in the chamber, or if not, where his prey might be hiding, and then he slowly followed the slice of light to a shiny object gleaming in the dark—it was a sword that was embedded in the cave's floor. Its blade was shimmering in the dim light of the cave. Holding the colt with both hands, he saw the niche in the wall and knew that it would be the perfect hiding place, but a slight noise off to his right drew his attention. Against his conscious judgement, his body instinctively reacted and swung to the right. Having tossed a tiny pebble up and over the shaft of light to Brannon's right to successfully distract him, Jack blindly swung the Whitworth. Brannon tried to compensate for his involuntary lapse of judgment, but it was too late. As the butt of the Whitworth connected with Brannon's skull, the Colt fired as he crumpled to the ground, sending a .45 caliber bullet bouncing off the walls and reverberations throughout the cave. The pistol popped out of Brannon's hands as he fell, and clattered on the cave floor. Jack jumped over Brannon to try and catch the Colt, but it bounced and skittered just out of his reach and tumbled end-over-end into the bottomless crevice. In the darkness of the cave, he couldn't tell if Brannon was still alive, but he knew that he was at least unconscious. Jack saw that the fallen scout didn't attempt to get up or try to stop him from grabbing his haversack, along with Andrew's sword and the Whitworth as he hurriedly scooted toward the cave's opening.

Jack knew that if the other scouts were still nearby, they would have definitely heard the shot—not even the sound of the waterfall could have covered it up. So, as he emerged from the cave and from under the waterfall, he tentatively looked around, but Brannon's horse was the only thing moving in his immediate vicinity. Once the rifle, sword and haversack were secured, he jumped upon the horse and was soon galloping through the thick and icy moss-pelted woods. Although his ultimate destination was Rubineville, Jack thought it would be more prudent to find a place to hide for the night and then wait until the next day to furtively head for the town—if there was a town still standing. He knew the territory well, and he thought that there may be some structure, barn or out building on his family's former property, so he headed in that direction, careful to stay in the thickest and least navigable parts of the winter woods, so as to best avoid Union scouts and companies.

He half expected the current owners to be waiting on the porch, and debated how he should approach them, but once he reached the old homestead, it was dusk and he discovered to his relief—as well as disappointment—that the house had been burned to the ground, with the exception of the various fireplaces and chimneys. However, his mother's first pottery shed was mostly intact, so he tied Brannon's horse to a tree in the nearby woods and scraped out a place to sleep on the floor of the shed. As he instinctively went through his pockets, he alarmingly discovered that his wooden tiger-head coin was missing, and he realized he must have lost it while dispatching the Yankee scout inside the cave. The discovery caused him a large degree of distress, even to the point where he considered riding back to the cave to search for it—Brannon or not—in the darkness. He eventually came to his senses and began questioning his very sanity. Gradually, however the bittersweet memories of his homeplace and boyhood lulled him into a fitful slumber.

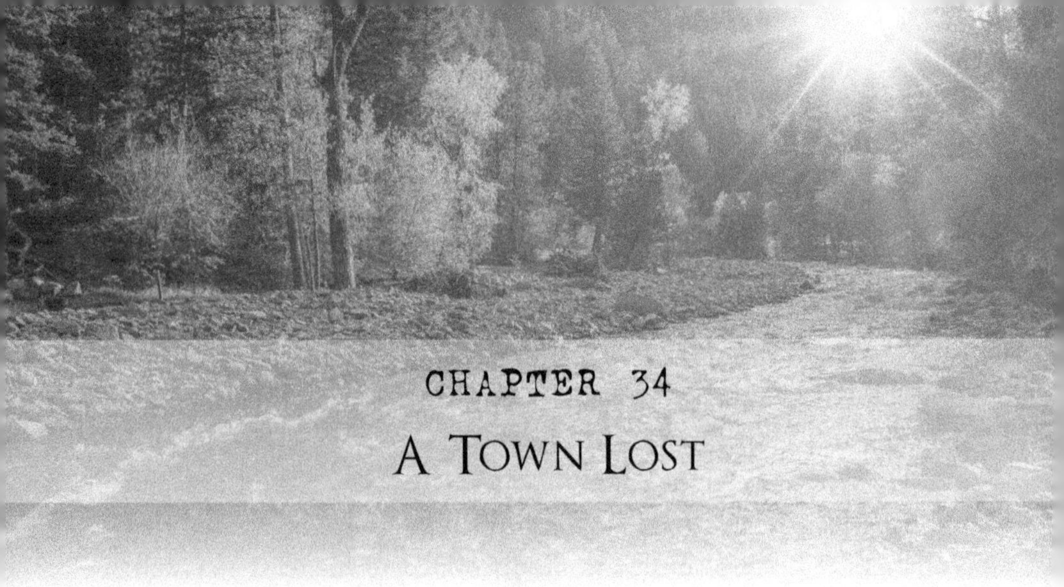

CHAPTER 34
A TOWN LOST

It was early afternoon when Lieutenant Cheswick and the raiding party reached the edge of Rubineville. The cotton factory stood silent and apparently abandoned. Nevertheless, the mounted soldiers cautiously approached the large wooden gates that protected the entrance to the large stone building. As the lieutenant turned to give an order to the corporal beside him, he saw him abruptly jerk up and roll off the saddle as a rifle crack drifted through the air. Spinning around, Cheswick saw a puff of smoke slowly floating away from the steeple of the little church in the distance, sitting next to the factory on the bank of the Rubine River.

"Again?!" he shouted, "Where are these shooters coming from? Sergeant, pour your fire upon the steeple of that church, there! You! You, men! Secure that factory!"

"Then what, sir?"

"Then, burn it to the ground!"

A sharp pop hit the ground beside the front hoof of the lieutenant's horse and the horse veered slightly to the left. Then, again, the rifle's report followed a split second later.

Cheswick instinctively looked up toward the direction of the steeple. "If that's what they want, then we'll be more than happy to oblige. Get that shooter!" he hissed through his clinched teeth. "And burn that church to the ground. Burn the whole town! Don't leave anything standing!"

Within minutes, there was the sound of crashing windows inside the factory's bottom floor and several of the raiding soldiers inside the building were silhouetted by the fires they had set. Another group of soldiers had cautiously surrounded the little wooden church and had tossed torches into an open window. Above, inside the small steeple, a rifle peered over the edge, as the shooter stood up to survey the scene below. His appearance was answered by a volley of rifle fire from the bluecoats surrounding the now-burning church. The shooter got off one shot, which found its mark, knocking one of the soldiers off his horse. This was answered by even more rifles aimed at the steeple. The bullets pinged off the small bell and tore holes in the white wood, which framed the structure of the steeple. There was a brief moment of silence, and then the shooter and rifle both fell chaotically to the roof of the church and clattered and rolled onto the frozen ground in the shadow of the burning building. One of the soldiers quickly dismounted, with his saber in hand, and he sprinted to where the shooter had landed, face down, on the frozen ground, slowing only when he was a few paces away. With his pistol drawn, he slowly approached the small, broken body and flipped it over with his boot. A young boy, clearly dead, stared back at him. A small, red circle stained the fabric of his torn and dirty cotton shirt, just above his heart. As the soldier gazed down at the youth, a light rain mixed with the occasional snowflake drifted down around them. As he prodded the boy with the toe of his scuffed and muddy boot, a single snowflake danced in the wind and softly tumbled its way down, slowly spinning, and finally settling on the blue iris of the shooter's open right eye, before melting into a single teardrop.

The soldier's mind immediately flashed to his own son back in Ohio—he would have been maybe just a year or two younger than the shooter.

"He's just a boy," he said as he slowly sheathed his sword. "What is it with these people? Don't they understand they've been beat?"

"Maybe not," said another, "But they ain't gonna have a town to hide behind, anymore."

"They also ain't gonna have a state to hide behind, anymore. We're gonna burn it to the ground. Maybe that'll teach 'em not to start somethin' they can't finish."

"Like what?"

"Like a war."

By then, the cotton factory was immersed in flames and columns of soldiers were galloping back and forth through the town, throwing torches and shooting at anything that moved. The town's two churches, on each end of town, were also on fire; the eerie flames from each building danced and licked at the sky, serving as crackling bookends to the businesses lining the main street. Soon, the entire town would join the growing firestorm, the windows of the businesses, shops and offices shattering and inside, their furniture popping in various degrees and sizes of explosions.

Just beyond the town, Neemy and Rev. Barre hid in the shadows of their barn and listened as their town and their church were being razed. As the soldiers began torching the cotton factory at the far end of the town, Neemy had managed to get a few peels of the bell before Rev. Barre insisted that they find a quick shelter. The winter afternoon had quickly faded into night, yet the sky maintained an eerie, sunset-like orange from the fire, as the sporatic snowflakes floated down and mixed with the rain and the rising ash from the burning town. There was a large field that ran from the barn where Neemy and Rev. Barre were hiding up to the top of the hill which bordered the road that led back into town. Behind the barn was the Rubine River that ran beside the town and past the burning cotton factory, and the minister had hoped that the two of the them would not be forced into the freezing river, but he knew that might be the only escape, should the soldiers torch his house, barn and field.

Suddenly, a soldier on horseback appeared in silhouette at the crest of the hill above the field. He was illuminated by a torch that he held above his head, as in a tribute to the destruction behind him, on the road into town. As Neemy and Rev. Barre held their breath in their hiding place in the barn, the soldier surveyed the field, barn and house, as in contemplation of whether or not to investigate the premises. Almost as an afterthought, he slung the torch into the corner of the field at the top of the hill, waited briefly to watch it catch fire, and then turned his horse back toward the burning town. As the edge of the field began to flame up, Neemy and Rev. Barre crept from their hiding place in the barn and crawled into the weeds in the field in front of the barn. When they felt sure the soldier on horseback was safely away, they quickly climbed the hill toward the flames, but to their surprise and relief, having hit several large patches of ice at the top of the hill, the flames had refused to advance down the hill. Through the smoke they saw the smoldering torch and, on down the road, their church—as well as the rest of the doomed town—fully engulfed in the fire, with dozens of men on horseback galloping through and around the streets. Neemy turned to look at the minister's face; it was lit in flickering patches of light that danced around his sad eyes like drunken fireflies.

"Revrun," Neemy said, "…the church…"

"There's no sense losing our lives over a burning building," Rev. Barre slowly said, "We can go and see what's left of it tomorrow. Once they've gone."

"Why'd they burnd the church building?"

"There is no accounting for evil, Neemy. If there's one lesson to take from this, it's that we've been given a glimpse of the fury of hell."

"But dere's no rebels in da church. Why they have to burnd it?"

"Because…like I said, there's no accounting for evil, Neemy."

CHAPTER 35
All is Vanity

At sunrise the following day, a dense cloud of smoke hung low around the town and as far away as the barn where the two lay hidden in the loft. The overcast clouds only added to the darkness of the dawn. As it became light enough to see the surrounding area, Rev. Barre peered out of the cracks in the barn's loft to make sure the soldiers weren't present. Neemy lay asleep in the corner, on several bales of hay that they had pushed together as a makeshift bed. The minister slipped down the shaky ladder and pushed open the barn's double doors. After making sure it was safe, he climbed the hill to the road and headed toward town and his smoldering church. Expecting to find nothing but rubble, he was surprised to discover that two of the structure's walls remained intact, including the one behind the alter. It framed the stained glass image of Jesus with his outstretched hands. To his amazement, he saw that the mosaic was largely untouched. It seemed to glow and illuminate the ruins of what was once the sanctuary. He slowly made his way around the ruins of the sanctuary, occasionally pausing to pick up some remnant or broken fragment. As he trudged through the debris toward what had been the podium, he noticed that one of Elizabeth's pots had survived the fire, unscathed. He fished it out of the icy mud and turned it in his hands.

Along the street outside the smoldering church, several flames continued to burn in some of the destroyed buildings. The church on the far end of the town was totally gone, much like the boy sniper who had lain in wait in its steeple at the onset of the soldiers' advance. The smoke from the burnt and burning buildings lining the town's main streets billowed and wisped throughout the ruins like an angry ghost. A lone dog barked and several shop owners and their families were combing through the remains of their various businesses.

None of them noticed the solitary figure walking slowly through the smoke, or if they did, they were too consumed by their losses to pay him any mind. The man, however, was careful to survey the ruins of the town and the activities of the survivors. In one hand, he held a large rifle, and in the other, an army pack. A sword in its scabbard was secured through his belt and it clumped awkwardly against his hip as he made his way toward the church, which was still enveloped by smoke from the previous night's fire. The smoke wafted through the ruined sanctuary and joined the morning's fog.

The man's plan was to find a place where he could wait in hiding; he figured it was only a matter of time before the minister would eventually show up at the burned-out church. As he stepped into the ruins of the smoldering church, he put down his pack and leaned the big rifle up against what once was a pillar. He heard the minister before he actually saw him and for a few seconds, thought that he had been spotted, if not recognized. Then, however, he realized that Rev. Barre had his back to him and was addressing the still-standing stained glass. The man slipped back behind the pillar and watched the minister as he held the surviving pot up to the light, turning it over and over in his hands.

"So?" Rev. Barre asked, glaring up at the window. "Where's the answer? What's left? A pot and a window? Are you listening? What's the answer? We just build a new church around a pot and a window? Is that it?" The minister stared up at the stained glass image. "What am I—what are *we*—supposed to glean from this lesson? *It is a lesson? Yes?* A sermon, maybe? A sermon in the ashes, perhaps? Dust to dust? 'Vanity of vanities, saith the Preacher, vanity of vanities; all is vanity.' Is that what you're telling me? We live through four years of a war, we live through starvation and boys that will never come home. Fathers, brothers…sons. Just last week, Widow Hendrix—you remember her, right? She was the one that would put her last dollar in the collection plate. Remember? An' if you were here last month, you'd remember that she got word that both her sons were dead. But don't worry—there was room for 'em out there. They joined their daddy out there in the cemetery. Col. Hendrix didn't even make it past Manassas in '61. And just when we think we've survived the bloodfest of that damnable war—I mean *we can almost see the light of day*—just when we think the worst is over, and we think we can rebuild what we lost in the war… just when we get to that point of…*hope*…a horde of bluecoat locusts come streamin' out of the Nile to destroy your temple? Or, rather, *the Rubine to destroy your sanctuary.*"

By this time, the minister was screaming, with tears of rage in his eyes, already red from the wafting smoke. "Is that the message?" he screamed. "Well, is it? So, that was the message? The sermon? That all is vanity? Well. Well. Well, here's my reply!" With that, Rev. Barre drew back and threw the pot with all the strength he could muster. The vessel hit the stained glass image directly between the hands of Jesus, and the sound of the broken glass displaced from the frames of the mosaic joined the hissing of the smoldering embers.

"There's my answer!" the minister screamed up at the window. He then cocked his head and looked at the new effect that the broken glass presented, with the large triangular hole between Jesus' hands. "Apparently, even the Lord, Himself, wonders what the message is! It's a mystery, ain't it, Lord?"

"So much for fire and brimstone, eh, Preacher?" The voice came from behind the pillar as the figure emerged.

CHAPTER 36

The Prodigal Returns

The last thing Rev. Barre expected was an audience for his outburst of rage. Shocked and surprised, he quickly wheeled to face the voice's owner. There was a lone figure at the back of what once was the sanctuary, but with all the smoke drifting throughout the burned-out structure, he couldn't make out who it was.

"Oh, my apologies," he said, collecting himself and straining to identify the visitor, "I thought I was alone. You must excuse me. I was just, uh, *overcome* by the situation. All the destruction."

"No, no, no. Preacher. No need for excuses."

Rev. Barre stared through the drifting smoke. The raggedy man looked vaguely familiar, but he couldn't place him. "Don't I know you, sir?" he asked.

"I don't expect you to remember me. Name's Maddau. Jack Maddau."

"Jack Maddau?" he said, "Of course. I knew your mother. I knew you, too. As a boy. You grew up with my sons."

"Yessir. I knew your sons. Both of 'em. Served with one of 'em. Served against the other'n," he said.

The minister stared at the man and made out the ragged remnants of a butternut grey Confederate uniform. "You must have served with Curtis," he said, "How is he? Do you know? Do you have any word about him?"

"Oh yes, I know. I'm sorry to tell you, Curtis is dead," Jack said, bluntly, "And your other son—the Yankee captain—he's dead, too, Reverend. They're both dead."

The minister stared back at him for a moment without speaking. "Andrew? Curtis? No," he finally said, shaking, "That can't be. That can't be true. Not both of them…"

Jack pulled the sword out of the sheath held by his threadbare belt. "I know it's a shock, and I hate to be the one who has to deliver the news, but there was no easy way to say it."

"Why? What…?"

"But, I do have something for you. I got one of 'em's sword here and the other one's rifle over there. Thought you'd like to have 'em." Jack paused to let the news sink in. The minister could only stare at him in shock and disbelief.

"Is it really true?"

"'Fraid it is," Jack said. "I gotta say—I liked Curtis much better than his brother, the Yankee captain—Andrew. You can thank his unit—your boy, Andrew's men—for all the nice renovatin' they did to your town. They weren't too benevolent to the town, nor did they take too kindly to the Lord's house, here. Buncha blue devils, the whole lot of 'em."

The minister still stood there, hands at his side, staring back at Jack in shock. "Andrew? Curtis?" he repeated. "Is that why you're here? Why are you here telling me this?"

"I was with Curtis when he died."

"And Andrew?"

"Um…he was kild by a rebel soldier. One of ours. And, uh… Curtis got his sword."

"This is horrible news."

"I can imagine."

"You were with Curtis? When he died?"

"Yep. I's right there."

"Did he say anything?"

"Well, yes, he did. He, he, he talked about forgivin'."

"Forgiveness?"

"Yeah. He said…uh, that he hoped you would forgive 'im."

"Me forgive him? For what?"

"I don't know, Preacher! He didn't go into a lot of detail as he died."

"Did he say anything else?"

"Well, as a matter of fact, yes. He asked if I would promise to find you and tell you what happened. And…to tell you to give me the money that was supposed to go to him. He said…uh, he wanted me to have it."

"Money?" the minister said, suddenly stiffening, "What money?"

"Uh…Jack said that, uh, you had some sort of treasure."

"Treasure?"

"Yessir. And he wanted me to have it. His portion. Oh, an' he thought he'd be gittin' his brother's portion, too. Since he was kild."

"Really?" Rev. Barre said through pursed lips. His grief had begun to swirl into a growing anger.

"Yes. Curtis was my closest friend. An' he said, 'Ask my father to forgive me and tell him that I want you to have my portion. My portion of the…treasure.'"

"So, he really said that?"

"Yessir. I know the timing is unfortunate. And all this must come as quite a shock, but I think—"

"I think that you are a liar," the minister angrily said, moving slowly toward Jack, "And it's only out of my respect for your memory of your mother that I don't kill you right now and right here with my bare hands!"

Jack pointed Andrew's sword at the minister, who was only a few feet away and still moving toward him in the debris, "Don't make me hurt you, Preacher. Jes' gimme the money and I'll be on my way."

"Give me that sword, you scoundrel," Rev. Barre shouted, lunging toward Jack.

Jack sidestepped the minister and defensively slashed at him with the sword, grazing his right ear with the blade.

"Now look what you made me do, you old fool," Jack said, "At least now you know I'm serious. I'm not leavin' without that money. I *wuz* just askin' for their portion. But now I think I'll take the whole thing."

The minister stared back at him, his hand up to his ear, which was seeping blood through his fingers, "I'm telling you. I don't know what—in the blazes—you're talking about. I don't know anything about any money, or whatever you're blathering about."

"This is what I'm blathering about," Jack said, holding the minister at bay with the tip of the sword's blade, "You are going to get whatever money you have squirreled away, and you are going to put it all in my bag." Jack turned to point at his army pack that he had left by the fallen pillar that he had initially hid behind. To his surprise, there was a black man carefully navigating toward him through the smoke and debris. The man had picked up the big Whitworth that Jack had left beside his pack and was slowly approaching with the rifle pointed at his head. He held the rifle not like a sharpshooter squinting through the sights, but rather, at chest level, like one would hold a shotgun. It took Jack a few seconds, but then, through the smoke and debris he recognized Neemy, and he smiled grimly.

"Well, as I live and breathe! It's our old houseboy. How you doin' brother?" Jack laughed.

"I ain't your houseboy, no more. And I sure ain't your brother," Neemy said, stopping at a safe distance, but still pointing the rifle at Jack.

"Hmm," Jack said, grinning and rubbing his chin with his free hand while gesturing the sword toward Neemy. He began to laugh. It was a rueful laugh, pitched with meanness. "Well then, brother. I guess you're the last one to know."

"I don' know whut you talkin' 'bout, and don' rilly care. But I's tellin' you. And listen good. You gonna git. An' right now."

"Oh," said Jack, still laughing, "Now I see it. You really don't know, does ya? How perfect is that?"

"Git on outta here and leave us be."

"That's no way to treat your kin."

It was Neemy's turn to laugh. "Whoo-whee," he said, still holding the rifle, "Sum ol' Yankee musta done shot you in yo head. You dreamin' up yo kinfolks, now."

"Hold yer horses, brother, I ain't the dreamer here. As I recall, you's always the one wid your head in the clouds," Jack said, mockingly. "Looks like you still don't know truth when it kicks you in yer old black bottom."

"Git, I said. 'Fore I open up a pichure winder in yo belly."

"Let me ask you sumpin'—Neemy."

"You can ast it on yo way out. Git, I said."

"Did you ever ast yerself why you's so light-skinned, when yer mama and yer daddy and yer brother wuz all as black as tar? Chu think it wuz they spent more time in the sun whilse you wuz making pots with the lady in the big house?"

Neemy stared back at him, and slightly lowered the Whitworth, but with his finger still on the trigger.

"You crazy. You always had th' devil in you."

"Maybe so, brother." Jack said. "There's good and bad in all us. I will give you that. But I'm thinkin' that somewhere real deep down in your light brown soul, you knew. Din ya? You had to know. Yessir, Neemy. Devil? My daddy was the real devil Neemy...'specially when he drank. An' he drank a lot. An' he liked the women. Color didn't matter. He specially like your mama."

"Don't listen to him, Neemy," the minister said, "He's a liar. He's trying to trick that gun out of your hands."

"Hush your mouth, Reverend," Jack snapped, still waving the sword, "Neemy, here ain't gonna shoot me. He don't even know how to shoot that thing, do ya, Neemy?"

Neemy had been looking back and forth, between Jack and the minister, and he hadn't realized that Jack had slowly been inching his way closer to where he stood with the gun; the ragged man was actually almost within striking distance. Eyes widened, Neemy tightened his grip on the Whitworth, and with his finger still on the trigger, pulled the hammer back with his thumb.

"Don't you come no further. Git, I tell ya," Neemy said with resolution.

"Oo-whee, Neemy. So, you know how to cock a Whitworth," Jack said, "That don't mean you know how to shoot one. 'Specially one that's got blood on it from killin'. No tellin' how many Yankees that gun done kilt."

"The way I sees it, this here rifle's color blind. It don't know blue o' grey…and right now, it's got nasty ol' grey in its sights."

"I see. But, here's a thought…what makes you think I was fool 'nuff to load it and sit it down so you could jus' sweep in here an' pick it up?"

"Cuz you a coward," Neemy hissed, "Always wuz. You never be slinkin' round like a low-down serpent with a unloaded gun, 'long as all these Yankees underfoot, wandrin' to and fro. Hmm? Do I thinks you a fool? A *fool*? Why yes, Jack Maddau, you is a fool. You a damned fool. A fool that would ex-ac'ly leave a gun 'round for some ol' houseboy to pick up and blow yer fool brains out."

"Neemy, just—" the minister began, but Jack seized the opportunity, hurling the sword end-over-end at Neemy. As the sword grazed Neemy's left shoulder, Jack lunged toward him, a split second behind the sword. A single step into his lunge, he was met with a loud and fiery blast from the muzzle of the Whitworth, which sent a hexagonal soft lead bullet spiraling deep into his chest. Jack's body twisted and rolled, finally settling on the cold embers of what had once been a support beam for the church's roof. At the same time, the recoil sent Neemy backwards, landing in the debris.

As the smoke and ashes settled, Rev. Barre stood frozen in shock at what he had just witnessed. Neemy sat stunned among the ruins, surveying the scene. Finally, the minister seemed to come to his senses and he stumbled over to where Neemy was sprawled in the ashes.

"Nehemiah? Neemy? Are you hurt?" he said as he knelt beside the dazed youth.

"Yessuh. I's fine. His ol' sword mostly missed me. Jes tore my sleeve a little, but din cut me none. *But you's bleedin'!* Yo ear. One thang fo' sho...dat fool din deserve yo money," Neemy said.

"Yes, if there actually was some money, he most certainly didn't deserve it. Neemy, go down to the jail, and see if they can send the sheriff."

"Sheriff? Ain't no sheriff." The voice came from the direction of where Jack had landed. "Ain't nothin' left of a jail. Ain't nobody in town. It's all burned down, just like your church."

Neemy immediately scrambled to pick up the Whitworth and stumbled to his feet and over to where Jack lay in the debris. "Don't you move, now," he said.

"What? You're gonna shoot me again?" Jack said with a hoarse laugh, wincing in pain, "Don't worry, boy—*brother*—you done kilt me. 'Sides, ain't no more bullet in that gun. Gotta give you that, brother...I din think you had it in you to really pull that trigger. Life shure is full o' surprises."

"Yes, like the surprise that there ain't no money here," Neemy said, still pointing the rifle at Jack.

"I said there isn't any *money*," the minister said, kneeling beside Jack, "I didn't say there wasn't treasure here."

"What, the winder? The broken winder? Is that your treasure? You throwing pots at your treasure, preacher?" Jack coughed.

"The window wasn't—*isn't*—the treasure. It just *represents* the treasure. The window and the images on the window aren't real. They just represent what is real and they symbolically watch over the treasure. There's no supernatural qualities of the window—it's just a beautiful image made out of stained glass. The actual treasure—the one that my sons always heard me talking about—is not silver or gold, but rather the message that the people who worship here find and embrace. Your mother understood the concept of the treasure, Jack."

"My mother was a good person," Jack said. Before he could finish his sentence, he was overcome by a coughing fit.

"Hold on, Jack," the minister said, "We'll go and get the doctor."

"Doctor? Where's a doctor? Not in this town. In Columbia? By now, they done burnt Columbia down, too. Includin' all the doctors. Don't you get it? They're gonna burn this whole state down. Ow! That hurts! 'Sides, its too late for me," he laughed, ruefully, "My brother kilt me."

"I din wanna kill you!" Neemy said.

Jack looked up at Neemy who still held the rifle. "She loved you, you know," he said.

"What?"

"My mother. She loved you."

Neemy seemed taken aback. All he could do is stare down at Jack. "Miz Lizbeth wuz good to me," he finally said, slowly.

"Yes, she wuz good. Shame I took after my pa and not her. But she wuz good to everbody. But 'specially you. She knew you wuz her own son's brother. *My* brother. I don't know if she was good to you 'cause o' that or in spite o' that. But she loved you. Thas what I've been tellin' you. Don't know what she woulda thought 'bout you killin' me."

"I tol' you, I din wanna kill you!" Neemy said, *"You come in here all crazy!"*

"How can we help you?" Rev. Barre asked. He was kneeling beside Jack in the debris of the sanctuary, and he put his hand on his chest over a growing patch of blood—as if he could heal the wound. "Can we notify your family? Is there anybody waitin' for you?"

"Jus' a wife an' boy. They ain't waitin' for me, but I'd 'preciate you lettin' 'em know," Jack said, grimacing, "Also I'd 'preciate you leavin' out the part about me tryin' to rob 'n' kill you." he said, laughing and coughing. "I even failed at that."

"Where are they?" the minister asked.

"Chicago. Stayin' with her sister and her husband. Name's Shelbertson. On Water Street. Her name is Emily. Wife is Emily. Boy's name is Ethan."

"I'll let them know. It may be after this war, but I'll try and locate them to tell them."

"Also, my folks are buried in the church graveyard. The other church, Preacher. Other graveyard. No offense," he coughed. "There's a Maddau plot there," he finally said, "Thas where I need to go. Rest o' my people's saved a seat fo' me."

"We can make the arrangements," the minister said, "Even if we have to do it ourselves. Jack?"

"What? Oh! That hurts."

"Jack, were you really with Curtis when he was killed?"

"Yes. That part was true. Oh!" Jack grimaced in pain, his hand over the widening red patch on his tattered coat.

"You killed him, didn't you?" Rev. Barre softly asked.

Jack sighed, painfully, "Yes. Yes, I did."

"Why? Why, Jack?"

"'Cause I'm mean, an' I'd-a said or done anything to git that treasure. The one you say you don't got," Jack said, his eyes closed, "I've lived a life of meanness an' a life a-lyin.' You know that, Preacher. You knew that when I was a kid though, didn't ya? That's my nature. Thas why my wife and boy is gone up…Chicago. They hate my meanness an' my lies. I'da kilt you too if my brother din kilt me first," he said, struggling for breath. "I saw so many die. All 'round me. Men drop beside me, in front, in back. Never me. Like bullets scared o' me. Preacher?"

"Yes, Jack?"

"I'm sorry I kild your boy. I'm sorry."

Rev. Barre just stared down at Jack as Neemy stood behind him and watched.

"Preacher? Reverend Barre?"

"Yes?"

"I'm sorry I kild Curtis. He didn't deserve it. He was a good boy."

For a moment, Jack was silent with his eyes closed, grimacing in pain. "Preacher?" he finally whispered.

"Yes, Jack. I'm still here."

"I lost my tiger-head coin."

"I'm sorry to hear that, Jack."

"Lost in the cave, I think."

"That's alright, Jack."

"If you find it, can you put it back in my pocket?"

"Sure, Jack. Is there anything else? Jack? Jack?" Rev. Barre asked, but Jack was silent, his lifeless eyes staring at the broken stained-glass window.

CHAPTER 37
SERVICE WITH A SMILE

"Here we are. You can stow your bag here until after you eat, if you want," Silas said as he parked the Ford in the large parking lot. The Ford's wheels screeched as he turned them into the parking spot.

"So, where are we?" Clay asked.

"We're here," Silas said.

"Where's here?"

"Here is wherever you are. I woulda thought you woulda known that…smart boy like you."

"Well, it don't look like a jail, so that's a plus, and there's people everywhere, and, it being Sunday, I'm guessing it's not an office building. So my final guess is it's some sort of church," Clay said, frowning.

"Actually, the church is inside the building," Silas said, smiling, "If you want to get all dogmatic about it."

"Wow, after a night like I had, to be at a church only a few hours later. That's what I call karma."

"Who said anything about karma? Unless my dogma's chasing your karma," Silas said, laughing.

"So, that's the idea," Clay said, grimacing, "You're taking me to church. I'm not so much of a churchy guy. That's not how I roll."

Silas laughed, "Oh yeah. I heard about how you roll…right down to the river."

"Ouch," Clay said, "All I'm sayin' is I shoulda known there's no free lunch. There's always strings."

"Ain't no strings, brother, and it ain't lunch, unless you wanna call it that. I like to think of eggs and bacon as breakfast," Silas said, "But, either way, it ain't no obligation to it. I jus' asked if you wanted to join me in a bite. You're free to go. You don't have to eat. An', by the way, we do have a medical tent if you want a doctor to look at your head. Sometimes head injuries can be worse than you think."

Clay looked over at Silas. Although he had detected annoyance in his response, he was still smiling.

"I'll skip the doctor, if you don't mind, but I ain't exactly in the mood to turn down a free meal," Clay said, "I just didn't—"

"—didn't think it would be at some do-gooder's church," Silas said, finishing his sentence. "Listen, man. I ain't judgin' you, so I'd ask the same from you—don't be judgin' me. Ain't no strings. You can eat and run, iffen you want. You can eat and hang out, if that's your thing. As I said, you can talk to the doc, if you want. Now, yes, I'm gonna eat and then go inside for the service, and yes, you can come with me, if you decide to, but nobody's forcin' you or askin' you to do nothing."

"So...you don't care."

"If I didn't care, I wouldn't have scraped you up out from under that bridge, so, no, I wouldn't say that I didn't care. I would, however, say that it is your decision what you do. It's between you and..."

"Me and who? God? Jesus?"

"Your conscience. Your inner voice. Whatever you wanna call it."

"Oh, so you're gonna just guilt trip me, right?"

"Brother, you're overthinkin' this whole thing. I just ast you if you'd join me for a bite and now you're lookin' for some sort of congressional bill for me to sign. It ain't forcin' church down your throat; it's just eggs and bacon."

"An' bandaids."

"Right. Eggs, bacon and bandaids...sunny-side down."

The two men crossed the street, walking toward the church's main building. The building was large, but not gaudy. There was a bank of glass doors, just under a sand-blasted marquis that said: "Rubine River Church" with a round icon of two intertwined circular red threads. On the main lawn, there was a large tent, with a number of tables set up. A banner that hung from the tent announced, "Breakfast." Underneath the banner, there were other banners, and Clay could make out part of an "L" and surmised that it said, "Lunch." *There's probably a "Dinner" under there, somewhere,* he thought. In another tent there were some medical banners and some casually-dressed men and women with stethoscopes, talking to several ragged men who Clay surmised were vets or homeless, or both.

At the far end of the "Breakfast" tent, on the other side of the tables, there was a row of portable cook stoves manned by a dozen or so women and men, and the smell of breakfast drifted out from under the tent and across the lawn. The tables were filled with a menagerie of people—men and women, old and young, black and white, fancy and shabby. The common denominator was the casual air. Everyone seemed to be in a good mood and enjoying themselves.

Great. I've wandered into some kind of cult, Clay thought, *There's probably a mother ship around here somewhere, just waiting to whisk everyone away to the good planet, Oz.*

Silas watched Clay as he surveyed the people inside the tent and guessed what he was thinking. "Consider it a breakfast club," he said. Silas directed him to the far end of the tent to the serving tables. There were plastic utensils and paper plates beside stacks of styrofoam cups, each of which were circled by intertwined red threads below lettering that read, "Rubine River Church," in simple serif letters. There were also food warmers on the table with eggs, grits, sausage, bacon, biscuits, and gravy, along with bowls of fruit and small boxes of cereal. And, there were pots of coffee. A short black man poured coffee into one of the styrofoam cups and handed it to Clay.

"Cream? Sugar?"

"Uh, yeah. Both."

The man handed Clay a couple of creamers and bags of sugar, and Clay opened all of them and poured them into the cup at the same time. When the cream hit the coffee, it swirled into animated cloud shapes.

Wow. There's another lion. This time in my coffee, Clay thought, *how strange is that? Or maybe it's an "afterglow" from last night's adventure.*

Moving down the line, Clay filled his plate, and Silas went over to speak with a group of people. Clay observed that it was actually quite loud under the tent; it was the buzz of conversation, peals of laughter and squeals of children. *I guess this ain't so bad,* he thought. As he finished his second plate, he noticed that the crowd had begun to thin out some, and Silas motioned to him.

"I'm goin' on in to the service," Silas said.

Here we go, Clay thought.

"Look, brother," Silas said, reading his expression. He pulled a card out of his shirt pocket and wrote a number on the back. "This is my cell number. You can call me anytime. Feel free to stay as long as you want. Or, if you need a ride, I'll be glad to drive you after church. You can come in with me or stay here and drink coffee, or roam around and meet me back here in an hour or so. There's a park a few blocks down, and these guys will keep serving food 'long as you're eating." Silas shook his hand and then turned to follow the line of people moving toward the entrance doors.

"Okay, okay, okay," Clay sighed, "I may as well come with you. I ain't sittin' here drinking coffee waiting for you to get out of church. But I ain't exactly wearin' my Sunday-go-to-meetin' suit. Take a look at me, if you ain't already—I'm a mess. I look like I've been kicked out drunk from a moving car and had to sleep under a bridge. But now that I think about it, I believe I'd enjoy embarrassing you in front of your church people."

"Suit yourself."

"Some of these people are wearing coats and ties. An' I gotta be smelling and lookin' like a railroad bum."

"Suit yourself."

"What? So, now you don't wanna be seen with me? There's still time to withdraw your invitation."

"Brother. You are overthinkin' once again. Come on, if you're comin'. We gonna be late."

As the two joined the line of people entering into the church, Silas watched as Clay surveyed the surroundings. Clay observed that the exterior of the building was not a traditional-looking church. It could have just as easily been a nice office building or school. There was a long single window that ran the length of the side of the building. He guessed that gazing out the window from the inside, you could see the banks of the nearby river that curved around the property. Once inside, he was surprised by the hustle and bustle and the contrast of both the people and the décor. With the high-ceiling atrium, and the crowds of people rushing to and fro in all directions, it reminded him of a metropolitan airport. A young mother with her fretting red-headed daughter was quickly headed down the hall under the "Nursery" sign. An older black man smiled over a cup of coffee as he talked to a stringy-haired college student, who was showing him something on his iPad.

"Whatchu thinkin'?" Silas asked.

"Well…I was thinkin' that you were taking me into a black church, and it's…"

"Ecru? Ivory? Off-white? Yeah, we know, but we thought black would make it look too Halloween-y"

"Now, you're just making fun of me. You know what I mean. Those guys serving us breakfast were all black."

"Actually, the first guy you saw was Indian…from India, not Cherokee. And the second guy was Hispanic. Puerto Rican, to be exact."

"The guy with the coffee was definitely black."

"Actually, his grandfather was a klansman, but yes, he is just very, very tan. He just returned from a month-long Caribbean cruise. Before he left, he was whiter than you."

"Wow, you really are making fun of me."

"Okay, you're right. He is a brother."

"You call everybody 'brother.'"

At the door to the sanctuary, they were greeted by a man in an electric blue polo shirt, embroidered with the Rubine River Church logo, a deep red "R" with an embedded cross, encircled by two entertwined ribbons of red.

"Well, well, what have you dragged in this time?" he said.

Silas smiled, "Hey, hey, hey! Don't be dissin' him—this is Clay."

"I ain't dissin' Clay," the man said, "That's who I was talking to!" Then, turning to Clay, he laughed and said, "What have you dragged in, this time?"

Silas rolled his eyes and said, "Sorry 'bout that, Clay. Forgive his manners. This is Jay. He's my brother."

"Another brother?" Clay asked, rolling his eyes.

"Yeah, well this one shares a mama with me!" Silas said.

"Actually, I can see the resemblance," Clay said.

"Yeah, I've been meaning to get that fixed," Jay said, "Welcome. We're happy to have you. Even if you're with Sy."

"Yeah, well, 'Sy' here is pretty convincin'."

"That I know, brother. I've been around him all my life. Make yourself at home, Again, welcome! Glad to have you!" Then, looking at his watch, he said, "Oops, gotta get going. I'll see y'all after the service." Then, to Clay, "You gonna hang around, Clay?"

"I supposed so. He has the car keys."

Then, with a final handshake, Jay melted into the crowd moving into the inner sanctuary, leaving Clay and Silas to find a seat.

CHAPTER 38

FROM THE ASHES

When the sun came up the next day, it revealed a town in ruins, but the smoke was gone. An all-night rain had driven it into the ground and left the town with an air of calm and renewal. Rev. Barre had a cup of coffee at the parsonage and then left to dig—once again—through the remnants of the sanctuary. Trudging through the rubble and the mud, he approached from the side of the wall with the large stained glass mural. The morning sun was shining in from behind the glass, and it lit the image up and cast colors on the ground beneath the window. Staring up at the window, Rev. Barre felt a twinge of shame when he observed the triangular hole in the window, which had been made by the thrown pot. As he walked and stared at the mural, he tripped, but caught himself before he could fall and roll down the hill beside the church. Instinctively looking back at what had snagged his foot, he was surprised to see the shiny object that he had tripped on. The object was sparkling in the sun and bathed in the colors from the illuminated stained-glass window. Glowing out from under the icy mud, the minister could make out the intertwined red threads circling the pot that he had thrown through the window. He reached down and picked it up, amazed that it was perfectly intact.

"Thas the beginning," said Neemy, who had followed him from a distance and was standing behind him. "Thas a hard pot to break."

The minister slowly turned at looked at him. Neemy was holding a rough wooden cross that he had apparently made from some of the surviving wood from the sanctuary.

"Beginning of what?" Rev. Barre asked.

"A new church. Outta ashes."

"You can't build a church on a pot, Neemy."

"Go 'head. Throw it agin. It ain't breakin'."

The minister looked at him guiltily.

"Yas, I know. You done throw that pot thru dat wender. Jack say he see you throw it. I knew it anyway. Jack or no Jack. That winder wadn't broke the first I saw it. The soldiers didn't make that hole in it. Das a preacher hole. Lemme see dat." Neemy set the wooden cross down and took the pot out of the minister's hands and turned it slowly to inspect it.

"You throwed it at God, not dat wender. You mad at God," he said.

"Of course, I'm mad at God, Neemy. How could I not be? It's all gone, Neemy," the minister said, sadly, "Our town, our church, our people, our families—my family—my sons..."

"God din burnd this church down. That took Yankee soldiers. God din kill your boys. That took dis war. I'm gwine tell you a secret, Preacher. See this pot? You know why it din break?"

The minister just stared back and slowly shook his head.

"'Cause I made this here pot. When I wuz helpin' Miz 'Lizbeth. An' I din make no pots to be breakin.' I makes 'em to be fine and sturdy vessels. Now, you git up and look around." Neemy montioned with this hands. "It ain't all gone. There's still one wall—that one with the beautiful wender..."

"With the preacher hole."

"Yassuh. We fix dat hole 'tween Jesus' hands. We jus' patch it up and add three more walls."

"And a roof."

"Yassuh."

"And a floor. And a pulpit. And pews."

"Yassuh."

"Then all we'll need is parishioners. You got them, too, Neemy?"

"'Spect I might be able to stir up some. My ma and pa. My brother, Jonathan. Thas jus' for starts. Got all kinds o' kinfolk. Only wish Unka-Jobee coulda bin here. He coulda help wi' the preachin'."

Rev. Barre pulled his pocket watch out of his jacket pocket, "Come on, Neemy," he said, replacing his watch, "We need to get on down to that cemetery to take care of Jack."

Neemy set down the pot and picked up the wooden cross, and the two men made their way down the street to the opposite end of the town, where the smaller church used to stand. They continued past the ruins of the church to the little cemetery, not too far from the western bank of the Rubine. They stopped at the far end of the cemetery, where there was a fresh mound of dirt with a shovel stuck in it, handle up. They stood next to a stone monument with "Maddau" etched in it, and Neemy grabbed the shovel and pounded in the cross next to the mound of dirt.

"Do you want to start, Neemy?" Rev. Barre said. "Would like to say something?"

"Only seem right, sincen' I kilt him. But I do gotta question. Not fo' him. Fo' you."

"Yes?"

"Think he be talkin' true?"

"What do you mean?"

"You think he be talkin' true? What he say?"

"About what?"

"Me bein' his brother an' all."

Rev. Barre paused a moment. "I don't know, Neemy," he said, finally, "But, let me ask you something."

"Yassuh."

"Look around you. At this point, what does it matter?"

Neemy was silent for a moment. "Why you say dat?" he finally asked.

"Well, think about it. There's only two directions it can go. If it's not true, you'll be where you are now. And if it is true, then you'll still be where you are now. So, if it's true, then what would you do different?"

"I needs to think on it."

"Neemy, listen. You can't change the past, nor the truth. You just have to find a way to live with both of them. Just throw 'em both down on the table and let the chips fall where they will. I'm not just directing that toward you; I'm reflecting it back on me, as well. You saw me. I have moments of weakness, just like everyone else. We all need to be there for each other."

"Guess you sayin' t'morrow begins t'day," Neemy said, scanning the horizon in the direction of their ruined church on the far end of the town. Amid the rubble, the stained glass window flashed in the morning sunlight like a flickering beacon.

CHAPTER 39
THE FIRST MIRACLE

As Clay and Silas entered the auditorium, a short Hispanic man intercepted them. "Hey, Silas," he said, "There's a couple of seats down close to the front."

"Juan, good to see ya. It's as full as Easter today," Silas smiled.

"Yes. The service don't start for another 10 or 15 minutes and those are the only seats left. You know what Rev. Meadow says," Juan said, smiling.

"Rev. Meadow says a lot of things," Silas said, and then turning to Clay, "He has a Bible verse or pithy remark for every occasion."

"So this Rev. Meadow is going to be preaching?" Clay asked.

"Today ain't his Sunday to preach. He preached last week, an' he'll preach next week. Today, it'll be Dr. Patrigno behind the pulpit. Definitely worth the price of admission."

Clay started to remind him that they hadn't paid anything, but then Jay, the man that had greeted them at the door, crossed the podium and stood behind the pulpit.

"Wait a minute, isn't that your brother?" he asked Silas.

"Yes. The Reverend Jonathan David Meadow. We always called him Jay. Short for Jonathan."

"Now, I really feel stupid. I had no idea he was the main man."

"Don't know that I'd call him the 'main man,'" Silas said, "But I 'spose you could call him *one* of th' main men. He's one of the associate ministers. Like I mentioned, he ain't the one preachin' this morning."

"Right. Dr. Patrigno will be preaching."

"Wow. You are a fast learner."

"Yeah, I figured there'd be a quiz after the sermon. How long has he—have you—and your brother—been at this church?"

"Since we were both born. Like our father. Like his father. Like his father. And so on. Our great-great-great-great-great grandfather was like the second minister after the Civil War. I think it's *five* greats. Anyway, our g-5 grandfather, Nehemiah, and his brother, Jonathan, helped to rebuild the church back after it was destroyed during the war. It was a white church before the war."

"That figures."

"Yes, but after the Union troops got finished with it, the only thing left was that stained glass window up there. My brother, Jonathan—*Jay*—was named after Nehemiah's brother. Jonathan—*the first Jonathan*—really started the choir. He was the musician of the bunch. Wait 'til you hear the present-day choir."

"I hear 'em. They've been singin'."

"No, they're just gettin' warmed up. Wait 'til you hear the special they gonna do."

"So, why weren't you named Nehemiah?"

"That's our older brother. He's Nehemiah. He came first. Then Jonathan. Me and Dinah came last. And yeah, we all had Bible names. I was named after Paul's buddy."

"That makes sense, theologically, I suppose. So, Silas, where's your brother, Nehemiah? Is he here in the church?"

"No, unfortunately. He's at large. MIA. We're still waitin' for him to come back from wherever he is. New York or California, last we heard. But that's God's timin'. Nehemiah'll show up, eventually."

"Looks like the place is doin' okay without him."

"The church is doing well. However, we could always use another Meadow!"

"Lord, we don't need another mountain…just send us a Meadow."

"Thas' right. Now you talkin'."

"So, the church has always had one of your ancestors for a pastor?"

"No, not at all. It's not like some sort of church dynasty, if that's what you're asking."

"I wasn't going to use that term."

"Right," Silas said, "But I saw your thought balloon. You were thinking it."

"Maybe. All the Meadows in the mix make it sound conspiratorial."

"Actually, the position of minister has skipped some of the generations in my family, and there have been other families that have been involved through the years, as well. Not always black. Not always white. But always mixed. And, as casual and logical as that sounds, in actuality, it wadn't always easy or safe. Sometimes it was downright dangerous to worship."

"Wow, that's a little dramatic, ain't it? We ain't exactly livin' in Nazi Germany or Communist China."

"Yeah, but it is the deep South."

"Yeah, up in Chicago, we skipped a lot of that crap."

"I ain't even gonna comment on that. Chicago's got its own issues. For many years, this church was led by a white preacher, Dr. Patrigno."

"The one that's preachin' today?"

"No. The Dr. Patrigno preachin' today is his grandson, though."

"Ah, another dynasty-sounding, non-dynasty, right?"

"I never thought of it that way, but it does sound, uh…"

"Conspiratorial?"

"Sure, why not," Silas laughed, "But not really. The first Dr. Patrigno was born up north—New York City, I think—but raised down here. He grew up in a blend of cultures, and I think he embraced the best of both, and cast off the worst of both. Anyway, he encouraged a multi-racial church, against the wishes of the law and the local culture at the time. He felt that to deny the multi-cultural and multi-racial heritage that this church was founded on would dishonor our founders and be spiritually hypocritical. To people on the outside, it appeared as there were two churches—white in the morning and black in the afternoon. But, oopsy, sometimes the services got all mixed up together."

"No?!" Clay gasped in mock horror.

"Right? Ain't that crazy? Some people read between the lines and grasped what was goin' on. People on both sides—white and black. He had more than a few rocks thrown through his picture window in his livin' room. He kept every rock ever thrown through his windows. Kept 'em on a shelf in his study. Painted a Bible verse on every one of 'em. My grandfather was also involved in that *blending* process. Dr. Patrigno treated my grandfather as an equal, rather than just a 'colored preacher.' That may seem and sound condescending now, but back then, it was a pretty big deal in these parts. So, yes, the Meadow family has always been involved in this church, from the Civil War on up to now. Well, for the most part, that is. Not always as preachers. Sometimes in the leadership. Sometimes as regular parishioners. And, sadly, there have also been some generations that *weren't* involved, but that's another story for another time. In fact, to be perfectly honest—I grew up in this church, but I drifted away for more than a few years."

"Wow. You were one of the 'lost Meadows?'"

"Guilty."

"So, it is Silas *Meadow*, right?" Clay asked. "I'm assuming that, since you never mentioned your last name when you introduced yourself this morning. You just said 'Silas.' I didn't even think about that until just now."

"Actually, that was intentional. I didn't want to freak you out."

"Why would 'Silas Meadow' freak me out? Because I would know your brother was the preacher? How would I have put that together when you found me under the bridge? Besides, preachers don't scare me. I got used to chaplains in the Army."

"No, that's not what I thought would have freaked you out. It's because I was *Meadow* and you're *Maddau*."

"Okay. So. It sounds similar. Both start with an 'M.' So what?"

"It's more than 'similar.' My g-5 grandfather, Nehemiah, and his brother—"

"Jonathan."

"Right. You're a good listener. The 'original' Nehemiah and Jonathan—they changed their surname after the war. It was originally Maddau—that's *Maddau*—like yours. And like you said, it ain't exactly an ordinary name. They considered it their slave name. So, after the war, they 'freedomized' it to 'Meadow.'"

"Freedomized it?" Clay blinked as the statement set in. "Wait a minute. Are you saying *my* family owned *your* family?"

"Actually, in the case of my g-5, Nehemiah, it's more than that, but it's a little bit of a long story. I had this gut feelin' that you were more than someone flyin' out of a pickup in the middle of the night—Superman, or not. I'm also saying that there ain't no coincidences, but we can talk about that after the service. We gotta quieten down now—I don't want my brother fussin' at me from the pulpit. He's already shot me a 'look of doom' from his podium throne up there. He may not call me down today, since I got me a guest, but I'd rather not chance it."

"Thought you said he wasn't preachin'…"

"He ain't, but he ain't above 'borrowing' the pulpit to chastise his little brother."

"Has he really done that? Called you down from the pulpit?"

"Nah. But there's always a first time," Silas said with a mischievous grin.

Clay sighed and sat back in his seat as the praise band's music filled the room. The sun shining through the stained-glass window painted patterns on his torn pants that shimmered on the wrinkles and torn creases in rhythm with the music. The colors from the window were projected to all the corners of the auditorium. He stared at Jesus in the picture. He was wearing a bright white robe with a blue sash that ran between his outstretched hands. His hands seemed to caress a beautiful pot. He recognized the design on the pot—it was the same as the church's logo that he had seen on the styrofoam cup that had held his morning coffee.

Silas noticed his gaze and whispered, "Water into wine. First miracle. And, the pot is a vessel. We're *all* vessels."

"Okay," Clay said.

As the music from the praise band continued, it seemed to serve as the soundtrack for the lightshow of color that bounced across the multi-colored congregation. Clay patted his shirt pocket and reached in for a stick of gum and was surprised to feel something sharp lodged beside the pack of Wrigleys. Glancing down, the sparkle of the object in his pocket caught his eye. He reached in and pulled out a good-sized, triangular piece of glass. As Clay held it up to the light, he had to smile—it was electric-blue, the same hue as Jesus' stained-glass sash. He recognized it as being one of the broken pieces of the empty whiskey bottle that he had used to christen the kid in the pickup truck. The incident from the night before seemed like an eternity ago. To the right of him, his eye was drawn to the side windows where, outside, a bright red patch of color screamed for his attention. It was a line of nuttall oaks in a fleeting display of brilliance before the onset of the winter. Clay then recalled that he had noticed a sentry row of the red oaks on both banks of the river that morning when he first woke up, and then later, when they pulled into the church's parking lot. *Hm-m-m, Rubine,* he said to himself.

EPILOGUE
From a Distance

From a bird's eye view, looking down at the Rubine River Church, it's as if there are connectional spokes, all leading to and from the main building in the form of booths and tables and people and cars and buses. The landscape is a colorful patchwork quilt of activity, almost appearing pulsing and electrical, at least from the vantage point of the clouds. Toward the eastern horizon, you can see the peeking spires of a small city's subtle skyline. You can trace the roads spider-webbing back and forth from the city to the church and the suburbia that has now enveloped the area that used to be the little four-block village of Rubineville. It still lends its name to the area, but, as a town, it never quite recovered from the inertia of the devastation at the hands of Sherman's army, as he slashed his way from Savannah through the Carolinas on to Columbia. There's an old federal highway that runs north and south, hugging and crossing the interstate off to the east that was built in the early 1960s. There's not an exit called "Rubineville" on the interstate, but there are several exits that give access to the area that used to be the town. Nowadays, there are several motels and a couple of gas stations, including an old '50s-era Gulf station that glares across the street through a maze of rusty pumps at a brand-new gas, convenience and fast-food center. There's also a lush new golf course and a few tourist traps, including the Bridgefield Civil War Museum.

The museum was built in the mid-'60s by Leonard Bridgefield, a New Yorker who came from old money and owned a string of beauty shops in New Jersey. After years of dreaming of moving and building a business in Florida, Leonard and his wife, Estelle, drove down to scout a location in the Sunshine State. On the way, their car overheated, breaking down on the exit to the highway which ran by the area which had once been the town of Rubineville. While staying at one of the motels, they noticed a flyer advertising a Civil War re-inactment to honor the 100th anniversary of the ending of the conflict. Even though their car was repaired the following day, they decided to stay to see the reenactment; as a descendant of a Union major, Leonard mainly wanted to be among the minority cheering for the boys in blue. The Bridgefields stayed another day after that event, and visited the church. There, they heard about yet another event scheduled for the following week, and since they were fairly comfortable in the motel, they stayed the next week, and another week after that. They found themselves falling in love with the area and the people, as well as the church, and they never made it to Florida. Wearing a worn Atlanta Braves cap, Leonard now sits silently in the front lobby of the museum and Estelle sells the tickets. Their son and daughter-in-law (and occasionally, their college-age grandchildren) point their visitors toward the various sections of the attraction.

The museum sits high on a bank over-looking the Rubine River, and boasts a good-sized collection of both Union and Confederate uniforms, drums, bugles, battleflags and guns, including a rare Whitworth with a scope and a scuffed and scarred riflebutt. It has detailed maps and telegraphs and messages sent back and forth from Sherman as he burned his way through the state. There are also some interesting and unique items from the area and that particular time, including a delicately-carved, wooden coin depicting the tiger mascot of a Confederate unit from Louisiana. The museum's centerpiece is a treasured collection in a climate-contolled room which features a number of yellowed wartime letters—all in various stages of controlled decay, but all brimming with long-forgotten passion and yearning.

And, running parallel to the old highway and behind the museum, the Rubine River runs clean and fast. If you climb high enough into the electric-blue sky, and the clouds are not too overbearing and stubborn, you can actually see how the river twists and turns and branches off and rejoins itself in a crescent as it dances around the far end of the church's property to the north. Better still, if you have the rare and incredible opportunity to observe its ebb and flow on a bright and sunny Sunday in October, there is always the chance to witness the nuttall oaks giving their seasonal farewell. *Look!* Their brilliant red reflection refracted in the rushing water gives the shimmering appearance of a pulsing artery upon the land, the lifeblood of a people who have weathered generations of joys and sorrows and hopes and disappointments, as well as the blood and uniforms of its storied past. The river skirts past the cemeteries, churches, schools, shops and parking lots. *Look!* It flows past those just beginning their lives—*babes in strollers and toddlers on swings*—those in their prime—*young fathers and mothers holding hands and making plans*—and those who are possibly in their last season—*watching the river catch and transport the falling leaves one final time.* The Rubine runs clear and swift, much like the memories of long-ago departed persons and families whose existence, like a current-swept leaf from a thinning nuttall oak, is soon forgotten as it makes its way slowly, but certainly, to the shining and patiently-awaiting vastness of the sea.

CPSIA information can be obtained
at www.ICGtesting.com
Printed in the USA
BVHW070044250720
584433BV00001B/35

9 781648 032622